What could go wrong? I just have to get two kids out of the house and get myself to work before my 9 a.m. meeting. Did I mention that I'm leading the meeting?

I grab the diaper bag, the laptop bag, the breast pump, my patent leather handbag, and the enormous, ridiculous, red Lands End beach bag that I use to carry all the other bags; I pick up the baby and grab my two-and-a-half year old's chubby hand, and we are out the door.

Awesome. Plenty of time to run to Dunkin' Donuts, get to the baby-sitter's house, and be to work by 8:45. Then I smell something. Something terrible. I look down.

The arm of my jacket – my best jacket, my Dolce bad-ass boho mama jacket – is covered in the unmistakable green-brown sheen of baby poop. It has penetrated the fabric.

I look at the baby. She smiles her cutest chubby four-tooth smile at me. I swear, they have that smile just to guarantee that we won't kill them.

www.lifemotherhoodhandbags.com

Emily Roberson

Life, Motherhood & the Pursuit of the Perfect Handbag

An Aster Book
Published by
Aster Amellus Books
12 Edenwood Lane
North Little Rock, Arkansas 72116

This novel is a work of fiction. Names, characters, places, and incidents either are the product of the author's imagination or are used fictitiously. Any resemblance to actual person, living or dead, events, or locales is entirely coincidental.

Copyright © 2011 by Emily Roberson

Cover design by Harriet Wu
Cover art © 2011 by Harriet Wu

All rights reserved. No part of this book may be reproduced or transmitted in any form or by any means, electronic or mechanical, including photocopying, recording, or by any information storage and retrieval system, without the written permission of the Publisher, except where permitted by law.

For Russell, Will, John Henry and Grant,
without whom there would have been no story

www.skyler-reed.com/inside-the-handbag

Skyler Reed + Boston

The Inside of the Handbag

Events | Our Obsessions | From the Creative Desk

Skyler Reed+Boston wins AAFD Award

June 15 - In a fabulous turn of events, Skyler Reed+Boston was picked for Accessory Designer of the Year by the American Association of Fashion Designers. Accepting the award, Skyler and I tried to be very high fashion about the whole thing – detached, cool, soigné. That was before we broke down in tears and smeared mascara all over our faces. We can't say enough about our customers, staff, designers, family, friends, and the editors, buyers, stylists and stores who have supported us. In other (related) news, a major fashion-friendly huge retailer (can't say who) has asked us to do a low-price one-time mini-line in honor of the award. Look for us soon!

Comments (25):

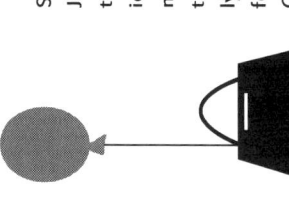

Creative Director – Tess Holland

Since I was a little girl, I have loved handbags – other things too, dresses, shoes, hats, the occasional scarf, but it has always come back to handbags. I'm all about making functional things beautiful. I call it the pursuit of the perfect handbag... I am lucky that someone pays me for my obsessions. I am the Creative Director at Skyler Reed+Boston, and I work for the original Skyler Reed. I live in a condo in a triple-decker in the Jamaica Plain neighborhood of Boston with my husband Pete, my son Jake and my daughter Gracie. We've been thinking of getting a cat.

JULY

1

Every working mother has the things she dreads, things that keep her up in the night – pink eye, an ear infection, the parent-teacher conference, the school play – all forcing her to remind the people she works with that she is not, in fact, wholly devoted to business enterprises, but has another secret life. For me, the night terror is the 5 a.m. phone call from the nanny.

A phone ringing at 5 a.m. always, always means nothing good – sweepstakes entities don't call that early, and no one ever calls at 5 o'clock to say they are on the way. So here I am, lying in bed with a warm baby, and there is my Blackberry in its orange skin, dancing across the top of the dresser like a tiny Carmen Miranda – minus the fruit.

The baby, who is not allowed in our bed, unless she wakes up when I'm too tired to remember bringing her into our bed, sleeps on my arm. I gently slide the dead arm out from under her – she burbles and growls, but doesn't wake up, and I tiptoe over to the dresser. On the way over, I step on a Matchbox car, which brings on a fit of silent cursing.

It's the nanny. Her stomach is bothering her. Funny, my stomach is bothering me too, now that I face getting two kids out of the house and getting myself to work before my 9 a.m. meeting about the high-profile launch of a mini-line of handbags, belts and shoes for a multinational corporation. Did I mention that I'm leading the meeting?

"Nanny's sick," I call to Pete in the shower.

"I'm sorry, honey," he says. He does sound sorry.

"Any way I could have the car?" I ask.

"Long call tonight, I need it to get home."

Great. My husband is a doctor and is in his final year of training after four years of medical school, three years of residency and a three-year infectious disease fellowship. In another year, he will officially be an infectious disease specialist and will help the needy and save the world. If I were to take the car, he would have to ride his bike home through sketchy neighborhoods at midnight. He already has an awful, brutal schedule of 80-hour week

Life, Motherhood & the Pursuit of the Perfect Handbag

after 80-hour week and rarely complains. That means I don't get to complain either. And I don't get the car.

It doesn't help my cause that I am only a handbag designer; true it is for a multi-million dollar accessories firm that is doing a small line of accessories for Mega Stores (a massive discount chain), but a handbag designer all the same. So now I have to rush my two small people to day care and myself to work by foot, bus and subway train.

I leave the baby asleep on the bed and get myself dressed before waking Jake, our two and half-year-old.

Thank God I laid my own clothes out the night before. This meeting is a really big deal – I've tried to rein myself in a little, down playing my normal boho mama vibe for a really beautiful black and white almost batik (but not) Derek Lam dress paired with an unstructured frayed edge jacket (Dolce & Gabbana, but I got it at a resale shop last year, just for things like this). I am an accessory designer, so I did decide to go with heart stopping yellow shoes and a flat yellow patent leather shoulder bag.

And now, here I am in all my finery, kneeling next to the bunk bed, trying to wake up my little boy. As a general rule, I believe that you should never, never, never under any circumstances wake a sleeping child; however, the wheels of commerce don't stop just because my little angel is about to turn into a grouchy, groggy monster.

"Jake," I whisper, and shake his arm.

"No, it's mine, my baby can't have it," he says, still asleep.

Just in case you wondered what toddlers dream about...

I stick my head into his bunk. His dinosaur pajamas are bunched up around his arm pits and his tummy rises and falls in his deep sleep – not quite the full round belly of a baby, but not the flat washboard of a big kid – and a lock of his blond hair clings to his face. That would be because his head is soaked with sweat. For some reason, he insists on going to bed in full long-sleeved pajamas with a blanket on, 80 degrees or no.

"C'mon Jake," I say, shaking his arm. "We've got to get up."

Finally I get through.

"You staying home today?" he says in a happy groggy voice.

"No..."

"Vanessa is coming?" he says, awake now, and a little apprehensive, but still okay.

Ah, I knew we would get to that. Vanessa is the nanny, and no, Vanessa is not coming today.

"Well, no, baby, Vanessa is sick; we're going to Sandra's house."

The tremor starts in his lower lip, then his mouth opens, and his chubby little face dissolves into a black hole of despair.

Do I need to add that this is accompanied by a howl of "NOOOOOOOO"?

Jake and baby Gracie have a clear hierarchy of care. Mommy (me) is Number 1, numero uno, best thing ever. Daddy is not quite mommy, but still pretty good. Vanessa is a close tie with Daddy, sometimes beating him, sometimes not, depending on how little he's been home. Sandra, the backup day care lady, is a distant, distant fourth, comparable only with strange old lady relatives. This is funny because they always seem to have fun at her house, but it is what it is.

At this point, I resort to nature's perfect tool in dealing with children – bribery.

"If you'll stop howling and get your clothes on, Mommy will take you to Dunkin' Donuts before we go to Sandra's."

"Sniff, sniff…"

"I'm serious though, we don't have any time, people will be mad at Mommy if we don't get moving."

"I can play?"

"Nope, nope, nope – clothes on right now. There's no time to dawdle."

I pull and push him into his shorts and t-shirt for the day. We have a brief scuffle over what color socks he should wear, but the promise of Dunkin' Donuts gets us through.

"I need my shoes to be tight," he says.

"That's fine." I swear my kid is not on the spectrum, but he is obsessed with the tightness of his shoes. They're a funny little pair of brown shoes with Velcro straps. Jake requires that the straps be pulled so tight that the Velcro will barely stick. When he runs, the straps flap like little brown flags on his feet.

Now he is dressed, and I am about to grab my bags, when I remember.

"Dammit. The baby!"

I run into our room, and there is baby Gracie, laying on the bed and pulling on her toes in a pink teddy bear sleeper. Great. She has become quite expert at rolling and could easily have ended up on the floor.

A trip to the emergency room would be a perfect addition to this morning.

I pick up the baby and hustle her into the kids' room. Lickety-split, she's changed and dressed in a cute little pink gingham dress and bloomers.

I grab the diaper bag, the laptop bag, the breast pump, my patent leather yellow handbag, and the enormous, ridiculous, red Lands End beach bag that I use to carry all the other bags, and we are out the door and down the two flights of stairs that take us to the front porch of our condo building.

Awesome – 7:30. Plenty of time to run to Dunkin' Donuts, get to Sandra's house, go to the train and be to work by 8:45.

Holding the baby, I bump the stroller down the steps, then get ready to put her in.

I smell something. Something terrible.

I look down.

The arm of my jacket – my best jacket, my Dolce, I'm a fashionable hip-happenin' bad-ass mama jacket – is covered in the unmistakable green-brown sheen of baby shit. It has penetrated the fabric.

Perfect.

I look at the baby. She smiles her cutest chubby four-tooth

smile.

I swear, they have that smile just to guarantee that we won't kill them.

"Honey, stay here on the porch and watch the cars go by for a minute, Mommy has to change the baby."

"Noooooooooo, I don't want to stay outside!!!! I want to come inside!!!!" He throws himself down in despair.

"Fine then, come inside, but no playing."

I put all the bags down on the porch and then run inside, and up the stairs. I put the baby on the changing pad and assess the situation.

The diaper has catastrophically failed. Poop covers her little pink back. Somehow she has managed to get baby poop in her hair.

I carefully roll the dress off of her, attempting to minimize the poop in hair issue.

After about 40 baby wipes and five minutes, she is finally changed and dressed. I'm aware that aggressive rubbing of baby wipes on the head is probably not the way you win a Good Housekeeping award for baby care, but there is no time for a bath.

I strip off my jacket and lay it on the mound of dirty clothes in the hamper, then pull on an old white TSE cardigan from the closet. Now a little more lady who lunches than power suit, but it's gotta do.

Finally, we are on the march.

Two kids, one mommy lugging an enormous bag, and one super-D-duper, high tech double stroller, headed off on our urban adventure.

"I need to walk," Jake says. In most cases, I encourage walking – healthy lifestyles, etc., but a toddler's stride is ill-suited to a break-neck rush to work.

I hand him a matchbox car and shove him into the stroller.

I wait until we are almost to Dunkin' Donuts to break the news that we will not be sitting inside.

"There's no time," I say.

Again the howl of despair.

"If you're going to cry, no donut," I say.

Crying stops.

Gracie starts laughing and clapping when we walk in the door. The ladies behind the counter wave. Perhaps this is a sign that we get donuts too often… I have friends that don't allow their children any sugar at all.

Clearly this is not my issue.

I get coffee for me, a strawberry donut no sprinkles for Jake and five glazed Munchkins for the baby. I hand them each a bag of treats and speed-walk to the back-up day care. It is about a mile away. I see the bus and start running, but the door closes before we get there. Looking onto the crowded bus, I'm glad we didn't make it – nothing is more harrowing than the looks of sheer hatred that you get bringing a big stroller onto a crowded bus. I wonder where people think you should put two of them? One under each arm, perhaps?

I have to shake them both off my leg to get out the door at Sandra's, then do a skipping near run to the train station. In heels – today truly should have been a Melanie Griffith working girl in tennies day, but no such luck.

8:30 – it'll be close, but I am probably going to make it.

The train stops once between stations for a good minute and I stand there stomping my feet, and looking at my watch before it gets moving again.

Finally, after a ten minute speed walk, I arrive at work. I throw the enormous bag down in my office, grab my portfolio and slow myself down before walking to the conference room, where everyone is probably waiting for me.

2

I'm the last one in the room, but not by much. The handbag designers who work for me, our shoe and belt teams, art direction, and a few marketing people are all just settling down into their seats. Skyler Reed (my boss and our resident fashion visionary) sits at the front of the room. She jingles under the weight of her bangles and the chandelier earrings that touch her shoulders. Skyler is five-three and curvy with long wild honey hair, and she has the utter sexiness that only comes from having no fear of embarrassment. She is a creature of obsessions and lately, her focus has been on India – I keep expecting her to come to work in a sari, but it hasn't happened yet.

She's been distracted recently, and we've been fighting unsuccessfully to get her to look at our ideas for two weeks. So she's going to see the whole thing an hour before we show it to the Mega Stores people coming in on the commuter flight from New York.

I stand while my designers pull out the samples and sketches. We have fabric, drawings of a girl carrying the bags, mock-ups, man-hour estimates and price points. The whole collection will only include five bags, two belts and six pairs of shoes, but we did more prototypes so that they would have a range to choose from. I started with handbags, because that's where Skyler's heart is. (Mine too…)

"I thought this was an opportunity for us to return to brass tacks – to show what we can do," I tell her. "Skyler Reed is about interesting fabrics, great lines, timeless style."

Before we have a chance to show her anything, the front desk buzzes in – "Skyler, your guests are here."

I look at my watch – it's only 9:15. They are early.

She calls reception and asks to have them sent over.

It's too soon! Our beautiful dippy intern isn't even back from Dunkin' Donuts.

"Skyler," I say, "Caitlin isn't back with the food. All the samples are lying out on the table. Don't you think you should meet them in your office first?"

"It's not them," she says.

"Who is it?" I ask. She didn't tell me about any other meetings today.

Skyler looks a little embarrassed. She is wearing the smile that means she's done something I won't like. It's the smile she brought in with the boatload of Indonesian batik fabric in '97. It's the smile she wore when she told me that she was running off to Argentina with her polo playing suitor in '03. It's the smile that she had on a month later when she came back. I'm sure that it's the smile she used when she told her dad that she'd taken the $20,000 he gave her for the down payment on a condo and used it to start a handbag company. She won't hold eye contact. I'm just going to have to wait to see what she's up to – the same as everybody else.

"Boys and girls, I'm mixing it up today," she says. "I've been thinking we need to learn to hunt with the big boys, or fish or something, go where the wild things are… Whatever it is that they say. Anyway, I brought in some new blood (or new old blood maybe, blue blood?), whatever…" She waves her hand in a floppy way that I don't find very promising.

Everyone looks at the door to the conference room.

In stride two men in boring expensive suits and a woman who looks like a sliver of ice; thin, blonde, sharp and dressed all in crème and pale blue. Everyone at the table seems as bewildered as I feel.

"These are Jim Allen, Tom Finnigan and Katrina Aspinwall. They are from OmniBrands."

The rest of us look at each other – we don't know any of these people. I do know OmniBrands; they hold a lot of fashion houses that used to be independent but now are under their corporate umbrella. I look at Skyler. We've known each other a long time. She gives me a wry look that I don't much like. Then she puts on her brightest Judy Garland/Mickey Rooney "let's put on a show" face and kick starts the meeting.

"Tess, I think you should tell Katrina, Tom and Jim about

your ideas for the mini-collection," Skyler says.

Just then, Caitlin comes in with the Dunkin' Donuts and sets the boxes down on our knock-off mid-century modern blond wood and stainless steel credenza.

Katrina, the sliver of ice stands. Her blonde hair is professionally blown out in a long layered style, and her crème-colored pantsuit is pristine. What kind of person can keep an off-white suit and pale blue blouse uncreased and unstained?

"Excuse me," she says. "I hate to interrupt, but I simply must ask a question."

She glides the two feet over to the credenza. She looks accusingly at the two cartons of Munchkins and Box o' Joe. She turns and points a manicured finger at Caitlin.

"Are you responsible for this?"

Caitlin gives her the patented look of doe-eyed blondie innocence. Caitlin is not intimidated. Caitlin is a tame little bunny who has never known fear. This is clearly an inadequate response.

"What does this look like to you?" Katrina demands.

"Um, breakfast?" Caitlin says. You know she's worried now because she takes the omnipresent iPod bud out of her left ear.

Katrina draws herself up and waves her skinny hand.

"Breakfast? Breakfast?" Her voice is full of outrage. Caitlin is not a bunny; Caitlin is a murderer of bunnies. "This is not breakfast. When one is entertaining, presentation is all. An occasion such as this one demands a true Continental breakfast."

She pauses and turns to the room.

"What do you see when you imagine Continental breakfast?" her voice turns dreamy. She does not wait for us volunteer our thoughts on baked goods. For myself, I see a chafing dish, doughy bagels with lukewarm cream cheese, and the ratty coffee maker in a Holiday Inn lobby, but that clearly isn't what she's going for.

"Coffee in a carafe, brioche, scones, a selection of preserves. Juice. There is still time – it is imperative that you call a reputable caterer immediately. An occasion such as this one demands true style, panache. I insist that you call them. Surely there are caterers in Boston."

She points toward the door.

Caitlin looks at me.

I look at Skyler.

Skyler looks down.

Shit. Looks like I'm going to be the bad guy vetoing brioche.

"Fashion people don't eat." I say. My tone is flat. I'm not wasting my budget on continental breakfast.

"Pardon?"

"No one will eat brioche. We like spending our money on other things." Like the margarita party that I am going to throw the whole group once this piece of work leaves.

"And you are?" she says.

I raise an eyebrow at Skyler. Apparently, the OmniBrands guys weren't shown an organization chart. I consider telling her to go find one, but instead I make nice. I do have a family to support.

"I'm Tess Holland. Creative Director and handbags."

Life, Motherhood & the Pursuit of the Perfect Handbag

She sniffs. She looks me up and down. She is not impressed. Perhaps it is my cardigan.

I look at Skyler. Skyler says nothing. At least she doesn't tell Caitlin to go get brioche. It looks like I've won on breakfast, so I'll go back to the purpose of the meeting.

I repeat my spiel about brass tacks, simple fabrics, great lines, timeless style.

I've barely started when Skyler puts on a make-nice smile.

"Tess, I know that you had said we were going to do a version of the Tinies for Mega Stores. Can you show us what you've got?"

Last year's breakout design, the one that likely won us the AAFD Award, was something we called the Tinies. Tinies are three bag sets (each sold individually) that are variations on a theme. Theoretically you could buy just one of a set, but if you are fashion conscious enough to pay $1,950 for a handbag, you are fashion conscious enough to care that your friends will know that you only bought one of a set. Actresses and style magazines love them because they are recognizable and collectable. I love them because you get to see all the creativity of the women who wear them. How do you carry three small bags without looking silly? The ingenuity of our customers is truly amazing. We did a limited run of each set. We had a vastly more expensive set in python – purple, gold and green, a set that referenced Tibetan prayer flags (in a not-tacky way, I hope), and five other groupings around themes.

For the tinies for Mega Brands, I used fabrics that were inexpensive, but still interesting - a burlap with really great texture, a white linen, and a red/gold made from sari fabric.

Katrina picks up the samples and quickly sets them back down on the table. She barely looks at each one and her bearing conveys boredom and indifference. She walks over and looks at the sketches on the wall. Finally, she looks at Skyler. She picks up a piece of burlap, and her frown deepens.

"I thought this was a high fashion firm," she says.

Just then, the front desk calls to say the Mega Stores people are here.

Skyler stands to go and I put down my papers and get ready to follow her. Katrina heads for the door.

"Tess, stay here and make sure everything is ready," Skyler says.

My face is hot. This is my project; I should be there to greet them.

Once Katrina and Skyler are gone, we all look at each other, but nobody says anything; the suits are still in the room.

We sit in silence for what seems like hours, but is probably only five minutes.

Finally, the Mega Stores team comes in with Skyler and Katrina, and it's a lovefest with the OmniBrands guys. They're all shaking hands and slapping backs. Apparently these people all go to the same boring suit conventions. I have that feeling you get when you call each of your friends to do something, and everyone's busy, and then you find out that they are all busy off having a party together.

Everyone except Katrina settles and enjoys their Munchkins and Joe before we start our show. She doesn't eat at all. Her face suggests profound indigestion. I consider offering her some Mylanta.

How can this go well now? With Katrina's words hanging in the air? Of course we're a high-fashion firm. Who the hell else makes $2,000 handbags? Not that money is everything, but isn't that the definition of a high fashion firm? You make incredibly expensive luxury items, and people buy them. As far as I'm concerned, that's the barrier to entry, and we've long since passed it.

I try not to present like someone with a chip on her shoulder. I probably use my hands too much, and my smile feels forced.

Meanwhile, Katrina's mouth is frozen in a tight line. It's hard to see how that is different from how it's been since she came in the room, so I hope for the best.

We wait.

Skyler looks down at her notes, and looks back at me. I'm ready for her careful mix of criticism and loopy praise.

"I have notes." Katrina leans forward and shakes her long hair.

She's not going to go after us now, is she? She does know that the Mega Stores guys are sitting here in the room?

"Again, I don't see high fashion in this. I see ordinary. Surely this isn't what you offer your customers? Where is the flash? Where is the bling?"

Emily Roberson

The bling? You know a hip hop term has truly lost its bearings when a 40ish blonde woman is using it in a conference room.

"When I think of Skyler Reed+Boston," she says, "I see luxury, details, fabrics – this is homespun."

Again nobody speaks. I guess it has to be me.

"We are artisans," I say. "If you push the price point down to $30 a bag, homespun is what we can do." I want to say something about pioneers and patriots and the virtues of homespun, but I don't think I can do it without sounding ridiculous.

"You are thinking of this backwards," she says. "Tell me what you want to do, and I'll tell you where you can do it for the price point you need."

"Believe me, I know what we can do or not do," I say. "We've been at this a long time. Why don't you ask them what they think?" I point at the Mega Stores guys.

She smiles and leans back in her chair.

I try not to close my eyes really tightly. It is clear by the look on her face that I have made a strategic error. Think Siamese cat, canary feathers barely visible in the corners of his mouth. That canary – that's me. Yellow bag and all…

The Mega Stores man coughs. "Well," he says. "It is true that we were hoping for a bit more pizzazz."

"And we were hoping to see some python," the woman says.

"Where is the beading?" he says.

"And the pockets? I love all those pockets," she chimes in. "And what about the rivets? The rivets from last season seemed so fun and, you know, contemporary."

"Pockets and rivets and sequins and python are expensive!" I say. I know that I sound like a righteous 17-year-old, but I don't know what else to do with this kind of idiocy. Python for $30? Come on. "New Bedford won't be able to make anything close to that."

Katrina laughs. It is a tinkling sound, the very polite laughter offered in response to early-in-the-evening cocktail party bullshit.

"You didn't think, [ha, ha, ha, ha], that Skyler Reed was going to be manufacturing the collection?"

Horribly, the Mega Stores people laugh too.

We manufacture all of our collections, how else would we have any control over our products? Facing the peals of laughter in the room, I decide that now is a good time to shut up. I look at Skyler – she is still the boss, it was her job to tell me things like this when she gave me the assignment to lead the collection.

She says nothing.

Finally, I say, and my voice is unforgivably hesitant, "Who will be manufacturing the collection?"

"Malaysia, I think," the man says.

"Isn't it Guam?" says the woman.

"Doesn't matter," the man says.

My gut says back out now. These things are going to have our name on them. These people think it doesn't matter who makes them. I'm not the boss. Skyler still doesn't say anything.

Crap. I look around the conference room. Katrina's half smile, the OmniBrands guys looking at their Blackberries, my people shell shocked, the Mega Stores' folks open-faced complacency, and Skyler wearing the look that she always wears when she just wants things to go away.

That appears to leave me. I speak very carefully, but firmly.

"We make our own things, that way we can have complete control over our product. Our reputation and brand are built around quality, and that cannot waiver…"

Katrina interrupts – "I'm sorry, Jim, Tom, I have wasted your time," she says and she stands. "I had thought that Skyler Reed+Boston was serious about becoming a worldwide brand."

"Wait," Skyler says. Her voice sounds genuinely nervous. This is not the Skyler Reed I know. This is certainly not the Skyler Reed who started a company with an idea, two handbag designs and twenty grand of her daddy's money.

"We're serious," Skyler says.

Katrina sits down.

"Well," she says, and she draws it out as though she is really considering picking up and leaving the room. "If you choose to benefit from my experience, I will say that being wedded to an old-fashioned mode of design and production will ensure that you never move beyond the status of a niche brand. We are living in a flat world – it is basic economics. We are in the twenty-first century; the time for mercantilism is long past."

Finally Skyler ends the suffering. "Katrina, you've given us a lot to think about," she says. She turns to the Mega people, "I'm sorry that our designs weren't what you wanted – How about we present the revamped designs to you next week? Does that work for you?"

The Mega Stores people get out their iPhones, and they agree on a date and time for next week. Katrina also confirms her availability, although it continues to be unclear to me why she should be there. They all choose Friday – the day that I always stay home with my kids. Nobody asks me about my availability, and Skyler doesn't notice, so I don't say anything.

3

Everyone avoids looking at me as they leave the room except for Stacey from stationery, who gives me a meaningful look and a soulful arm squeeze – worse, in its way than the downcast eyes of the others.

As soon as Skyler rounds the corner on the way to her office, I grab her arm.

"Can I talk to you?"

She smiles. It looks half-assed and defeated.

"I'm pretty busy," she says. "Can we do it tomorrow?"

"Skyler!"

"Okay, but don't yell at me."

There's the Skyler I know.

"I'll try to keep it in check."

We walk back to her office. She moves a stack of fabric samples off the chair in front of her desk and I sit down.

"What's going on?" I ask.

"What do you mean?"

I look down at her handbag on the floor next to the desk, and I see a book sticking out. It looks ominously familiar. I grab it before she can get it back from me.

"You're reading *Eat, Pray, Love*?"

My book group read *Eat, Pray, Love*; it's the kind of book that makes middle-aged ladies decide to leave their families and change their names to Peace Blossom.

Skyler blushes.

"So? A girl can read, can't she?"

It suddenly dawns on me. The book. India. The ganesh on her desk. Turning 40.

"You're selling the company." I don't even have the energy to add an exclamation point. I suddenly know what we just witnessed. "I just thought that you had finally lost it, but that's not it, is it? – you're selling out to OmniBrands."

She clinks and jingles as she shifts around in her chair.

I feel like I'm talking to Jake, my two-year-old.

"Skyler, look at me. You owe me this – are you selling Skyler Reed?"

She nods.

"What are you thinking? We're only half-way finished with the collection. We show in less than two months. What are we going to do in September in New York? Who will go to Paris? Everyone will be expecting you. For all we know they'll want to start the whole collection over. Why not wait until after September and finish what we started? Then you can sell it to anyone you want."

She shakes her head. "No, this is the best time... With the award and everything... I'm so tired of everything... And this is the best price I'm ever going to get for it... You won't believe how much they are willing to pay! Daddy would be proud – buy low, sell high."

She gives a little laugh. Her dad hated the whole idea of her putting money into handbags. He would be very proud of her for turning a profit on her crazy scheme.

I'm not.

"Skyler, they are going to ruin it. And it has your name on it!"

"I thought of that," she says.

She looks at the book in my hand.

"You can't change your name," I say.

"But Parvati's pretty, right?" she says.

"Parvati?"

"What about Kali?"

"The goddess of destruction sounds about right to me just this minute."

"Tess – don't be that way."

"Why not let me run it? I thought that's what was going to happen. We have the same vision, the same ideas…"

"They are going to make it huge, Tess."

I don't know what to say. I'm not going to cry here, but I sure will at home.

"But why?"

She touches my hand.

"Listen, Tess, a few years ago, I would completely have let you buy in and had you as a partner. But lately, you just haven't been all the way in it. Skyler Reed just hasn't been your priority."

I close my eyes tight and open them again.

"You mean since the kids were born?"

"I didn't say that. It's just that when we first started, you were involved in everything, you were there with me 100 percent and I could always count on you to say yes, and lately it's just been different – that's all."

I am really mad at her, and my feelings are hurt. It must show on my face.

"I'm not saying you're not great at your job," she says. "You are. I just don't think you could be the President. Tess, that's why I'm selling it – you just can't have any other priorities when you have this position. All these people depend on me. It's just too much."

"Skyler I could do it, I swear." I say.

"Tess, you are great at handbags – you are the handbag guru, the diva, the star – but everything else? Tess, in the past three years you have lost track of everything else."

"That's not true," I say. But as I'm saying it I wonder if I'm wrong…

"Okay fine, what about the trouble we've been having with the Chicago store? The shoplifting? Our needing to hire a new manager and a new team? I had to go to Chicago for a week to get everyone back on track. Are you ready for that?"

I am silent.

"Admit it," she says. "Did you even know that we were having a problem with the Chicago store?"

Honestly, over the last few years, I have kind of let my attendance to meetings about the brick and mortar retail side slip a little. They didn't really need me there, right?

"Do you even know how many stores we have?" She looks at me with sharp eyes.

"Um, 16?"

She shakes her head. "Thirty – we have 30 stores now, and the President has to know what is going on with all of them."

"I'm a quick study – I was there when we opened the first store and the fifth, remember? I worked in retail all through high school. I could figure it out. Plus, you've hired some great people, I'll be able to delegate."

"Okay, let's say you are great with the retail side. What about the manufacturing? Did you know that one of our cutting presses just broke down - do you think it would be better to invest in a new one or repair the old one? What are the tax consequences? As we expand the line to make more and more, and to make more mid-priced items, should we consider offshoring? How should we find reputable manufacturers who will uphold our brand values? There are consultants who help with those things – do you know what is a reasonable price to pay one, or what the best way would be of choosing one?"

I hang my head a little and don't say anything. I don't know very much about these things. She's not done. I think at this point, she's just trying to show me how crazy her life has become over the last few years.

"And what about designer appearances and trunk shows?" she asks. "I was on a tour of the South last month with one at Neiman's in Dallas, and another at Barbara Jean in Little Rock, Arkansas, and six or seven others – that's the sort of thing you have to do to keep your stores happy. The big ones want you, the small ones want you, and there's never quite enough of you to go around. Are you ready to do that? Tess, when was the last time you did a trunk show?"

I scan my memory. I seem to remember standing in a Dillards in St. Louis when I was about eight months pregnant with Jake. That would have to be the last one – I have barely traveled anywhere for anything since then. I just haven't been able to figure out the logistics. I wish we had family in Boston…

I try to lighten the mood - "Would I really have to do trunk shows? Couldn't we get someone to impersonate you and do them? The ladies wouldn't even know who I was; they'd be expecting Skyler Reed…"

"Ha, ha," she says. "Yes, you have to do them – unless you don't want to sell any bags, or shoes, or belts. If people are paying this much for something, they want individual service. And that doesn't even include flying to Paris to kiss up to designers; or going to Hollywood and convincing stylists and starlets to carry Skyler Reed bags. Are you really ready to do all that?"

Emily Roberson

I remember the beginning. When I answered Skyler's ad looking for someone who was energetic and loved handbags. I remember us driving all over the northeast in Skyler's faded silver Isuzu Trooper, trying to convince people to stock our bags. I was involved with everything. When we started we both were – we were cutting and sewing the bags ourselves in her apartment and then in the first small storefront we rented in the South End, back when it was right next to the combat zone. I visited all those old mill towns in Southern Mass before we decided on New Bedford. I helped to set up the factory. I even wrote the first letters to find out if we were eligible for any special funding for starting new manufacturing work in New England. But then we figured out that my special gifts were for design, and that Skyler was great at everything else. We had already started to divide the labor before Jake was born, and since then it's just gotten more divided.

"But Skyler," I say, in a last effort to defend myself. "I've done everything you've asked me to do, and you've always been happy with my work."

She pats my hand.

"Of course I'm happy with your work. I love the work you've done over the past few years. Your designs are amazing. But I haven't asked you to do more because I've been afraid that you would quit if I did. Believe me, I know how hard it has been with Pete in residency – hell, I think it's been two years since I've even seen his face. This is the right thing, Tess, you'll see. Nothing's going to change."

"When is it going to happen?"

"I don't know," she waves her hand in her old breezy way.

"Skyler?" No way she doesn't know.

"The end of the month. They'll take over the first week of August. It looks like they'll probably have Katrina leading the brand. Don't worry, I told them all about you. They promised me that things would be just the same. You'll still have Creative Director and the handbags. Don't worry Tess, things will be fine."

"August is two weeks away! How long have you been planning this?"

"I don't know… Six months? A year?"

She can tell my feelings are hurt.

"I couldn't tell you, Tess. I never meant to hurt you. I know it's been a great ride, and I've had fun, but I'm just so tired. I promise, I'll call you from India and check in on how everything is going."

Sure. I stand up and leave.

I walk into my office and close the door.

I call my husband.

"Honey, I'm on rounds, can I call you later?" he says, before I have the chance to tell him anything.

"Sure. Love you."

He hangs up. I understand that you can't say I love you when you are standing in a circle of 20 doctors looking at some kid with RSV, but I could have used a little I love you today. Someday we should set up a code. I'll say, "I love you" and he can say "that'll be just fine" or "strawberries and potatoes" or "Iway Ovelay ouyay".

Somehow I make it through the afternoon. I meet my demoralized design team, and I don't even try to give a pep talk; we have no idea where to begin. I ask them to think of themes.

"Bling?" one says.

"Sure..."

The one nice thing was that I got to talk with Tera from marketing about a few more ideas for our blog.

We have worked together on a feature for our website. It's called From the Creative Desk and I do a little blogging about whatever it is that has me fired up. We've had Caitlin scan images of fabric, sketches and other stuff. Just to get our customers excited about the next season's ideas.

My technical skills are iffy and my time limited, so I've been sending my writing to Tera for her to clean up and post. It's been fun and we're hoping to expand it to include the other product lines down the road.

Of course, who knows what's going to happen now that Skyler is selling us.

I resolve to take back my little handbag sketch before the sale. I did it when we first started the web feature, and now we like to dress it up in different ways. If they take the blog from me, I'd hate to think of someone else using my little bag.

I can't tell Tera or anyone else about Skyler's plans. That's really hers to do. As I leave, a suspiciously large number of people carry their portfolios out of the office with them.

4

What a terrible week. At least Skyler announced the upcoming sale on Tuesday so I didn't have to keep lying about it.

We have still not really figured out how to bring our level of quality to a $30 price point. None of us knows a damn thing about low-cost production. We all try to get around our ignorance without calling Katrina Aspinwall. I Googled and I went to the library, but nobody makes Fashion Outsourcing for Dummies.

Finally on Wednesday, I go to Skyler and tell her that she has to call Katrina. Skyler hangs up looking shell-shocked. However, it seems there is nothing to worry about – Katrina said to design without regard to price and she promises to come in next Monday, look at what we have, and voila, she'll make it happen – fairy godmother style (with an assist from Guam). I'm sure that Katrina didn't say the fairy godmother part – that sounds like Skyler's pixie dust.

Great.

I now realize that this awful person is going to be my new

boss. How can I transition from working for a flibbertigibbet to a block of ice?

I feel sick at the prospect, and I decide that the best medicine is for my husband to take me to dinner.

I call our favorite restaurant – Oleana in Cambridge. Of course they don't have a reservation, but the host confirms that you don't need a reservation for the patio. So the nanny agrees to stay for a few more hours and Pete comes over from the hospital after work to pick me up.

When I come downstairs to meet him, I get a thrill just seeing his face. We met when we were both still in college, and I thought he was very cute then. I still do. He's sandy haired and strong with tan skin and bright green eyes. As usual, his wavy hair is a little long on top and he looks ragged around the edges. He barely manages to meet the doctor standard of clothes, and that's not saying much. I know that he's had the khakis he's wearing for at least 10 years, and he's got the standard dark blue shirt and yellow tie. His white coat is wadded up in the back seat. I look at his feet – of course he's wearing the Dansko doctor clogs, today it's the brown ones. At least he doesn't have scrubs on. I smile a little thinking of the body underneath his clothes. He played varsity soccer in college and he had a beautiful body – strong legs and ripped. He's slipped a little since then, since he can only squeeze in a few pick-up games and occasional trips to the gym, but even with a few extra pounds he is still a handsome man.

The only thing that's missing is his sparkle of fun. It comes on when he smiles at me or the kids, but in repose, his twinkle is absent. Pete is the kind of guy who could make a friend anywhere, and who can always be depended on to be up to something. Or at least that was true before he got swallowed by the grueling work hours and expectations of medical training. We're both so busy, we don't really have time for fun anyway, but I miss it. I hope he can recover it when he's done with all this.

He looks at me and suddenly, I see the sparkle.

"Are you up for a little something when we get home?" he asks with a smile.

We are so busy and with Pete's terrible call schedule, we haven't had time for sex in about five weeks. This may be the longest dry spell in our marriage. He takes my hand as we drive across the bridge to Cambridge. Then I feel his hand start to move. I remind him to concentrate on managing the traffic.

As always, he follows way too close and cuts people off and generally makes me slam on the imaginary brake in the floor and hold tight to my oh-shit handle.

Inside the restaurant, fashionably dressed people sit at the booths and tables indoors and the bar is packed. I am salivating thinking about the food.

"We'd like to sit on the patio," I say to the host.

"The patio's under construction this week," he says. He barely looks at me. This is definitely the same man that I talked to this afternoon.

"But, I talked to someone today, and nobody said anything

about the patio being closed…"

I know my tone is radically uncool and verging into the Yuppie whine, but I can't help it: I feel like I'm flying alone with kids and I find out that I have to spend the night in the Newark Airport. I need fine dining and a glass or three of wine and scrumptious food and a stress-free evening with my husband.

The maître d' shrugs and turns back to his conversation with a young woman with blonde hair and a nose ring. She is very pretty, and I can't tell if she is a server or the arm-candy stand-in hostess.

Pete smiles his big crinkling smile. This is the smile that gets kids to take shots, old people to tell their life histories, his mother to give him the last piece of cake.

"Excuse me, is there any chance you could get us a table? Look at my wife; she's desperate for the Baked Alaska. I see that small table over there in the corner."

The maître d' is made of stone.

"That table is reserved."

I usually never do this, but Pete's right, I am desperate for the Baked Alaska.

"Do you follow fashion at all?" I ask. Pete cringes, but he must understand that the situation is desperate.

The woman perks up.

"Sure," she says. "I love fashion."

"So you know about Skyler Reed?"

"You're Skyler Reed?" she asks, hopefully.

Life, Motherhood & the Pursuit of the Perfect Handbag

"No, no, but I am the Creative Director and lead designer."

I look optimistically at the reserved table. I know it is not really reserved for anyone in particular, just for any VIPs who might show up. Like I said, I rarely do this, but that's because I save it. Skyler Reed is the restaurant silver bullet.

"I read in Boston Magazine today that they got acquired," the woman says.

Ooof. And that quickly, the door slams, the silver bullet falls to the floor. I feel like Superman in a room full of kryptonite.

"You can sit at the bar if you would like," the host says.

I look past the host station to the bar – there are two stools right next to the kitchen door. This is not what I imagined for our romantic dinner.

We trudge back to the car.

We decide to try a wine bar/tapas place in Brookline that has the benefit of being on the way home. As we are driving it starts to rain. Pete laughs.

"Good thing we aren't outside," he says.

As Pete weaves through the narrow wet streets, we still don't talk. With my life collapsing, I don't even know where to start. My company is getting sold. I will not have Skyler watching my back anymore. I can't quit, we need my income. There are not any handbag jobs in Boston that are not with Skyler Reed. I don't know if I'll be able to keep my Fridays off. I've thought someday I would run Skyler Reed, and now I know that is never going to happen.

We park on Beacon Street then run together through the rain to the restaurant. Once we get beyond the fogged windows, it looks delightful. Full glasses of wine, people laughing, wonderful smelling food. Unfortunately, there is a crowd inside the front door and a two-hour wait.

With a baby-sitter on the clock, there is no way that we can do a two-hour wait.

Finally, we end up at Café D, two blocks from our house. We seem to go out to dinner there every time either of our parents is in town and watching the kids for us. It's cute. I always forget how cute it is. Very bistro. Old newspapers on the wall, large store front windows, a big blackboard covered with the day's specials. Most importantly for tonight, it's only three-quarters full so we have no trouble getting a table. We sit by the window so we can see the rain.

I finally have my glass of wine when Pete starts talking.

"You remember my friend Gretchen?" he asks.

Gretchen? How could I forget Gretchen? She is Pete's "friend" from his lost year and a half. To make a long story shorter, Pete and I dated for most of college and all of medical school – then right about the time that he was planning to ask me to marry him, I got spooked and broke up with him. In response, he followed his lifelong dream to Nigeria to work with a medical non-profit. While he was there, he met a wonderful, amazing, beautiful and saintly kindred spirit named Gretchen. I have met her twice. She is a German physician who looks like Franka Potente. I've yet to

Life, Motherhood & the Pursuit of the Perfect Handbag

tell Pete that I hate her.

"Yes, I remember Gretchen," I say.

"She's committed for another month or two to Doctors Without Borders, but she's thinking of coming to Boston to look for work. You don't mind if she stays in our guest room for a week or so, do you? She might be able to help out with the kids a little when she's not interviewing."

"Sure," I say. What else can I say? Our spare room is the way station for friends passing through Boston, so I can't very well say no to this one just because I'm a little jealous. Of course it is connected to our bedroom by French doors, but what's a little intimacy between friends? Perhaps I'll finally get around to hanging curtains on the doors. I want to ask if he ever slept with her in Nigeria, but it's so long ago, and our romantic dinner seems like a bad place to find out if the answer is yes.

"You know it's been almost six years since you came back from Africa?" I say.

"It's been that long?" he says.

"Yeah," I say. "Remember that Christmas?"

Peter smiles a smile that makes me want to box up our food, go home and jump him.

When I broke up with Pete, it was during his intern year. I knew things were headed toward us getting married, but Pete still wanted to save the world. He dreamed of going to work for Doctors without Borders or Partners in Health. I didn't want to go – in fact, most of those organizations wouldn't even let a girlfriend tag

37

along, even if I'd wanted to. I couldn't be the one destroying his dream; especially because by then I was working for Skyler Reed and living mine.

So Pete went to Nigeria. And I lived the single girl whirl in Boston. Little apartment in Harvard Square, lots of flirtation, working until late in the night and then drinking until much later. Then came the fall of 2001 and everything crashed to a stop.

After September 11, Boston felt different. Everything was slower, more inward, and people were grasping for connection. I suddenly realized everything that I was missing, especially Pete. I was getting closer and closer to 30 with no prospect of love, family or home. How would I ever find something like that again? I certainly wasn't meeting any likely candidates in the fashion industry.

Then, right around Christmas, two years after we broke up, I ran into him at the Border Café in Harvard Square. I didn't even know he was back in town. I stopped in my tracks. Here was a man…

He sat at a table with his friends and he hadn't seen me. My friend Kerry pushed on my back and pinched me until I finally walked over to him.

I could tell his friends weren't happy to see me. None of them had forgiven me for breaking up with him and driving him to Africa. Pete stood up from the table and gave me an enormous hug. I realized how much I had missed him; how much I hadn't felt really whole without him.

We stood there awkwardly trying to figure out what to do. Neither of us wanted to go back to our seats, but at the same time everyone was waiting for us. The food was getting cold on the tables.

"Um, see you later," I said finally, pointing at the table where my girlfriends were gathered. I turned to leave.

Kerry jumped out of her seat.

"I'm sure you two have things to talk about. Don't they have things to talk about? You guys just go on, we'll see you soon."

Kerry says the electricity was visible. I know neither of us worried about the food we left on the tables as we walked out into Harvard Square, covered in snow.

We hugged again for a long time standing by the T Stop.

"I missed you," I said.

"Shhhhh."

"I was wrong," I said.

"Shhhhh."

Then he kissed me.

I took him back to my apartment and that was that.

It turned out that Pete had already decided to complete his training and had come back to Boston.

We got married the following summer.

He worked very hard, and I worked hard, and we were happy, but we had never exactly hammered out how he could be married to me and save the world.

Then we had the babies and I put off worrying about it.

It occurs to me that Pete might wonder about the path not taken.

"Has Gretchen been working for non-profits this whole time?" I ask.

"Yeah, she did a while longer in Nigeria, but she's spent a lot of time in Darfur since things have gotten bad there. Just talking with her makes me think, what the hell have I been doing? So much needs to be done, and here I am just dicking around."

He's looking at me intensely as he's saying this. Clearly it is about fellowship, not about our life together. Surely it is…

I nod, not really trusting myself to say much.

"I miss that feeling of eating and sleeping something. In Nigeria, especially during the measles outbreak, the need was so great; we just poured ourselves into it. I had to write myself a post-it note that said 'eat, sleep, drink, and bathe'. That's how all-consuming it was. We were really making a difference. And Gretchen's still doing it: I mean, there's a crisis, she can just jump up and go. But I've just got to, you know, hold down the fort."

He smiles and it's that smile that I love, and I keep hoping that he'll throw me a line – something.

Instead he says, "I just feel…"

He trails off; the words I'm filling in the blank with are not happy ones – trapped, chained, tied-down, boxed-in…

We sit in silence for a moment. He looks out the window at the rain.

"You feel what?" I say. I need to know.

"It's like my horizons are smaller. Like maybe I won't be able to do the things I really want to do in the world – in public health, in making the world a better place – because I don't have that freedom of action."

I have nothing to say here. I look down at my steak. Maybe I should have another glass of wine.

I can't figure out how to tell my husband that raising two little children into moral people may be the best thing that he can ever do. I want to tell him that he'd be half a man if he poured all of himself into work with no life outside of it. I want to tell him that his ambition to change the world is adolescent and unrealistic. I want to tell him that if that was what he really wanted, he never should have come home, and he never should have married me, or had our beautiful babies. I want to tell him all these things, but I don't, because if he doesn't already understand these things, how could I possibly make him?

My book group read a book called *Beyond the Sea*, and everyone but me loved it. It was about an amazing man (and one of Pete's supervising physicians at Mass General) named Dr. Gerard van de Berg who fights AIDS and tuberculosis in Africa. He has transformed medicine. It also tells the touching story of his late-in-life courtship and marriage to a young Malian doctor, who after having been educated in the U.S. returns to her homeland and works in Dr. van de Berg's clinic. From the beginning of the book, we know that his wife and little girl live in Geneva, and that they see him as he travels between his clinics in Africa, his responsibilities at MGH, and his work leading the nonprofit foundation he started (which is at least based in Switzerland).

In other words, on the occasional weekend. I couldn't even finish it. The vision of that little family waiting for daddy while he changes the world made me want to cry. How to grow up knowing that your father was pulled away from you by the most urgent needs? You couldn't even be mad about it without feeling guilty – I mean who begrudges the desperately poor their healthcare? In fact, here I am in the same boat. How can I really argue with my husband about his priorities when he wants to be saving people's lives in Darfur? That's a loser of an argument – hundreds of thousands of suffering people against me and two little blond first worlders.

I came to dinner wanting to talk about my fears for the new acquisition and my future and our hopes, but it seems silly now. What to do when your husband has just let slip that his hopes and dreams don't even include you and your children?

When we get home and let Vanessa go, Pete wants to have sex, but I get under the covers while he's brushing his teeth and pretend to be asleep when he climbs into bed.

5

Friday night is girls-night-out – since we've all had kids we've migrated from bars to our own houses, but we do the same thing we always did – drink and talk. Tonight is a wine and cheese night.

We are my friend Mira's house, a monstrous Victorian on the swankier Pond Side of our neighborhood. The house is rambling and lived-in, and although they only have two boys right now, it seems like it could hold five or six more children. They have done minimal renovations, so the house is a palimpsest of all the different owners – the Victorian old ladies, a dash of 70's harvest gold, and the objects from around the world that Mira has collected in her years as a fashion photographer. Like Mira herself, the house is eclectic, a whirl of colors, fabrics and styles, but all brought together with the same polished eye.

She meets me at the door, barefooted in a green sundress with gold embroidery and her long black hair pulled back in a ponytail. As usual, she looks beautiful.

Her husband Raj waves at me from the top of the stairs as he chases after their two naked boys with a towel.

Kerry follows me in the door a minute later, carrying a bottle of wine (although she has just told us that she is pregnant and can't drink it). Kerry has just come from work as a corporate attorney, her pantsuit is tailored, her red hair blown straight, and her figure is slender – no sign of a baby bump yet.

Mira, Kerry and I have been friends since college, and I have promised myself that I won't high-jack girls-night with the tales of my sorrows. I must look awful, though, because after leading me into the kitchen, plying me with cheeses and an extra-large glass of wine, the girls begin pumping me for information.

I've just gotten to the part about Katrina drawling 'I thought this was a high fashion firm,' when Mira asks, "What does she look like?"

"The evil ice queen in Narnia," I say.

"Long dress? Green fingernails?" Mira says.

"No, no, maybe more like Heather Locklear in Melrose Place," I say.

"Very short skirt? Crazy eyes?" Kerry says.

"Wait," I say, "Let's Google her. Then you'll see."

We fire up the computer in the kitchen and crowd around. I type in Katrina Aspinwall.

Gold mine.

Since she is beautiful, youngish, socially connected, and has a sharp nose for business, she is a star. She is all over the internet – profiles, pictures from society events, and press releases in corporatese.

From the first picture, my friends say – "Oh…" and understand.

"How old do you think?" Kerry asks.

"Does it matter?" Mira says. "Isn't it important how old you feel?"

"It matters," Kerry says.

"Can't tell," I say. "Oh wait, this article from last year says 44, which makes her around 45."

"Married?" Kerry asks.

"If so, she doesn't wear a ring," I say.

"Does she have kids?" Mira says.

"I can't imagine that she does, but who can say," I say.

"I'm betting no, and bitter," Kerry says. "They are always the worst. Especially the ones that haven't resigned themselves to it, gotten fat, and become wonderful aunties with a houseful of cats."

"That's a nasty thing to say," Mira says, absently petting the cat in her lap.

"Maybe so, but I'm telling you, as an attorney, I've seen my share of bitter women, and the fat cat lovers are better than the ones who are still maintaining that girlish figure. Bitter and starving…"

We buzz through the posts. For the past ten years, she has cut a swath through a series of old line luxury accessories firms carrying words like positioning, brand momentum, and aspirational marketing. The press releases speak glowingly of growth, profit, expansion and share-holder value. Nobody says anything about quality, value or the decency of work, but I wasn't really expecting that in the fashion or financial press.

"What's aspirational marketing?" Kerry asks.

"Convincing people to buy stuff they can't afford," Mira says.

I roll my eyes. I don't love the term, but for someone who makes her living photographing models wearing outfits worth thousands of dollars, Mira can be very naïve about the industry.

"It's getting people to want to be a part of a brand, and to buy lower-end entry price items," I say.

"Gateway drugs," Mira says.

"Hey, you are the one making the images that sell them," I say.

"I make my pictures," she says. "What people use them for isn't up to me."

We look at few more articles.

"If she had a husband or kids, it would say so," Kerry says. "Stories always mention that if it's part of someone's life. See, this one says she has a beloved bichon frisé – if they are going to mention a dog, they would definitely say something about a husband and kids – or even just kids. Single moms making it big sell papers. It's human interest."

"Okay," I say. "Her only soft spot appears to be dogs. Too bad I don't have any."

"You could pretend the kids are dogs, she might give you a

bit more sympathy – I've found that's often true with dog people, they like their dogs more than most parents like their children, and they love to hear about the traumas of other people's dogs," Mira says.

"Thanks, so should I switch out the pictures on my desk?"

As we look at the articles, though something is bothering me…

"Wait a minute," I say. "She's Creative Director for all these jobs. Skyler says that I can keep Creative Director."

"But you say this Katrina woman doesn't even know who you are," Kerry says.

"Well she doesn't admit to knowing who I am," I say.

"Same difference," Kerry says. "I expect that you can say good-bye to Creative Director."

"Not really? But Skyler said…"

"Sweetheart, you don't own anything – promises she makes to you mean nothing."

I know she says this from her years of experience as a corporate attorney, but it doesn't make it sting any less.

"You know what really bothers me, though?" I say. "Skyler didn't even consider making me the President. She says I haven't been connected enough with the whole operation over the last few years since the kids were born."

"That's terrible," Mira says. "You are too involved."

Kerry looks at me hard.

"No she's not."

"What?" I say.

"Come on, tell yourself the truth, Tess. We've talked about this since Jake was born. Your whole goal has been to maximize the parts of the job you like and minimize the parts you don't like. Fridays off, no travel, only design… Skyler likes you and you are great at what you do, but don't deny that you've been cherry picking."

"I have not!" I say. "I do lots of stuff that stinks – like this Mega Stores thing. I did that."

"How is it different? You just designed more handbags. Have you taken over anything for her? Made anything easier for her?"

"But I can't!" I say. "You know what my life is like – we have two kids, Pete works all the time – parenting has to add up to 100 percent, and with Pete only able to give five percent at home, who is going to make up the difference? It has to be me. I'm doing the best I can, Kerry."

She shakes her head.

"You're like the new associates who come in right out of law school and immediately want to negotiate what they will do and not do. Oh, she wants to work three-quarters time, but she wants to make Partner in the same time-frame as someone who is busting her ass. I answered email messages on my Blackberry from the maternity ward. I'm not complaining – I'm just saying that's how it is. Sure, I wish I could be at more dance recitals, but I think we're doing pretty well by Madison. If I wanted something different I could back off tomorrow, but I want to be a partner. I'm not going to apologize for what it takes to get there. She'll understand, and when she does the same thing, I hope I can be as helpful as my mom has been."

"But Tess doesn't have any family here," Mira jumped in, trying to make me feel better.

"Hire a night nanny," Kerry says. "There are college students who would be happy for the work. Get an au pair, then you have someone on call all the time."

"But then who is raising the children?" Mira says, her voice is scandalized.

Kerry laughs.

"Mira, you can only say that because you have Mr. Mom here looking after everything. Without Raj staying home, what would you do when you have to jet off to Marrakesh for a shoot?"

"I'm just saying that Tess shouldn't have to have strangers raise her children in order to be successful in her career."

"Tess is successful in her career," Kerry says. "Even if the ice queen takes Creative Director away from Tess, she's still the lead handbag designer for a company with $20 million in annual sales."

"$35 million," I say – my tone is a little pissed.

"See, she does know that," Mira says.

"Don't get mad, girls," Kerry says. "I'm just saying that if what Tess wants is to be the President of a $35 million company, she's got to be ready to give up her Fridays off."

"You really are a bitch," I say to Kerry.

"Thank you."

My feelings are hurt.

Kerry comes over and puts her arm around my shoulder.

"I'm sorry, honey," she says. "I'm not trying to make you mad. I think you do a great job at work, and I understand how hard it is for you to balance everything. All I'm telling you is that you are in a dream world if you think you can keep your life the same and become the President of Skyler Reed. And honestly, it surprises me to even hear you say that you wanted it. I never thought you minded working for Skyler."

"I didn't mind working for Skyler: I'm happy with my life right now. I just don't want her to sell it. If someone else is going to be in charge of it, I want it to be me. They are going to ruin it."

"You don't know that," Mira says. "Why not keep a good attitude about it?"

"The eternal optimist," I say, and Kerry and I both roll our eyes.

Our conversation doesn't make me feel any more confident about next week's meetings with Katrina.

6

It's Sunday night and I can't sleep at all. Tomorrow is our meeting with Katrina so she can school us all on the dark arts of outsourcing. I toss and turn. What should I say? What should I do? What should I wear?

I was thinking of another pretty black and white geometric dress and jacket, but we saw how well that went. Maybe I can blame the whole disaster on the baby poop explosion and me being stuck in a damn cardigan. This time I'm going professional, conservative, businesslike - a pantsuit.

I am out of bed rummaging through the closet. I try to be quiet, but I hear Pete toss in the bed. I get quieter.

Unfortunately for the businessy image I'm hoping to put across, I'm just not much of a pantsuit person. There is that D&G jacket from last week, but it's buried somewhere here, baby poop and all. I know, I know, I just haven't had time to get it to the cleaners. Don't tell my mother.

I pull out a several seasons old Gucci jacket (another consignment find). It's fitted and a little shiny with a big herringbone pattern and some cool stitching details on the shoulder and a modified military collar. Nothing like the tasteful Armani Katrina is likely to show up in, but hey once I add the black pants and boots, it is technically a pantsuit. I grab a fat red patent leather handbag with buckles and a few rivets. I am an accessories designer, after all.

I lay this whole collection next to the Lands End carry-all full of breast pump, laptop, lunch bag, and such. I try not to cringe when I think about how this behemoth destroys the effect of everything I've just picked out. Better than an old lady rolling shopping cart, I suppose.

The phone doesn't ring at 5 a.m., so at least the nanny is coming. That's something. I take the time to straighten my hair, so I still don't get to work until almost 9:00.

Our meeting isn't scheduled until 9:30, but Katrina is already there when I arrive. She is wearing a tan Armani suit with a shawl collar and a silk blouse. Her hair is again perfectly coiffed. She is standing in my office when I come down the hall. It is right next to Skyler's. Her laptop is open on my small table.

"Good morning," she says.

"Hi." I put down the massive bag behind my desk.

"You have a laptop?" she asks, looking at my docking station. "I will need a certain amount of privacy today, so it would be best if you could find some other space to work."

She waves airily as though we are in an expansive suburban

Life, Motherhood & the Pursuit of the Perfect Handbag

office park where there are dozens of empty offices.

I feel my eyebrow rise. Did she just kick me out of my own office?

"In addition, I think we can agree that it is of the utmost importance that I be close to the President's office, so that I can effectively manage the transition."

"The President's office?" I ask.

"Tom, our Executive Vice President for Direct Brands, whom you met at last week's meeting, will be serving as President following the transition next week," she says. "It's temporary, until a new President can be chosen for the brand."

"But this is my office," I say.

"Of course," she says. "However, it will be necessary for me to occupy this space following the transition. I am sure you can find someone to help you move your things over the next week. I'll be in on Wednesday to order office furniture."

She looks disdainfully at my Ikea desk. I like my desk.

I look at my bag. Let's leave aside the whole professional question of someone taking over my office – the totem pole, chain of command, etc. - but I need my office. Not for status, but for the sole fact that I can hook myself up to a machine and pump breast milk three times a day. There is a sign on my door, with a picture of a baby and a message – "if the door is closed, please call or email, but DO NOT OPEN THE DOOR".

"I need my office," I tell her.

She smiles, "I'm sure there is some other space where you

could work. I, in fact, prefer that team managers be on the floor, overseeing their people."

Team managers? I thought I was going to be Creative Director and handbags? That is an issue for another time. Right now, I need to get this office thing figured out.

"I have other, personal needs for the office," I say and point at the sign.

She looks at me uncomprehending.

"I have a baby at home," I say.

"Skyler had mentioned something of the sort," she says. Still clueless.

I am deeply uncomfortable talking about the pump. I have read enough breast-feeding propaganda to know that I should not be, but I am, so there you are. I feel like a cow hooked up to it, and I am excited that Gracie will soon be one and I won't have to do it anymore. But in the meantime, I am doing it, and I need somewhere to do it.

"I need the office to pump breast milk," I say, finally.

Her face has a look of utter disgust. Wow, so much for sisterhood.

"Surely there is some other place where you could manage such matters. The ladies room, perhaps, would be more appropriate."

The ladies room? The bathroom is an appropriate place for filling baby bottles?

I don't know where to begin.

"The bathroom is not a valid option," I say.

"Then a supply room, perhaps?" she says. "There must be somewhere more appropriate than my office."

We have a dark, small supply closet. It has a light bulb with a pull chain hanging from the ceiling. I doubt there will be room for a chair. I don't know if there is an electrical outlet. There certainly will be no space for my normal multi-tasking of designing, pumping, phoning and emailing using the hands-free double barrel features of my high-tech pump.

Just then Skyler comes in. She is actually wearing the full sari today. Just a few more days until her flight to India.

"Katrina is going to be using your office while she is here," Skyler says breezily. "Oh look, it's time for our meeting. Let's go to the conference room."

I defiantly carry my bag into Skyler's office. Skyler will have to find somewhere else to be for the 11:30, 2:00 and 4:00 pumpings.

The entire design team, handbags, shoes, belts and stationery, is crammed into the conference room, and Skyler introduces Katrina to everyone. Katrina sits at the head of the table, Skyler is at her right. I'm randomly stuck in the middle of the table.

Skyler introduces Katrina briefly. She calls her a leader in the industry and explains that she will be the new Creative Director and head of the brand. She explains that Tom Finnigan of Omni-Brands will be the President and that he will be coming up from New York two or three times a week to manage the new company. Jim Allen, who was also at the meeting last week, is the CFO.

55

Katrina stands primly.

"I'm here today to talk about offshore assembly and licensing of many of Skyler Reed's product lines," Katrina begins. "In my experience, offshore assembly is a crucial element in brand growth and profitability. Our goal is to concentrate on what we do best in this country – design, creativity, branding, and synergistic lifestyle optimization, while leaving the actual production to those who are less skilled and less developed."

She spends another half hour talking about case studies, manufacturing, and explaining how merchandising works.

I look at my watch. It is now 11:00. In a half an hour, I will need to go and pump. This meeting is showing no sign of slowing down.

This seriously goes against everything we've been telling our people for more than ten years. We've been saying that our value comes from our workmanship. That our price point makes sense because of the quality that our customers are guaranteed. That we are contributing to the common good by producing our handbags locally. We have received tax breaks from the Commonwealth of Massachusetts for just this reason.

Finally, I have had enough. Skyler is already checked out, but I'm not. There's no way I'm going down this road without at least registering my concerns.

"Skyler Reed was built around creating something different, about quality," I say.

"Pshaw," she says. Wow, I didn't know that anyone actually

ever said that.

"You are living in the past. You have to leave behind this old-fashioned model or else you can expect to be out of business within the next several years. This work is simply too capital intensive to perform as a cottage industry. Unless you are all hobbyists?"

She waits. As though one of us is going to volunteer that we're looking at this whole fashion thing as a macramé project.

"Off-shore facilities will provide the quality that we require at a much lower price point."

I can't keep quiet. "By nine-year-olds chained to their looms?"

"Of course you might feel that way," she says. "I understand that you have no ownership stake in the firm?"

Count on her to find my one weakness. It's true. I was the first employee, I've been here for eleven years, but Skyler has never made me an owner.

Katrina doesn't even need to see me nod. She knows already.

"That's what I would expect from someone who does not have a proprietary interest. What does the future mean to you? I can tell you the future: you grow, or you die. You can't stop growing your brand."

I'm not giving up – "But our customers expect…"

She smiles broadly for the first time today, showing a line of perfect bright white Chiclet teeth. She has me. I don't know how, but she does.

"Not to question your knowledge, but I submit to you that you have no idea about your *customers*." She actually makes air quotes as she says the word.

Nobody is looking at me now. I focus on a scratch on the middle of the conference table. I look at my watch. It's 11:30. My breasts are uncomfortably full. I had taken off my jacket in the hot, crowded conference room, and now I only have on a pale blue shell. I cross my arms in front of my chest and will them to stop the tingling feeling. There's no way I can leave the room now.

"Look at Burberry," she continues. "Gucci, Fendi, the list goes on. You can continue to deliver the same level of quality to your existing base – no one is suggesting that you change that – but you will be failing in your responsibility to the future of the firm, to these young people, if you ignore the opportunity to capitalize on your luxury image to develop lifestyle products for a larger, fashion-conscious demographic; yes they may not have $5,000 for a handmade leather baguette, or $20,000 for the version in python, but they can manage a $350 pair of sunglasses."

She stands and addresses the room.

"I understand your concerns, but I promise you that this is the way to build Skyler Reed into a worldwide brand. Trust me and look at my record of success."

At this point, she gets Caitlin to hand out a glossy reprint of an article about her and the brands that she's transformed. The mood of the room has changed; they all have dollar signs in their eyes.

I would love to say more, but I can feel the two circles of leaked breast milk on the front of my shirt. I can't even drop my crossed arms to put my jacket on without looking like a contestant in a wet t-shirt contest.

As everyone raises hands to ask Katrina questions, I rush out of the room and speed walk to Skyler's office.

I've got my kit going and I am focused on the picture of Gracie when I hear the knock at the door.

"Tess, are you in there?" It's Skyler.

"What do you want?" I ask.

"Can I come in?"

"No."

"But I need to talk to you."

"Dammit Skyler, I'm pumping."

"I'm coming in anyway."

I am facing her credenza with my back to the door anyway, so when she opens the door nothing is indecent.

She sits in the chair in front of her desk. I don't turn around.

"It's going to be okay, Tess," she says.

"After that? Jeesh, Skyler, synergistic lifestyle optimization? $300 sunglasses? Don't you remember that we just wanted to make handbags that women would love? Pretty, well-made, hip handbags, that would be great for working girls like us? Our bags are expensive because they are expensive to make, not because we want to make a lot of money…"

"Tess, I know, but it's just a company. Things change; we are a dying breed anyway. We can't change the world all by ourselves, can we? Also, I'm not sure if expensive handbags are really world changing."

"We certainly have done something nice for 100 women in New Bedford who wouldn't have much of a chance of a good paying job if it wasn't for us."

That slows her down. She loves the factory. She loved going down there and getting all noblesse oblige with the workers.

"They wouldn't close the factory; I'm sure of it," she says. Her voice sounds like a little child's trying to convince herself that Santa is truly real. "They're just talking about outsourcing for the other things, the new things they want to do."

"Skyler, there's still time, you can back out of this," I say.

She has a substantial pause as though she's really thinking this through. I've got her, I'm thinking. There's no way that she'll really do this. More than a decade of her life is tied up in this company. She loves being Skyler Reed and having her name mean something. Finally she shakes her head no, and I hear the bells in her earrings jangle.

"No, no, there's really not any way out. I've signed papers. Plus my condo's sublet. I already have my tickets for India, and it was a total pain in the ass to get a spot at the ashram. In fact, I'm leaving tonight. I came to say goodbye."

I turn off the pump, sure that perhaps I heard her wrong.

"You're leaving today?"

"Yeah, I just have to go home and pack."

"Well hold on and avert your eyes while I disconnect from this damn thing. I can't let you go without a hug."

She waits.

When I'm covered, I go to give her a hug.

"Tess, you're crying," she says.

"No, no I'm not," I say, covering my face with my hands. I don't want to tell her about all my fears. She has already said that she's not changing her mind. Also, Skyler hates crying. It makes her feel guilty even if she hasn't done anything wrong, and this time, she's definitely done something wrong.

"You're going to be fine. They'll love you. You always land on your feet."

I nod, afraid to say anything.

She pats my arm, grabs her bag and flees, closing the door behind her.

I sit down at her desk and weep. I'm crying for the girls we were when we started the company, I'm crying for the future of our firm, I'm crying at how much control I'm about to cede.

I hope Katrina can't hear me through the office wall.

www.skyler-reed.com/inside-the-handbag

Skyler Reed + Boston

Events   Our Obsessions   From the Creative Desk

The Inside of the Handbag

Big Changes at Skyler Reed

August 1 – It's all in the OmniBrands press release: OmniBrands, Inc. has agreed to purchase Boston-based Skyler Reed+Boston for an undisclosed amount. "We are pleased to add Skyler Reed to our family of brands," said Tom Finnigan, executive vice president of OmniBrands and acting president of Skyler Reed. "Skyler Reed is iconic, and the potential for licensing arrangements and multi-channel brand expansion make this acquisition an important part of OmniBrands' ongoing strategy for growth." Skyler Reed+Boston designs, manufacturers, markets and sells fashion accessories. The company sells its products through 30 stores, e-commerce and distribution through high-end department stores. OmniBrands has also announced that Katrina Aspinwall will be Creative Director and lead the brand expansion strategy. "Skyler Reed has great existing brand value that has never been effectively tapped. We are excited to bring Skyler Reed from a niche brand into the first level," Ms. Aspinwall said. Skyler Reed founder Skyler Reed will maintain an advisory role, but will not be active in daily operations.

Comments (15):

Lead Handbag Designer – Tess Holland
I am the Lead Handbag Designer at Skyler Reed+Boston. I live in a condo in a triple-decker in the Jamaica Plain neighborhood of Boston with my husband Pete, my son Jake and my daughter Gracie. We've decided we're too busy to get a cat.

AUGUST

7

You know how it is with old friends? You start off all fired up to talk about what happened to you, and then somebody else has something going on in her own life, and you end up talking about that, and then you get to the end and you realize that not only did you not talk about what was bothering you, it doesn't even seem like such a big deal anymore. Until you remember that it is.

That's what I'm hoping for today… I want to think about something other than my crazy life. I want to forget for an afternoon that Pete is working nights again, Gretchen is coming to stay sometime soon, and it's been seven weeks since last intimate contact; that next Monday is the first day under the new regime and I am terrified; and that this morning there was a cloud of fruit flies over my kitchen sink. Instead, I am hoping that someone else has something going on in her life that will take my mind off of my petty problems. Thankfully, my friends aren't likely to disappoint – not everyone has friends that can turn a three-year-old birthday party into high drama, but I do.

So the kids and I walk up the hill to Kerry and her husband Kevin's house – their little girl Madison is three today.

Their large green Victorian sits high on the hill that overlooks our condo. Back in the day, the people in their house owned the factories where the people who lived in my apartment worked their 18 hour days. I tease Kerry about that sometimes.

As we walk up, I see that there is still a blue tarp over the back of the house. They got the house as a steal, but it has been a lot of work. After its heyday, the house took a progressive path downward; single family house divided into nice apartments, then less nice apartments, and final conversion into flop house. In the three years that they've owned it, there has always been some kind of construction. Kerry says that the delay is because Kevin is very scrupulous and they have had trouble finding a contractor who measures up to his high standards. There are other words that I can think of to describe Kevin, but I'm not married to him, so I keep my mouth shut.

A ladder leans against the side of the house, and I see a guy in

Life, Motherhood & the Pursuit of the Perfect Handbag

paint-splattered carpenter jeans getting some things out of a van parked on the street. This must be the new guy. I get a look at him as we come down the street. He doesn't look like any of the guys that we've had do work on our condo. First he looks well under 50. Next, he's not carrying a huge gut over his belt. Third, he's pretty good looking if you go for the Celtic armband tattoo type.

He nods at us. "Good morning," he says, and it is clear he is mother-country Irish. I bet Kevin and Kerry love that. Kevin has a discreet shamrock tattoo on his ankle and Kerry has already enrolled Madison in step-dancing classes.

I smile, and Jake waves excitedly as he always does when he sees someone with a vehicle that is clearly used for work.

As soon as we turn the corner, Jake starts bouncing. Kerry and Kevin have rented a large inflatable pool with slide and sprinkler system. Landscaping is last on their list, so the front yard is still an expanse of asphalt left over from flophouse days – but you would never know it with the transformation that Kerry has worked. The party decorations are beautiful, like something out of a lifestyle magazine – flowered table cloth, a large wicker basket tied with a pink bow and full of party favors, a beautiful spread of food, two decorative buckets full of ice with drinks, alcohol in one, juice boxes in the other. I wonder how on earth she did all of this? Somehow she makes it look easy: high-power attorney on partner track at one of Boston's most well-known firms, party planner and fixture of the society pages. It helps that they have a full-time nanny, and Kerry's mom recently moved into a condo two houses down.

I am very glad that I went with the knee-length poplin skirt, crisp white shirt and belt instead of the shorts I was thinking of. It looks like I should be expecting photographers from Boston Magazine.

We are a few minutes early and as I park the stroller, I hear voices through the screened side door.

"Mommy, I need to go potty!"

"Kevin, would you please take Madison to the bathroom? I have to finish getting the food outside and the clown should be here in a minute," Kerry says, her voice has a pleading tone that you would never hear at work or in conversation with her friends.

"Dammit, Kerry, can't you see I'm in the middle of something?" This is unmistakably Kevin's bellow. "You were the one who insisted on having this damn party anyway, I have a lot of shit to do before I go out of town on Sunday. The fucking clown can wait."

I blush and feel like I've witnessed something I shouldn't have.

A second later, Madison spots us and streaks out of the house.

She has on a pink halter dress and a tiara sits in her strawberry-blonde hair. From a distance she looks like a little princess, until you look in her eyes. They show the real girl: a tiny daredevil, wild, hilarious and up for any adventure. Jake lets go of my hand and runs to her. They hug, yellow head next to red head. Every time they see each other, they do a hugging dance that always looks like it will result in both of them toppling to the ground, but most of the time they stay upright. This is especially good today because they are standing on a very unforgiving surface. Baby Gracie begs to be taken out of the stroller and allowed to crawl around on the asphalt. I hold her instead.

Kerry follows Madison outside. She looks like she came out of the magazine where her party is featured. She is tall and slim in a white and yellow sundress with her red hair curly and in a ponytail. If I didn't know she was pregnant, I would never know she was pregnant.

Kerry asks me to watch out for the clown while she takes Madison into the house to go to the bathroom. We don't say anything about Kevin and his bellowing.

I don't actually have to talk to the clown, thank God, and I avoid talking to Kevin, and pretty soon all of our friends are there and I'm just having a great time. And sure enough, a photographer actually is taking pictures for Boston Magazine.

I'm on my second beer; Gracie sits on the asphalt, her cupcake clutched in her dimpled hand; and Jake is making his 200th trip down the bouncy slide into the pool. No one has mentioned the fact that Jake is naked. I forgot his bathing suit, and it seemed like too much trouble to go back for it – I know, I know, but would you want to walk a half mile back home with two screaming children who are guaranteed to disturb your sleeping husband? No, I didn't think so. So my decision was: let my kid swim in his birthday suit or in one of Madison's many swimming suits? With the photographer there, I figured that down the road, Jake would hate me a little for naked ones, but that would be nothing on the trauma of pictures of yourself in a girl's bathing suit. That is rehearsal dinner joke material.

Mira's husband Raj is standing next to the pool directing traffic as six three-year olds and their little brothers and sisters fight for a turn. When we first met him, Raj worked in consulting and he was a suit-wearing, frequent-flying, corporate reorganization warrior. Since he got laid off and became a stay-home dad, however, he's gone off the reservation. He's grown a little pot belly, his hair is touching his collar, and his summer uniform has devolved to Cuban shirts, long shorts, Birkenstocks, flip flops. Next comes the sarong…

Mira is looking at him too. "You aren't going to believe what Raj said the other day. He said, 'me and the other moms went to J.P. Licks after our playdate.'"

"The other moms?" Kerry laughed.

"As a parent, I feel okay about it," Mira said. "I certainly couldn't travel to shoots all over the world if he wasn't doing it. As a daughter and daughter-in-law, I am terrified," she adds.

"Why?" I ask.

"Raj's parents are coming next week; what if he says something like that to them?"

"So?" I say.

"Tess, Raj's parents don't know he's not working," Mira says. Her tone says this is something I should have known for months, but it's the first I've heard of it.

"Wait a minute," I said. "They don't know? Raj has been home for almost 2 years – Amit is 3, Ravi's 1 – how can they not know?"

"We didn't tell them," she says.

"They've been to visit how many times?" Kerry asks.

Mira shrugs. "Four or five times, maybe? When we first started it was a really small lie – it was only going to be short term. Raj didn't feel like telling his parents that he'd been laid off from his consulting job, and we were sure he'd find something different. And then he liked being home, and our lives were going so well. Neither of us really wanted him to go back to work. But by then, we'd already been lying for a while, so we couldn't figure out how to bring it up."

"What do you do – how do you fool them when they come to visit?" Kerry asks.

Mira is one of those people who always looks perfectly at home, but right now she seems as uncomfortable as a pimply 8th grader looking for a seat at the lunch table.

"He puts his suit on and pretends to go to work," she says.

I let out a crow of laughter imagining Raj, putting on his suit like a kid playing dress up.

"What does he do all day?" Kerry asks.

"He goes to the library, coffee shops, takes long walks around Back Bay – he just avoids the kind of tourist destinations where our parents would be likely to take the kids," she says. "We've got to tell them this time, though – his parents are coming next week, and mine will be in town a few weeks later. They know each other, so once we tell one, the other will definitely know."

"Why end the charade?" Kerry asks.

"He's gained 20 pounds since he started staying home and none of his suits fit," Mira says.

Just then I hear shrieking coming from the direction of the pool. I have a bad feeling that my child might be involved. Jake is just that kind of child… Not that he's bad at all, he just always seems to fall into trouble.

No, Jake is going down the slide same as 200 times before. Still buck naked and dripping wet. His skinny shoulder blades jut out of his back.

In trying to figure out what the trouble is, I notice that suddenly, Jake is not the only naked child. Two or three other ones are out of their suits – in fact one of the boys is peeing in a flower bed before running back to the pool.

And then I notice Madison taking her little pink bathing suit off. This strikes me as a terrible idea. Jamaica Plain is a very liberal neighborhood. Most people would not blink at a naked kid, or even a naked kid peeing in the bushes. But some families are different, and sometimes things are different for boys or girls…

"Madison! Get the hell out of there! What are you doing! Get your damn clothes on!" Sure enough, there's Kevin's roar.

Kerry and I make it poolside at about the same instant.

Kevin turns and looks at both of us – his face is calm, but I feel terrible anger. Something about the set of his jaw…

"What in the hell, Kerry, why weren't you watching her? I mean, Jesus, she's just taking her clothes off in the middle of the party – what kind of girl does that? You've got to get her under control." He points his finger at Kerry. "I don't care what your friends do, my daughter will not expose herself to the world."

Throughout this tirade, Kerry is quietly apologizing – "I'm sorry, I'm sorry, I'm sorry, I wasn't paying attention, I'm sorry, I'm sorry…"

He stalks inside, clearly so angry that he can't remain social at the party. The whole time he's been excoriating Kerry, he's been looking at me. I watched Kevin steadily drinking all afternoon and I have the definite feeling that he wishes he could rip me a new one for letting my piece of crap kid give ideas to his perfect little girl.

I look at Kerry – She is red in the face.

"What just happened?" I ask.

"You know, he's just old-fashioned," she flutters her hand. Then she smiles, "I blame his mother."

"Well, yeah," I say. "I mean really, what kind of person lets their kid run around a birthday party naked anyway? The gall of some people!"

That gets a laugh from her, but I definitely decide that it's time for us to head home.

At home, the fruit flies are much worse. I decide to take the kids to JP House of Pizza and think about the kitchen tomorrow.

8

When Pete gets home Sunday evening, we are sitting on the front porch. The kids in their pajamas, me with an enormous glass of wine.

He's holding flowers.

I barely notice.

"Hey family, what's going on?" he says.

"Mommy says we have to sit outside until the spray of death has gone away," Jake says.

"Excuse me?" Pete looks at me.

"We have a drosophila infestation," I say. "Maybe you've noticed?"

Pete sits down next to me on the front step.

"Did I miss something?"

After last week's night shifts he had yesterday off for sleep, but then had to go back in for a few hours (a few hours being eight hours in medical speak) on Sunday.

He's been sleeping and gone so much that I'm sure he must

have missed the fruit flies in our house. They started near the sink, but they've branched out. They are in rooms that have never seen a fruit. Believe me, my kids are not allowed to eat outside of the kitchen and dining room area for a reason. But now there are fruit flies in the bathroom, in the kids' room, darting around our marriage bed. In fact, there is one backstroking in my wine right this minute.

"They are everywhere in our house! Fruit flies everywhere!" I know my voice is hysterical and I don't care. "I've thrown away all the fruit; I've taken out the trash; I scrubbed the inside of the garbage disposal and can I just say, yuck, yuck, yuck. I just contaminated our house with flying insect killer while the kids and I waited out on the porch in our PJs. All to no avail. I'm Ahab battling the white whale…"

"They're just fruit flies, Tess, they don't hurt anything," Pete says.

The least I could ask is a little understanding…

With our crazy, crazy lives, I have given up on being the perfect housekeeper. We have a cleaning lady who comes once a week (it would be more, but at $70 a pop, it gets expensive). Every week, I look at our dusty floors and grimy sink and I feel happy that someone has charge of cleaning them. But I pride myself on a clean kitchen. We don't go to bed with dirty dishes in the sink – even if that means that I'm up at 1:00 a.m. washing them. So I don't appreciate a bunch of fricking bugs coming in and taking over my house. Bugs mean dirty and that's all there is to it.

73

Are the roaches next? I can see them, packing their bags, prepping for the move into our house – 'hey, guys, the fruit flies called, they said the new neighborhood is great – old house, lots of places to hide, and man those kids can drop about a ton of food on the floor…' Mice? Rats? Raccoons? The potential list of vermin is endless. It's enough to keep you up at night feeling things crawling on your skin.

I must look wild-eyed, because he suggests we go back inside.

It's been over an hour, so it's probably fine.

Just inside the door, Pete knocks over a wine trap with his bag. It's a coffee filter set in a cup full of wine to trap the fruit flies. I also have laid traps using baby food jars with holes in the tops and little pieces of fruit in them. What can I say; nobody says that the information on the internet is all completely correct. I have some garlic hanging over the sink, but I think that's maybe the wrong pest.

The house still smells a bit like bug killer spray.

Pete picks up the can off the counter and reads the list of ingredients.

"Seriously? Tess, this stuff is toxic, you sure it's the best idea to spray it around the kids? Gracie is still putting everything in her mouth."

"Thanks for the vote of confidence, do you have any ideas?" I say.

"Leave them alone?" he says. "They'll go away eventually."

"Not an option."

"Did you call your mom?" he asks.

Now that's an idea – unbelievably not one that I'd thought of. My mom knows everything. She is literally the woman who has it all – great job, great family, beautiful home. My dad does do the cooking and gardening. I resist calling her because I have seen her surreptitiously run her finger along the shelf of a bookcase to see if I've been dusting. I don't want to admit my insect failure to her.

"Hopefully the spray of death worked, so that will be unnecessary."

I finally notice the flowers.

"What are the flowers for?" I ask.

"You. I know I've been crazy busy, so I just wanted to let you know that I missed you. (And I love you)." He whispers the last part into my ear. I put my arms around him and kiss him on the mouth. Starts as a peck and moves deeper when we both remember the peanut gallery.

"Did you guys eat?" he asks.

"Mommy gave us some pizza before the spray of death," Jake says.

"It's time for them to be in bed, I haven't had anything though," I say.

"Why don't I run up to James Gate and get us something nice and bring it back?" Pete says. He whispers, "We can meet on the porch, make a date of it."

James Gate is the Irish pub close to our house, and they have wonderful food – not cheesy Gringo Irish, but well-thought out, modern Irish food. I would love to go in person, but with a 7:00 bedtime, our kids are not good restaurant kids (except brunch – they love brunch). Date night on the porch is a close second, however, so I put the kids to bed while Pete goes to get the food.

He comes back, and we eat our food and the kids sleep peacefully, and we laugh and talk, and I even get to tell him a little about my fears for tomorrow and Katrina and everything.

Then we go in and we're getting ready for bed. My clothes are off and his shirt is off, and his body is just as strong and beautiful as I remembered, and we turn toward one another, taking one another in, and then a fruit fly comes into my field of vision.

I concentrate. I'm not ruining this, not for a fruit fly. I just have to check the bathroom, just to make sure. In the bathroom there are a cloud of them over the sink. Nothing has changed. The chemicals have failed me. The spray of death was worthless.

Aaaarghhhhhh.

I grab my robe and my cell phone and go to call my mother.

"Tess, honey, what are you doing?" Pete calls from the other room.

"Go in the bathroom – it's full of damn fruit flies."

"Tess, leave it alone."

But my mom has already picked up the phone. I describe the situation, and she recommends a special trap that she's used for years. She tells me where she orders it. When I get off the phone, I get on-line and order a box of the traps. How did I not see this before?

I go back into our room. Pete is already asleep. His mouth still looks angry.

I should wake him up, apologize and get it on. The fruit flies have totally put me out of the mood.

Pete rolls away from me when I get in bed.

9

It's Monday with the new team.

First off, we have a firm-wide meeting. Tom, Jim and Katrina are all in the office for the day. Last week, our conference room was off-limits, subject to some corporate IT tinkering.

Corporate – which is what we are all suddenly calling the OmniBrands headquarters in New York where the suits, PR, and marketing sit, has decided that we – now known as Boston – need videoconferencing capabilities. It is considered important for us to work collaboratively and synergistically with our overlords in New York City and the whole other operation full of proles like us in an office park off the Garden State Parkway in New Jersey.

Soon there will be a large video conference.

According to the receptionist, sandwiches have been ordered.

For most of us, this is our first experience with a corporate video conference or corporate take-out. We generally get Thai food. I feel a little ridiculous in my outfit today. I had decided that I've had enough of dressing conservatively to please Tom, Jim and Katrina. I put myself into that kind of a little box, and see where that got me…

So today I have on a vintage 1970's tunic – with gold embroidery on a white background. Above the knee. With purple tights (I cribbed the idea from Chloe) and knee high tan leather boots. I didn't know we would be videoconferencing with New Jersey. I'm sure this outfit would look totally everyday in Manhattan. But Jersey?

So, here I am in my new cube, sitting with my team. Everyone seems a little nervous to have me working close to them. What should they tell me about? Should they talk about their weekends? Should they mention anything about the transition? Ask how pissed am I at Skyler? Inquire if that Katrina woman is as much of a bitch as she seems? They are all whispering about how hammered they got last weekend. I am hit suddenly with exactly how lonely I'm going to be at work now that Skyler's gone. And old – did I mention old? Everyone around me is 25…

I look at the picture of my kids on the desk. At least Mira took it and it looks all hip and fun and artistic – I wonder how the Olan Mills family pictures of my childhood would go over here?

At a loss of what to gossip about, I give them the brief update on Mega Stores. They like our new bling-coated designs, and they've sent them off to Malaysia or wherever to be manufactured. They should hit the stores around October 1. We'll see them when everyone else does.

I make this sound upbeat.

Finally, we all go into the conference room. It's packed. I sit on a plastic chair next to Stacey from stationery and Therrien from belts.

A conference room in New York City and two in New Jersey take up three quadrants of our huge screen. The fourth quadrant is a PowerPoint presentation. Unbelievably, it uses one of the stock PowerPoint backgrounds – they've chosen one with dark blue and yellow – not too far from the OmniBrands' royal blue and gold, but far enough off to be noticeable. Are there no design people at this company? Times New Roman for text and Arial for headings. I really should not be wearing purple tights.

Tom Finnigan, OmniBrands Executive VP and our new President, stands at the front of the room. He is wearing a nice grey suit. I suppose in a nod to our being a fashion firm, he also rocks a striped shirt/polka-dot tie combo – in pastel shades. I'm sure there's a name for his tie, but we've never gotten into menswear. No pocket square though. I have yet to hear him say two words, so I'm surprised to hear that he has an Australian accent. How on earth did he get here? He is handsome in a nondescript Ken doll way – not a face that makes an impression five minutes after it's gone.

A pretty young woman, hugely pregnant and dressed in Liz Lange-style maternity business casual, runs the slideshow.

I zone out while he indulges in some corporatespeak about exciting new opportunities and synergies. Then a picture of Katrina fills the screen. It is full length and she wears yet another

Life, Motherhood & the Pursuit of the Perfect Handbag

pantsuit. It is clearly a posed photo taken by a professional photographer with great lighting. She sits on a credenza, holding a portfolio and looking serious.

She stands and thanks all of us for coming. As if we had a choice.

"As we bring Skyler Reed into our corporate family, I thought it was important for all of us to connect the resumes, experience and faces of the very talented individuals on our team to the names that you will be hearing. So I will introduce my team."

A PowerPoint slide flashes up with postage-stamp sized of each the department leaders, me from handbags, Linette from shoes, Therrien from belts, Stacey from stationery and Tera, our marketing director.

We all smile. This is hard for me because the postage stamp picture of me appears to have been taken from a camera without a flash on a day when I have all of my hair piled on top of my head and a cardigan on. I have a hazy memory of Caitlin taking my picture sometime last week, but I had no idea that it was going to be used for anything.

"Linette D'Aubrey brings several years of leading the shoe designs for Skyler Reed. Her shoes have been praised at the highest levels of our industry and have been seen on the feet of major Hollywood stars and on the most exclusive runways in New York, Paris and Milan."

Linette blushes. I'm not sure that anyone notices since sitting down she is barely visible in the sea of people. Linette's specialty is impossibly high heels, which might have something to do with her being four-foot-ten and needing heels to see over the top of a bar. As always, she is dressed head to ankle in black with her shoes making the only color statement – today royal blue suede short boots in honor of our new corporate parent.

Everyone claps politely. Katrina moves on.

"Therrien McClure leads our belt design, and he has taken an obscure design backwater and transformed it into a major profit source. What Therrien has done for belts will be our model for the transformation of Skyler Reed. Therrien has made Skyler Reed's belts a must-have accessory, and almost single-handedly changed the fashion silhouette over the past two years. I credit Therrien's outreach with designers, his marketing of Skyler Reed's distinctive designs and his collaboration with creators and customers for the amazing growth of this product line."

Okay, that's a little much. Sure, Therrien certainly was on the leading edge of the belted looks of the past season, but to single-handedly credit him seems strong. I'm sure he had a hand in writing that little hagiography. The work he has done with rivets is very nice, though. Besides, I know that his real name isn't Therrien. Back in Ohio, he was plain old skinny misfit Danny McClure. Not anymore though. He wears black jeans, a fisherman sweater and a blue and white striped scarf tossed around his neck. His black glasses give him the look of a French New Wave director.

She goes on to politely introduce Stacey (what can you really say about stationery?), who is just a little plump and always looks just like a librarian, and it occurs to me: She isn't going to introduce me.

This woman is not going to introduce me. I take a deep breath. I'm probably wrong.

Stacey smiles at me when her praise song is finished, but I can tell she wants to do another arm squeeze.

I realize that I may not have remembered to put on deodorant this morning. Great. Because sweat stains on a white tunic dress are exactly what I need today.

Katrina wraps up her show with praise for Tera's marketing prowess, including a long discussion of the amazing web presence.

"Now, Jim will talk about the logistics of how the firm will operate, and after lunch, I have some exciting announcements about the future of Skyler Reed within the Omni family."

She sits down.

My picture is still sitting up there on the PowerPoint slide. I wonder, am I the only one who can see it? Maybe it's like Banquo's ghost in Macbeth: invisible to all but Macbeth. By that logic though, this evil woman would be the one haunted by the picture, not me...

Tom stands.

"Katrina, aren't you going to introduce Tess?"

Now I'm blushing.

She looks flustered and kind of pissed. Did she forget? I know about Freudian slips, and I know about having things slip your mind, but is it possible to have a Freudian mind slip?

She stands back up, flips her hand in my direction and forces a smile.

"Of course, Tess. Well, what can I say? Tess is a busy working mother. She's been at Skyler Reed for many years and we are grateful for her knowledge of the history and former processes and procedures at Skyler Reed."

She sits back down.

That's it? A busy working mom? Processes and procedures? It makes me sound like an admin, like the office manager, like the person who makes sure that timesheets get signed for accounting. I was the Creative Director for crying out loud. I'm so mad that I pay no attention to Jim's speech about corporate consolidation. Surely someone can brief me later.

Lunch is a haze. I eat my sodden turkey sandwich and mourn.

Therrien pats me on the arm. Linette smiles nervously.

Tera comes over.

"Do you think they'll want us to keep doing the blog?" she asks.

"I have no idea," I say. "You'll have to ask Katrina. I sent you an email last night with some more ideas."

"I saw it this morning and posted it – I just don't know what they'll want to do with the site. I guess I'll learn soon enough. I go to New York tomorrow for a meeting with corporate marketing."

"That should be fun," I say.

"A barrel of monkeys."

Life, Motherhood & the Pursuit of the Perfect Handbag

I skip the networking for a trip to my supply closet dungeon to pump milk.

When I come out, it seems that everyone has gone back into the meeting. I put my little cooler of milk in the fridge and think of skipping the second half of the meeting.

Just as I turn to go back to my cube, Tom Finnigan, our new President turns the corner. Damn.

"Sounds like Mega Stores is really happy with the effort your team put in," he says.

I manage a smile. "Thanks, Mr. Finnigan," I say. "It was very different from what we are used to, but I think everything should come together nicely."

"Tom, please," he says. "We're all on the same team here. Come on into the meeting, Katrina has a big surprise."

He opens the door for me and ushers me into the room.

Katrina is already speaking, and I see her eyes on me. I know that she's wondering why I'm late and what I talked to Tom about.

I see Stacey holding my seat for me, and I feel a rush of gratitude.

Tom goes to the front of the room while I make my way over to my seat.

Sitting next to Katrina is the single best looking man I've ever seen, and I work in an industry full of good looking men. Tousled sun kissed hair, light tan, blue eyes, tall. He's got on a suit jacket and black motorcycle boots. I look at Stacey, Linette and Therrien; it's clear that they are thinking the same thing.

Therrien passes over his note pad with a scrawl – 'look familiar?'

He does, but I can't tell why.

Then, just as Katrina says the name, I know. He's Leo Magnusson, the fashion designer. We haven't ever worked with him, but his story is well-known. California surfer kid, went to Columbia, fell into modeling, from that into fashion design. His designs have been innovative and fabulous, and he's got great presence in front of the camera. He got a rush of publicity last year when Reese Witherspoon wore one of his dresses to the Oscars.

Why is he here? Guess I'd better listen to Katrina.

"Leo will be charged with the most audacious part of our expansion of Skyler Reed. Many of you already know that we plan to expand our traditional base in accessories to include licensed products such as sunglasses, home fashions and lifestyle accoutrements, but we have a major announcement today. With the addition of Leo to our team, Skyler Reed will release our first small line of women's ready-to-wear at New York fashion week this September. If all goes well, we plan to have a full runway show ready for next February's fashion week."

Clothes? We're going to start making clothes? We don't know anything about making clothes. Clothes are a disastrous business to be in – the profit margins are insanely small; accessories are where all the money is. People design clothes as an excuse to sell accessories and perfume. What are they thinking? Like there aren't enough luxury clothing lines? Now a fragrance line, that

Life, Motherhood & the Pursuit of the Perfect Handbag

would actually be a good idea.

"Leo will be working with our women's wear design team as well as the Skyler Reed team here in Boston to expand the line while keeping in touch with the Skyler Reed aesthetic and the goals of each season. By adding apparel to our brand umbrella, we will draw interest and attention to the brand at the same time that we are expanding our other product lines."

She turns her attention to the room. I can't guarantee that she's looking right at me, but it sure feels like it.

"This will not be easy. There will be doubters. There will be those who suggest that Skyler Reed is attempting too much. They will suggest that we should stick to what we do and not expand our brand. To them we must answer boldly – OmniBrands is not afraid to lead. We must not listen to those who demean and disunite us. This brand has tremendous potential, it is our job to bring it out and create a new, prosperous and leading-edge Skyler Reed."

I try to get excited – it might not be a bad idea, and Leo Magnusson really is a great designer. I just keep wondering what was wrong with the old Skyler Reed? We were doing fine, we didn't need rescuing.

After the meeting, I go to the front to meet Leo. I do not intend to give up my position as a leading design influence of the Skyler Reed aesthetic, no matter what Katrina Aspinwall wants. As such, he needs to know who I am.

I put out my hand and introduce myself.

Emily Roberson

His beautiful blue eyes crinkle at the sides.

"Nice to meet you," he says. "Nice purple."

He nods toward my outfit.

He smiles.

I hope he uses his powers for good.

www.skyler-reed.com/inside-the-handbag

Skyler Reed + Boston

The Inside of the Handbag

Events	Our Obsessions	From the Creative Desk

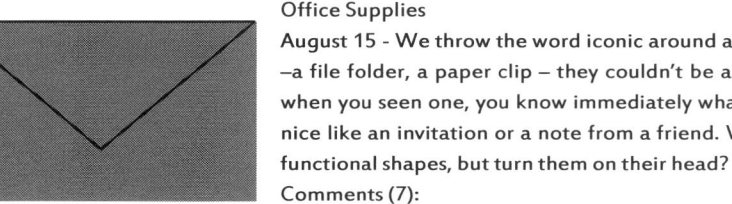

Office Supplies

August 15 - We throw the word iconic around a lot in this industry, but these designs truly are – a file folder, a paper clip – they couldn't be anything but what they are. I love envelopes – when you seen one, you know immediately what it is. To me, a small one suggests something nice like an invitation or a note from a friend. What about bags that reference these simple, functional shapes, but turn them on their head?
Comments (7):

Fashion Week Fast Approaching

September 1 - All is crazy here at Skyler Reed, as Fashion Week rushes in! You will all love the clothes.... (and handbags too, I hope!)
Comments (12):

Lead Handbag Designer – Tess Holland

I am the lead handbag designer at Skyler Reed. I live in a condo in a triple-decker in the Jamaica Plain neighborhood of Boston with my husband Pete, my son Jake and my daughter Gracie. Adding a gerbil to our family is currently under discussion.

10

Katrina does not believe me when I remind her on Thursday afternoon that I don't work on Fridays.

I stop by her office in a moment when the door is open and she is not on the phone. She doesn't stand up from her desk. I try not to remind myself how much I don't like the furniture she ordered – it's very 18th Century French. Not that I mind the 18th century, or the French, it just seems rather precious in our setting. I can't imagine anyone sitting in the spindly little chair in front of her desk. It looks sized for a child. I would likely break it and then have to pay for it or worse, endure a lecture.

She barely looks up at me as she speaks. "Certainly, we all need to manage our personal affairs from time to time, but the expectation is that we will all be here during business hours. I do wish that you had told me sooner that you would be out tomorrow."

I think about how best to answer this. I want to have this discussion without apologizing for my schedule. I'm not telling her that I won't be there this Friday, but rather that I don't work on any Fridays. I decide to go with the direct approach.

"I have always been very clear with everyone from Omni-Brands. I do not work on Fridays."

This is true. I have said it to every human resources minion, every person in my staff. It's on my voicemail and on my email messages. I am sure that I have even said it to her before, but I don't actually think she listens when I am speaking.

Fridays are my day with my kids. It's my day to recharge and to play at being a stay-home mom. We go to playgroups; we take the T to the aquarium and the Museum of Science. In the summer, we go to the beach sometimes. The three of us look forward to it all week long and Jake and I talk about what we might do – lazy home days or adventures. It makes all the long days with the nanny bearable. I do not want to lose my Fridays.

She purses her lips.

"I do not see how this can continue now that you are in a leadership position in the company."

Now that I'm in a leadership position? What the hell does she think I've been doing for all these years? Did Skyler tell them nothing about how this firm really operated? Sure Skyler was the heart of the operation, but all of the actual design tasks fell to me. Skyler didn't even know how to design the bags – she can neither draw nor sew. She brought in the ideas and the pizzazz, not to mention her incredible salesmanship and head for business; but the rest of it? The rest of it was all me.

I decide to be reasonable.

"I have held this schedule for several years of my tenure as creative director for Skyler Reed including three of our most successful years on record and the year we won a national design award. It has not been a problem."

I am still standing in the doorway to her office. People are starting to notice. I may have raised my voice a little there at the end.

She finally looks at me.

"That was when Skyler Reed was a small, parochial firm; we are now a part of a much larger world. I am afraid that it will simply not be possible to continue this schedule. It is unprecedented."

She has not raised her voice at all. She showed vastly more emotion during the brioche kerfuffle on the first day I met her.

I take a deep breath and calm down. I am on the right side of history. I know about the past ten years, the movement toward flexible schedules, best companies to work for, etc. I am going to embrace my role as an educator.

"There are several others at Skyler Reed who keep a flexible schedule, and it is written into my contract."

This stops her.

"You will be available by email and phone," she says. This is not phrased as a question.

"I always carry my phone with me," I say. "But I won't be at a desk working."

I turn to go.

"We will revisit this," she says. "I do not see how it is possible to have someone in a position of authority in this firm who does not keep a full working schedule. What sort of impression does that present to the staff? It is important that we set an example for those we lead; if we fail in our duties…"

She leaves the rest unsaid.

I do not say what I'm thinking, which is that we are not saving lives, just designing handbags.

I go into tomorrow knowing it is likely my last day of flexible schedule. What am I going to do, fight her in court? Get demoted so that I can prove a point? I wonder how much more the nanny is going to charge me for that additional day. I wonder if she'll even do it. Vanessa doesn't like working on Fridays either.

Katrina looks up at me again. She narrows her eyes.

"One more small matter, if I may have a moment," she says. "Please close the door."

I step into the office. I close the door. I have never been reprimanded. Skyler is the only boss I've ever had, and she's not in the scolding business, but the look on Katrina's face suggests something bad is coming.

She looks me up and down. She sneers.

I look down at myself.

I have on a new dress. It is Marc Jacobs. I will not say how much it cost. I'm not planning to tell my husband either. It was a treat, purchased to make me happy when so much else is not. It is jersey and blue, styled like a cap sleeved kimono with a wide belt and flower print on the skirt. I'm wearing it with high-heeled platform open-toed espadrilles, similar to the ones that Marc showed it with. I had a pedicure last week, so my toes can't be the problem.

"The world is watching Skyler Reed and OmniBrands," she says.

I nod.

"We are an important element of a major international corporation – in fact, this company is depending on us to grow and transform a sector that has been, quite frankly, lackluster over the last several years. You may not already know this, but Tom was brought in particularly to engage in a new strategy that would grow important segments of our business. He has promised that Skyler Reed will see a quadrupling in revenues within five years."

I nod again. This is all familiar from the meeting on Monday. Crazy in my opinion, but familiar.

"There are those who would say that he is not up for the task," she says. Her face is disapproving. She looks at me as though she suspects me of lurking among the naysayers. "There are those who would say that Skyler Reed is not ready to carry the weight of this company on its narrow shoulders."

"I would never say that," I say. I may not know what to think about OmniBrands, but I'll defend Skyler Reed's narrow shoulders to the death.

"I am glad to hear that. I tell you this, because going forward, it is important that each of us look like the representative of a major corporation. OmniBrands is traded on the New York Stock Exchange. Flights of fancy have their place, but not, I believe, in the leadership of this company."

Gosh is she glad I didn't pick out the bumblebee striped yellow and blue number I was looking at. I wonder what Katrina would have thought of Skyler's way of dressing? Maybe she would write her up for all her jewelry.

"As someone with director in your title, you represent Skyler Reed and OmniBrands whether you are in this office or out in the world. It is important that we show the utmost seriousness in our bearing and attire."

I feel that I have to throw something in here.

"I wear labels and designers who we work with and who reflect our aesthetic."

"Whom," she says.

"Pardon me?"

"Designers whom we work with."

"Sure," I say. I'm not going to be sidetracked. "This is new Marc Jacobs – if we can do half of what he's done with the clothing line, we'll be in great shape."

She shakes her head as though she is talking to a child. It is a look more of sorrow than of anger.

"I am not suggesting that you leave fashion to the side. No, rather, that you choose styles that are equivalent to your age and status. Look at me, I love fashion, but I know how to dress appropriately. Also, if one chooses to wear high fashion, it is important that one respect the designer and his vision, garder la ligne…"

I rack my brain for my high school French to try and remember what this means – watch the line? Oh, I remember. It means to stay slim. I am a size 8. By most standards, I already am slender. By my mother's standards, I am skinny. Katrina of the ropy arms and jutting collarbone must be a size 0. I have managed to work in fashion without developing a body obsession, but it's nice that someone is working to change that.

She has on Armani again today. I think I might have spotted one Arkis suit earlier this week and it wouldn't surprise me if she occasionally wears Escada on the weekends and Valentino for evenings on the town. I have never seen her in anything that is not a pantsuit. She has seen the one pantsuit-like thing I own, if you don't count a white Saturday Night Fever mistake at the back of my closet or a vintage Yves St. Laurent le smoking that I bought years ago in Los Angeles.

During this whole conversation I have been standing because of my refusal to sit in the tiny chair. Now I know how fitting models must feel. I leave the office feeling crappy about my Fridays and depressed that I won't be able to wear this dress to work again. Now I'm definitely not telling Pete how much it cost. Maybe I can sell it on eBay?

As I'm leaving, I run into Leo.

"You got a minute?" he asks.

I slow down from my breakneck pace and put down my enormous bag.

"Sure."

We walk to his office.

"Can you take a look at these sketches?" he asks. "I just want to see if they gibe with your vision of the Skyler Reed aesthetic."

"It's not really my vision you should be worrying about," I say wryly. How can he have missed that?

With a wave of his hand, he pushes away corporate politics.

"I know, I know, but believe me, other people will be happy with whatever I do. I just want to stay true to the brand that you and Skyler started."

I look over the sketches and swatches of fabric he has laid out. They have classic lines without being dowdy and interesting fabric choices. Just like old school Skyler Reed.

"These are good," I say. "I think they will really appeal to our customers."

"I'm glad to hear that. This whole practical design thing is a little new for me."

I remember some of his more outrageous collections and smile imagining Skyler's trunk show customers in his batwing jacket from last season... or in the fisherman net shirts from two seasons before. It's true that his client base has tended toward the very young, very fit, and ultra-fashionable. That's not totally fair though – he also has done some truly beautiful evening wear that anybody (or any body) could wear. However, $100,000 handmade gowns are not the market OmniBrands is shooting for.

He looks me up and down as I turn to go. A very different once-over than the one I have just endured from Katrina.

"Marc Jacobs?" he asks.

"Yeah." I wonder if I can tell him about the poor critical reaction...

"Good choice," he says. "I really like what he's been doing with shape."

"Thanks." I say.

He looks down at his desk.

"Hey," I say. "Do you think it's a little whimsical for the office?"

"Do you have another, secret, job as a banker? No, it looks great."

I want to ask if he thinks it's too young for me, or if I'm too fat for it. In my experience, though, a fashion designer will answer such questions with ruthless honesty. I decide that I don't really want to know.

On the train home, I receive this email from Katrina:

Review of your work by the Creative Director
I noticed that you sent an email with sketches and ideas out to the handbag team this afternoon, and I must ask that you clear everything with me before sending it out to the team. Please also cc: Caitlin, as she is tracking my correspondence for me. At this crucial time, it is of the utmost importance that I see everything that represents handbags, as it is our signature line. It would be quite a disaster if something were to get out that is not consistent with our brand image. Several of the designs seemed quite rough, and it

would be better if they were more polished before being sent to the team. In that way, the younger designers are not tempted to run off on their own. We are happy with the initial designs and we do value all your experience.

I don't even know what to reply. I'm supposed to clear brainstorming designs with the Creative Director and Caitlin? They are just the roughest first stages – will she want to see every single iteration? Wow, this is going to be a change from Skyler. And why Caitlin? Has Caitlin gone over to the dark side? I had noticed that she's been spending a lot of time around Katrina, always ready with her coffee, nodding vehemently in agreement with her pronouncements. I guess Caitlin is her minion now. I shudder to think what she will do when she finds out that I posted some of my ideas to the blog. Bad enough to share with the team, but with the world?

11

I get on the bus at 6:00 and I remember that we have nothing to eat. The idea of another meal of Trader Joe's burritos for me and Pete and frozen chicken nuggets and sweet potato fries for the kids deadens my soul just a little bit more.

I decide to call for sushi takeout from JP House of Seafood and pick it up as a surprise for everyone.

Dinner taken care of, I spend the rest of the bus ride rehearsing take-downs for Katrina and her evil plan to turn me into a corporate cog while she ruins my company (and I am grateful that no one is sitting beside me – although frankly I would hardly be the first person talking to herself on the bus).

When I get off, I notice a woman I've seen a thousand times, but never really thought about – she has a stand on the sidewalk where she sells jewelry, scarves and bags. Every day, she sits outside the post office on a folding chair, selling her wares.

I think about what would happen if I really told Katrina to

shove it. That would be me; selling handbags on the sidewalk. If I went out on my own, I would have no sales force, no marketing, no infrastructure, no factory even; just me and my stuff. Sure I know buyers and store managers, but that's no guarantee that anyone would buy anything. Also, there are all the up-front costs, and I don't have those. In fact, I have a family that is depending on the money I earn now. Without me working, how could we pay our mortgage?

So I get the sushi and come up the stairs dejected.

On top of everything else, I am petrified to tell Vanessa about Fridays.

She isn't going to like it. Vanessa is a 25-year-old artist, originally from Nebraska, who keeps herself in paints by watching my kids. She is working four 11-hour days for me as it is and she complains about that.

I smile when I see her, because I can still see the cornhusker, even though she's cropped her straw-blonde hair pixie short and has a collection of random earrings and a tattoo on the back of her neck. She's on the zaftig side, but that never stops her from showing a little skin. Today she has kind of an early nineties thing going on – halter neck sundress with a hot pink bra under it and heavy black boots. It scares me that I'm seeing things come around again so quickly. Can I really be that old? Based on Katrina's comments, I guess so.

"Cool dress," Vanessa says.

I left in such a rush this morning she probably only saw me as a blue blur.

"Thanks," I say. "The evil woman says it's too young for me."

"Dude, that's fricking crazy – you're only like forty, right?"

"Thirty-five," I say.

The kids are jumping and begging for my attention, but I still need to tell Vanessa about the Fridays.

"Mommy, Mommy," Jake pulls on my hand to take me back to their room to show me something that he found, while Gracie begs to be picked up.

Vanessa spots the bag. She often ends up sticking around to eat a little if we have take-out.

"Oh, sushi," she says.

"I got some extra dumplings, so you can stay and eat if you like. I have something to talk to you about too."

"I'd love to, but there's this thing – almost like a happening – and there's someone I think might be there… You know how it is…"

It's clear that the desire to avoid business talk has overcome the lure of free food. I don't want to press her, but it seems like a baloney excuse – what happening starts at 6:15 on a Thursday?

Jake pulls on my arm, but I will not be distracted. "Hold on, Jake, I have to talk to Vanessa for a minute."

So I'll just have to tell her. I tell Jake to bring whatever he found back into the living room; that should buy me a few minutes.

"Um, Vanessa, the horror show told me today that I can't take Fridays off any more."

"Balls!" Vanessa shouts and then the former-vacation-bible-school-student in her remembers to look sideways to make sure Jake didn't hear. "That's un-frickin-believable. Can she do that? Don't you have a contract or something?"

"No, it was always an understanding – nothing in stone." I decide to lie – better than explaining that I don't have the will or stamina to fight the Man.

"Damn."

She doesn't say anything else. No mention of how we might make this work. In fact her face has a look that suggests this is my problem, not our problem.

"Is there anyway that you could do Fridays?" I ask. "You know, Jake is going to start preschool soon anyway, and that should make things easier, and I'll definitely increase your pay to cover the extra day…"

Her face isn't softening.

"Please, Vanessa, please, how about only until after fashion week – it's that first week of September. I don't know what else to do. We need you. After I prove myself, I'll figure something out, I'll talk to people – I'll get the Fridays back."

"I'll do it until then, but after that, you'll have to figure something else out. I can only work so much before I can't create any more."

"Sure, sure, I completely understand. So we'll start next Friday. And I'll figure something out before the middle of September."

She's already halfway out the door as I finish.

I know, I know – I just guilted the baby-sitter into something she doesn't want to do – but I don't have another option.

Wonder of wonders, just after Vanessa leaves, Pete comes in the door.

"Daddy!" the kids both cry out, shocked to see him before bed time.

I put the food on the table, and then turn to Jake.

"Now what did you find that you wanted to tell me about, honey?"

"We were in the closet looking for umbrellas to play Peter Pan and I found this!" He holds out his open palm. It's Pete's hacky sack from college and med school. It's the crochet style, its colors faded from years of heavy kicking. Many of my memories of Pete from our early years together involve him coming up with elaborate moves to keep that sack moving, and whistling at the same time. Pete used to whistle all the time, just a constant habit. You could always hear him coming before you saw him. Funny thing, he hardly ever seems to whistle any more.

"Here, daddy," Jake says, and he throws it to Pete.

It's not a bad throw, and Pete catches it.

"Let me show you what it's for," Pete says.

He throws the bag up in the air and kicks it once, then again, like he's trying on the muscle memory. Then he does a whole routine with it – kicking, off the chest, off the knee, in some crazy move behind his head. By the end of it Jake is jumping up and down.

"Show me, daddy, show me. Let me do it. Please, please?"

Pete hands the bag back to Jake, and Jake throws it up in the air, but doesn't make contact with his foot.

"Can you show me how to do it, daddy? Can you teach me, please?"

I can see Pete take a look at his watch. I know he's thinking about dinner and bedtime and the amount of reading he has to do before tomorrow and how he can manage to get more than five hours of sleep.

"I'd love to, but it will have to be some other time. Look, mommy brought food, and then it will be time for a bath, she'll read you stories and get you guys to bed."

Jake's lower lip starts to shake.

"I promise, we'll do it another day, buddy," Pete says.

We eat together, then Pete goes off to read while I give the kids their bath and get them ready for bed.

After everyone's asleep, I find a beer in the fridge and go to look for Pete.

He's sitting at his desk in the spare bedroom. He looks exhausted as he reads from his huge textbook.

"Hey," he says, and I see a flicker of the light I love in his tired eyes.

He turns his chair around, and I sit across from him on the futon.

"How are you doing?" I ask. I realize that it's been a while since I asked.

"I'm okay. Tired, of course, but that's not new... Speaking of, I think I'm supposed to remember to tell you something..."

"That you love me?"

He smiles a little.

"No. Or yes, of course, but that's not what it is... Wait, I've got it – I got an email from Gretchen yesterday. She's definitely coming by the first of September."

Great, Gretchen. That's less than a month away. Just who I want to think about.

I can't be derailed by thinking about Gretchen. I only have a few minutes when Pete is actually home, awake and coherent. I have to use those precious moments to figure out what I'm going to do with my life.

"I don't know what to do about work," I say.

"What happened now?" He looks even more tired, and I feel bad about burdening him with all this – but I just don't know what to do on my own.

"The bitch took away my Fridays. Vanessa says she can do them until mid-September, but after that she doesn't know..."

"I'm sorry, babe. What do you want to do?"

"I don't know – do you have any ideas?"

"Why don't you quit?" he says. As though this was the most obvious idea in the world.

"Pete! I can't quit my job."

"Why not?"

"Supporting our family, for one thing."

"Don't forget, I'll be done with fellowship in June – then I'll be making more money. We can make due until then."

"Pete, this is Boston – there's no way we can support the four of us and pay our mortgage on your tiny salary."

"Hey," he says, offended.

"I know it's not your fault – it's just the way the medical gods make it; but it doesn't matter, we can't survive without my salary."

"I'm sure we could figure it out," he says. "I'll moonlight."

"You'll work more?" I say, incredulous.

"Fine, you could sell a bunch of these clothes and shoes on eBay. Mom told me all about it – she said her neighbor has turned it into quite a little business…"

"But what would I do then? I don't want you to support me while I stay home with the kids. I'm a designer!"

"I'm not saying you should stop designing purses or anything else you want. You don't have to work for Skyler Reed to be a designer. You've been doing it since the first time I met you, and that was years before Skyler Reed even existed. I'm just saying you should quit working for this terrible person if she is making you unhappy."

I bow my head and put my hands in my hair. I can feel the tears starting to run down my face.

"I just want things to be back to the way they were. I want to be the creative director for a major firm, and be making new designs all the time, and have happy customers, and a great relationship with my boss, and Fridays off to spend with my kids. And maybe an award thrown in now and then. Is that too much to ask?"

I'm trying to be funny, even as I'm half-sobbing, but it's all true. I do want all of those things.

Pete gets up from his chair and puts his arm around me.

"Tess, I don't know what to tell you. What I can tell you is that it doesn't matter to me where you work. I just want you to be happy."

I feel a long way from happy right now.

12

Friday morning, I don't tell Jake it's probably our last Friday together. Why spoil his day? Plus, he's two. Which I forget sometimes.

Anyway.

Gracie has heard a rumor that we might be going to our neighborhood playground, the Brewer Street Tot Lot, and she is bouncing in the stroller saying, "la la, la la," her baby word for Tot Lot. Keep in mind, she can't say mama or daddy, but man can she say Tot Lot.

But first, we stop for donuts. They had breakfast at 7:00, and it's snack time. Thankfully Gracie doesn't say munchkin yet.

Our favorite table is open, so Jake rushes over to grab it. This means that my kid knows how to get the jump on somebody and hold a table before he's even three years old. This and the fact that he gets excited about take-out Pad Thai mark him as an urban kid. I am almost entirely certain that I did not know how to hold a table anywhere when I was two and a half years old. In fact, I'm pretty sure that the only place my parents took us before we were ten was the drive-thru lane at McDonalds.

I get a massive ice coffee for me, a strawberry sprinkle donut for Jake (his pink aversion is ignored when it comes to strawberry donuts), and an assortment of Munchkins for the baby. After we eat, Jake throws away our trash, and then holds the door for me and the baby in her stroller. We walk out together into the sunshine.

I am so happy to be together and to have the sun on my face. Jake must be thinking the same thing, because he looks at me and says, "Mommy?"

"Yes, honey," I say.

"I wish you didn't have to go to work. I wish you could stay with us everyday."

"Well, I have to go to work to make money to pay for the house we live in."

He looks at me very seriously, like he has the answer to this problem.

"Mommy, stay home, we can live in the yard. That would be okay."

It occurs to me that this is the first time that I've answered his question this way. Before OmniBrands, before Katrina Aspinwall, I would have said that I go to work because I like what I do and that he'll feel the same way when he starts preschool in September – we each have something we do during the day and then we all enjoy our fun times together. Our time together is on Fridays and the weekends and holidays. And I am reminded again of how much I hate this woman for taking away my Fridays.

I don't have to rush him for once, and it takes us almost twenty minutes to walk the three blocks from the donut shop to the park.

As we walk, Jake calls out the types of cars that we see.

"SUV. Station wagon. Pickup truck. Car."

A few weeks ago, when we were all together as a family, Jake called out "station wagon" when he saw a Subaru Forester.

I said, "No, honey, that's an SUV."

Pete said, "It's actually a station wagon. Look, it's on a car body."

I looked. It looked just like an SUV to me. I decided it must be like handbags, something that some people care a lot about, and others not so much. So I've decided to trust the child's judgment on cars.

When we get to the Tot Lot, I see that Mira and Raj's two boys are already there.

Jake runs over to Amit and they hug quickly before starting a demolition derby with the riding toys. I lift the baby out of her stroller and take her toward the sand box.

I look for Raj. We don't plan it in advance, but he and the boys are often at the Tot Lot on Friday mornings too. It is a great opportunity for some adult, non-work conversation.

He's not there. Instead, I see his parents sitting on a park bench.

Or at least I have to assume that they are his parents. The man looks like the Indian version of the classic Midwestern parent visiting Boston in summer – shorts, socks pulled up, polo shirt, and a very large camera, while the woman has on a sari.

I go over to say hello.

"Hi, I'm Tess. We're friends with Mira and Raj and the boys. Where's Raj today?" I hope they are letting him have a break for a nap or a haircut. I wonder how they took it when Raj and Mira told them about Raj's decision to be a stay-home dad. It is promising that they are still here; if they were truly angry about it, perhaps they would have gone home.

"Yes, yes, nice to meet you," the man says. "I'm Raj's father. We are looking after the children today while Raj is on a job interview. We were quite surprised at the unfortunate news of his recent job loss – perhaps you had not heard? – it is a good thing that we happened to come just at this time."

They didn't tell them.

"No, I hadn't heard," I lie.

The baby is loudly complaining about the fact that she isn't in the sandbox yet, so I have an excuse to leave.

I call Mira from the sandbox.

"You didn't tell them!" I say.

"I know, I know, there just wasn't a good time…"

"What are you going to do now?"

"I don't know, maybe Raj won't have any luck finding a job…"

The Tot Lot is a park the size of one city lot; it has a sidewalk around the edges and a play structure in the middle. There is a sandbox, a see-saw and dozens of plastic riding toys that have been donated by neighborhood parents. The best thing about it is that there is nothing fun for anyone over five, so it is very safe for babies, toddlers and preschoolers. No marauding elementary school kids running around pushing little people.

I am helping Gracie push a little car around the sidewalk and watching Jake and Amit on the see-saw when my phone rings. I resent having to carry my Blackberry around on my belt like a stockbroker – not that a stockbroker would be caught dead in white capris and a melon-colored tank top with a ruffled collar that tastefully references the 16th century without looking ridiculous (I hope, although I am fairly certain it is not helped by the phone clipped to my hip). However, I don't have enough goodwill reserves to miss a call from work today.

It's Kerry. I had called her last night to tell her about losing my Fridays and the attack on my apparel, and to receive reassurances that at 35 I'm not actually too old for my clothes. She told me that I look fine and that Katrina was just jealous. Somehow I doubt that jealous is the problem.

"Great news," she says. "I called in sick this morning. Madison and I will be meeting you in a few minutes."

"Kerry, you never call in sick. You never get sick, and when Madison gets sick you make your mom take her to the doctor."

"I know, I know, but it's a special occasion. We have to honor your last Friday. Madison and I are taking you guys out for pizza."

She must have called from the car, because she and Madison park on Brewer Street two minutes after she hangs up.

There are four pizza places on Centre Street and after taking a poll of the kids we decide on That Same Old Place. That really is the name, but given how often we end up there, it's also the truth.

On the walk over, I complain to Kerry about my situation and my fears for the future. I try to make it clear that I'm really trying hard and not cherry picking at all. I'm just working for an evil, evil woman. Kerry hates complaining, so it isn't long before she starts throwing out potential solutions.

"Could you work for someone else at OmniBrands?" she asks first.

"Not if I want to keep leading handbags."

"Can you get her kicked out? How's the EVP? Kiss up to him and before long, you'll be Creative Director again."

"That seems awfully mercenary," I say.

She shrugs. "That's business."

"Besides she already knows everybody there. The CEO picked her. I've never even met him – just a video message, but apparently they are old friends. No way that they're booting her and putting me in her place."

"Would you do a better job?" she asks.

"Of course," I say.

"Then why not go out on your own?" she says. "You've been

part of something that started from scratch before. You just got through telling me the other night about how you wanted to be President of Skyler Reed. Why not be president of your own company?"

"But that was with Skyler," I say. "We were a complementary team – she has stuff I don't have: pizzazz, salesmanship, business sense, lots of friends, money. And I had a few things that she didn't have…"

"Like the ability to design a handbag?"

"Well, yeah, but that doesn't make up for all the other stuff…" I say. "I don't know how to run a company!"

"You are just scared. You know how to read a balance sheet and you understand how a business works. You're a good manager. You can design handbags people want to buy. You would do fine," Kerry says. She says it matter-of-factly, like I'm an idiot to not acknowledge that she is correct. She was very supportive and empathetic over an attack on my clothes, but this looks like business to her, and in matters of business, she has no patience for sissies.

"But Pete's gone so much, how would I manage it with the kids and everything?"

"Look at my friend, Corrine Downing Dailey – she has a successful design business, she has a daughter who is four, her husband works all the time – she does fine."

I remember Corrine Downing Dailey, I've seen her in Boston Magazine a million times and I met her at Kerry's. Her husband is a leading investment banker; they live in a row house in Back Bay.

"Kerry," I say. "They have millions of dollars. I could make this work too if I had that kind of money."

"Start your own business," she says, "maybe you will."

I can't bank on that. I have a family that is depending on the money I earn now. We need for me to have steady work, not dreams. I am in no position to go out on my own.

That does tell me what I have to do.

If Katrina wants me to wear a pantsuit, I'll wear the suit. If they need for me to work on Fridays, I'll work on Fridays. But I won't give up on Skyler Reed. If I can, I'll be the voice for quality and our values. That at least I can do (I hope).

13

If I'm going to wear a pantsuit, I need to own a pantsuit, so on Saturday morning I drop the bomb on Pete while he's drinking his coffee.

"Pete, can you keep Jake with you this morning?"

A long minute of silence.

"I have some reading I really need to do," he says. I appreciate that this reading is important – and yet, not quite 3-year-old boys make terrible shopping partners.

"I know, I know," I say. "But I have to do some clothes shopping and it will be easier if I just have Gracie."

He puts down his coffee.

"You have to do some shopping? We have two closets full of your clothes. My clothes are pushed into a corner in the children's closet. What could you possibly need?"

In the interest of addressing the current problem, I decide to skip this fight – one we have had more than once.

"My new boss doesn't think I look professional enough. I

have to get a couple of suits."

"That sounds expensive," he says.

I make a non-committal sound.

"You know we're well past the annual budget on this, right?" he says.

On the whole, Pete is understanding about the very large clothing expenditures required for my job. In this industry, it is expected that you will look a certain way, and there's really no way to do it on the cheap. I shop at resale shops and look for sales, but still it is a really massive portion of our annual budget.

"I'll be careful," I say. "So it's okay?"

"How long do you think you'll be gone?"

I make sure that Jake is out of hearing range.

"Pete, I don't know. It's not asking that much. He's your son. You know there are lots of families where the dad takes the kids every Saturday."

His face says, please don't start, but his mouth says, "Okay, okay."

"He likes to go to the Tot Lot, or you could go to Toddler Drumming."

"What's Toddler Drumming?" he asks.

"Just what it sounds like, a drumming class for toddlers. I know I've told you about it before. It starts at 10:30."

I write out the directions for how to get there, and wonder if they'll go. I stop myself from writing out a list of what to give Jake for lunch or his favorite activities. Pete is his father, not the baby-sitter.

As Gracie and I leave, Jake hugs my leg and cries, which I'm sure does nothing to make Pete feel better about the whole thing.

I decide that I am not going to rush home. For once, I can have a day alone with my little girl and Pete can figure out what to do with Jake.

I put Gracie in her small Maclaren stroller and we walk to the train. She giggles and sings the whole ride to Back Bay. She is a decoy-baby, the kind who makes people think that babies are easy – happy, easily entertained, independent.

Our first stop is a consignment shop on Newbury Street. I have to carry the stroller down the stairs to get in. Once I'm inside, it has that resale shop smell. I've been thrift shopping since high school, so it doesn't gross me out, but it's always there, cigarettes and different perfumes, a little bit of mothballs, and underlying all, the smell of people.

I ask if they have any high-end pantsuits in an eight.

I've seen the girl behind the counter dozens of times, but still she barely registers my presence. I'm not sure how much money you have to spend here before you get treated like a regular. Or maybe nobody gets treated like a regular.

She waves me over to the suits.

The very high-end suits are on one circular rack at the front of the store. Compare that to row after row of jeans at the back. There are three suits in my size. One of them is immediately disqualified by being tangerine orange in shantung silk with a mandarin collar – for $700. The other two are in black, and both are also very expensive. I understand that they are considerably marked down from the original price, but it still seems crazy to spend more than $500 on resale clothes.

I roll Gracie back to the dressing room and try them on.

I wore a jean skirt, flats and a tank top today so that I could try things on without too much trouble.

The suits are disastrous.

I do not have the right body for a suit jacket. I'm busty. Busty looks fat in a boxy suit, but in a one or two-button jacket that fits in the shoulders and waist, busty just looks smutty.

I put the suits back and wrestle the stroller up the stairs.

I walk into a few more stores and find affordable things that look cheaply made or things that are so expensive that I can't even think of buying them. In the expensive stores, the sales people pretend that they don't see me or the baby. I thought they were supposed to be alerted to cues, like the Skyler Reed bag hanging off the handles of the stroller, but the rest of my package must alert them to my amateur money-spending status.

I finally buy something in Banana Republic. It is black, it is boring, but at least it fits.

I drop by the Back Bay Filene's Basement and pick up two blazers that are really quite awful – seriously, one of them is silver sharkskin like something from Guys and Dolls and the other looks like it was intended for the Red Guard, but I just can't make myself try anything else on. It all looks so bad or incredibly boring and staid; not me. I decide that I will make due with the Banana Republic suit and put the blazers on over my normal clothes whenever I see Katrina approaching.

At this point the baby lets me know that she is hungry, so I buy us Wendy's and head over to the Public Garden to eat.

My handbag hangs off the handles of the stroller, the garment bags balance on top of the sunshade, and the Wendy's bag sits precariously on top of it all. I have a drink in one hand and am driving the stroller with the other. In theory, I could use my teeth to rescue the Wendy's bag if a strong wind blows. We make it across Arlington Street and into the public garden, and I am concentrating on not running the stroller into any of the children, small dogs or old ladies swarming around us. It is at this point of maximum distraction that I hear someone call my name.

I turn around and see Leo barreling toward me on a skateboard.

He jumps off inches away from us. The baby claps and laughs.

"Hey, what are you doing out here?" he asks and brushes his hair out of his face. He is still gorgeous – tan, big smile, hair streaked with gold. He's wearing knee-length plaid shorts that are recognizably from the same family of shorts my husband or his friends would wear, but transformed – a little tighter, a little longer, a little bit more detail. He has on a ribbed black tank top, tight enough to see that he is in great shape, and a black button down shirt, fitted, worn unbuttoned with the sleeves pushed up. He has a messenger bag with a thin strap over his shoulders, sunglasses hanging from the neck of his shirt and a big expensive-looking watch. He is also wearing black and white checkerboard Vans, a nod to the board, perhaps.

"I have a better question," I say, "what are you doing here? I thought you lived in New York and only came a few days a week?"

"I know, I know, but they put me up at the Taj, and I figured I'd enjoy the nice weather and stay in Boston." He points at the hotel across the street, the hotel that used to be the Ritz. It's still just as fancy.

I can understand why he'd stay in Boston right now. There are few things as beautiful as Boston at the end of summer. The flowers in the Public Garden, the tourists dressed up in their best clothes and headed toward Newbury Street, the Frog Pond on Boston Common, and the sailboats on the Charles. I like New York, but with Boston's intimate scale, you can see all of those things in a morning. I try to imagine the view from his window at the Taj in the morning. I try to imagine coffee from room service, not having a baby next to you in the bed, hey maybe just waking up to sheets that were recently changed.

"Rough life," I say.

"Well, there's not much bringing me home at the moment."

He looks momentarily sad. I wonder why. A breakup? Did the dog die? Did the housekeeper quit?

"You want to join us?" I ask. "You can eat Gracie's French fries – she only likes the chicken nuggets."

He shrugs. "Sure."

We find a spot in the grass, close enough to see the ducks and the big swan boats in the little pond, but not so close that the geese will try to steal our food. If Jake were here, I'd have to worry about him climbing trees or falling in the pond, but with just Gracie, the spot is perfect.

When I take Gracie out of the stroller, the whole precarious tower I have built topples over backwards. My shopping bags crash in a crumpled mess on the ground and my purse is squished by the stroller.

Leo jumps up to pick up the mess. "You have a bunch of crap balanced up here – what are you buying?"

"Oh, nothing fun," I say. "You can take a look if you like."

He frowns at the Banana Republic suit and then looks at the Filene's jackets like they are radioactive.

"In a word – why?"

"I have been informed that I must dress more conservatively to suit my age and status."

"Age and status? Who said that?"

"I shouldn't say," I say.

"You don't have to. There's only one person who would possibly say that. Well it's bullocks in my opinion - what is this, the Taliban?"

"Bullocks?" I say, teasing. "I don't know that I've heard Britishisms from a Californian before."

"My partner is British." He shrugs.

Well that answers that question. I would have leaned 60/40 not gay, but I didn't want to presume. I haven't even asked Therrien, who swears that his gaydar is flawless.

We eat in silence.

"You can't wear these," he says, finally.

"Why not? I thought I could just throw them over whatever I have on when Katrina is in sight. I'd be obeying the letter of the law."

He suddenly looks serious.

"Look, I'm doing a whole new thing here. I'm designing a ready-to-wear line geared toward working women who care about how they look but aren't models. I don't have a lot of practice in this. I am used to designing for models, actresses and socialites, who have full-time trainers, meals prepared for them, and bottomless dollars all at their command. What I do have is great design skills and a muse."

Just then Gracie pulls herself into my lap and starts nuzzling me. Crap. The baby is asking to nurse right in front of the world-famous fashion designer who is also my co-worker and could easily be completely grossed out by the whole baby thing.

I'm still trying to figure out what to do when Gracie starts whimpering while obviously and desperately pulling at my shirt.

"Are you going to feed her?" Leo asks.

"You don't mind?"

"Dude," he says with an exaggerated California accent. "I'm from Marin County; my mom nursed me until I went to kindergarten."

I pull the large scarf that I have for just this occasion out of my bag and toss it over Gracie's head as she settles into my lap.

We sit in companionable silence for a few minutes, looking at the garden, enjoying the day. Then he asks, "Do you know who my muse is?"

"No idea. I hardly know anyone in New York," I say.

"She's not in New York – she's in Boston – she works in our office."

"Who is it? Linette? It can't be Stacey? Maybe Caitlin?"

"The intern?" His voice is incredulous.

I shrug. "I give up."

"It's you, you idiot. You are clearly the imagination that produced the bags and your personal style is inspiring the line that I'm designing."

I am flattered for a minute, but then I think about all the things that he's just said about the Skyler Reed woman (busy, no time to exercise, no trainer, no meals made for her – in other words, kind of a chunk). Great.

At the same time, I'm blushing. I really liked the designs I saw the other day, and I'm kind of flattered that he was picturing me when he did them. Come to think of it, the woman in the sketches did look like me.

"So you have to listen to me," he continues. "I cannot change the fact that Katrina has instituted this ridiculous rule requiring you to wear suits, but I will not allow you to come to work dressed in this," he shakes the Mao jacket. "How will I ever design a whole collection if I have to draw my inspiration from thin air?"

"But I tried," I whine. "I looked everywhere and it was all, uniformly terrible. Dowdy, ill-fitting, ugly, awful."

"You weren't looking in the right places," he says.

I'm all buttoned up and the baby is now asleep in my lap.

"Let's take those back and do a little more shopping," he says.

I admit that I could use the help, transfer Gracie to the stroller and follow Leo back to Newbury Street.

He drops off his skate board with the valet parking guys at the Taj and they all act like this is the most normal thing in the world. I have a feeling that this is the default position of the world for everything that Leo does. How could he not have a sunshiny disposition? Between his amazing good looks and his California affability, people bend over backwards to help him. It must be a completely different view of the world than the rest of us get.

I see the same effect in Armani, where I stopped for two seconds with Gracie today before turning back around. Everyone pretended not to see me when I walked in. Not so with Leo. We have a salesman on us from the first second in the door. When Leo tells them what we are looking for, the salesman immediately makes the conversion from U.S. to European sizes and sets me up in a dressing room.

We are there for more than an hour. I try on suit after suit. Finally we try on the two best, and I see myself in the mirror in two beautiful suits. Both of them look like things I would wear, while also being infinitely more suited to a boardroom than the majority of my wardrobe. One is a belted blue and gray floral jacquard jacket with elbow-length sleeves and a slight puff at the shoulders. From a distance, the jacquard print looks a bit like snakeskin and I love the dissonance of something so beautiful looking vaguely badass from 100 feet away. The other one is a black skirt suit with ¾ sleeves and a black and white bow at the waist instead of the conventional button. The jacket has lapels and an open collar and it has a silky shell to be worn underneath that drapes without looking at all messy or slutty. The grey and blue jacket does not have lapels and is slightly open at the neck. Leo wants me to wear it without a shell, which seems scandalous, except nothing shows.

I have to admit that this is categorically different from everything else that I have seen. I also know that these things are tremendously expensive, far more than even my budget for such things.

"See, you look wonderful," he says, fussing with the collar of the grey and blue jacket as he looks at me in the mirror.

"Leo, I can't buy these," I whisper. "I can't afford them."

He turns away from the mirror to look at me.

"Who said anything about you buying these?"

Oh. I laugh in the way you laugh when someone makes a joke that you don't get. Was this just an educational exercise? I feel myself blushing.

"Okay," I say. "Well, I'll get changed. Are you going to tell them we aren't getting anything?"

I gesture toward the crew of salespeople who have now brought us drinks and offered snacks, and have rolled Gracie to a quiet corner.

"No, no, of course we're getting them. I was just saying that I never expected you to pay for them."

"Well who will? Not like I can charge them to OmniBrands."

"Me. I'm buying them."

This is thousands and thousands of dollars. Between the two suits and blouses, alterations and tax, this is at least $7,000, maybe $8,000. My mom would be horrified. I can't let him get them. Would I owe him something? Would I be prepared to pay him back if it turns out that he has nefarious motives? Maybe he's planning to blackmail me with Katrina, or something? Knife me in the back?

I look at that open gorgeous face and it seems unlikely that such scheming is going on. And the suits are so beautiful.

"I can't let you do that," I say, but perhaps not as forcefully as my mother would expect.

"I'm buying them," he says. "I'll put in a call to Giorgio and there's a good chance he'll pay me back – it's for a good cause."

"But…"

"If you leave this store without these suits, I will buy them for you and present them to you at work – in front of Katrina Aspinwall. How does that sound? Besides, you're a muse. I'm sure that I can write it off my taxes."

With that, I agree to let him buy me these beautiful clothes. I give my address to the salesman so that they can send me the suits once they've been altered to fit me perfectly.

I retrieve Gracie from the salesgirl who has been keeping an eye on her. The baby has just recently awakened, and she is gurgling and cooing. The hard Armani façade breaks for a moment when the girl says, "She is really a doll."

Gracie has that affect on people. I have wondered what it will mean for her future life, and I think that I have just seen it in the way the world welcomes Leo Magnusson.

"Where to next?" he says.

"No, no," I say. "Thanks for everything, but I have to take this little one home. I'm way later than I expected as it is."

"That's right; you have another kid, right?" Leo says. "Tell him I said hi."

He lopes back toward the Taj before he turns back around.

"What are you going to do with those?"

He points at the shopping bags balanced on the stroller.

"I guess I'll take them home. I don't really want to take them back right now."

"No, no, no, I'll take them. Keep the Banana one, but these Filene's monstrosities are going back."

"You don't have to do that – I'm sure you have other things to do."

"Nope, nothing else going on today. Dude, I like going to

Filene's. Here, give me the bag."

I hand over the shopping bag and head back to the T.

I call Mira from the train to tell her about the day. She says I have to take the suits back.

"No, no," I say. "It's okay – he says it's a business expense."

"You can't have a man that is not your husband spending thousands of dollars on you. It will make you look like a kept woman. Besides, how do you know there isn't some kind of quid pro quo?"

She sounds like my mother.

"No, no, it's not like that," I say, and I hope I don't sound too much like myself at 15. "He's gay."

"You're sure about that?"

"He mentioned his partner."

"Okay, fair enough. When are you telling Pete?"

"Soon. Just as soon as there's a good time to explain."

She is on a pretty high horse, so it seems like a good time to ask about Raj's job hunt.

"Well, there's great news, really," she says, her voice full of false brightness.

"Yes?"

"Raj got a job."

"Crap, you mean he's really been going on interviews? I thought he was just putting his suit on and going to town."

"That was the original plan, but his parents have organized the job hunt. They've been sending out the resumes. He has to go on the interviews or else they'll find out the whole thing is a sham."

"What did you tell them you've been doing for the past year and a half?"

"Independent consulting for two major clients," she says.

"Did you tell them the clients are two and four?"

She laughs.

"What are you going to do if Raj is working?" I ask. "Are you still going to be able to travel for shoots?"

"Um, it's a consulting job, but it's cool. It's for a firm that specializes in telling big companies how to go green. He's kind of excited."

I return to my earlier question. "What happens to your photography?"

"Does Vanessa work on the weekends?" she asks.

When Gracie and I walk in the house, Jake is jumping up and down with excitement.

"Mommy, mommy, look what daddy taught me to do!"

He takes the hacky sack out of his little pocket and tosses it up in the air, kicks it, and then catches it.

"Now try to hit it with your other knee," Pete says.

"Show me, daddy, show me," Jake says.

So Pete does a little of the routine he did the other day, but he does it slowly, so that Jake can really see what he's doing.

And I feel tears in my eyes.

We have dinner and put the kids to bed and fall asleep watching TV on the living room sofa and somehow the good time to tell Pete about a man I just met spending thousands of dollars on me never seems to present itself.

14

I walk in Monday morning with my new black Banana Republic suit and expect someone to say something. I do have on a vaguely silly sherbet-colored Phillip Lim tank top underneath, but it's barely noticeable. I am even carrying a rather subdued electric blue bag and wearing plain old black pumps. No ornamentation whatsoever. Not even an interesting heel.

I think at least someone should ask if I'm going to a funeral or a job interview, but no one does. As I make my cup of coffee and say hello to my co-workers, I remind myself that I'm not allowed to talk about my outfit with anyone because a) that would make me a whiner; b) no one else seems to have noticed that I'm dressed like a corporate minion, which means that no one pays attention to what I'm wearing, which means I've been wasting a simply tremendous amount of time and energy over the past ten years; and c) I have decided that I am in no position to bitch about Katrina Aspinwall, and any discussion of my wardrobe would lead, inevitably, to some amount of bitching about Katrina Aspinwall.

This decision not to complain about Katrina is almost immediately tested when I get back to my desk. There, as I unpack the mammoth bag filled with laptop, breast pump and other accoutrements, I hear a new voice.

"Medela?" the woman says.

I turn around and see the very pregnant woman in Liz Lange who was running the PowerPoint during the presentation when Katrina forgot to introduce me.

She points at my breast pump bag. It is unmistakable. The Medela Pump & Style comes with two carrying case options – a backpack and a shoulder bag. They are both black nylon and bear some small resemblance to early 1990's Prada bags, except they are not stylish at all. Partially this is because they are immediately recognizable to sisters in the know, and nothing says unstylish like dragging around lactation equipment.

"However did you guess?" I ask.

"Oh, I have my own, waiting in storage for whenever this baby decides to arrive. I'm Lauren, Tom's executive assistant. I'll be here this week getting the kinks worked out, then it looks like I'll be up here two days a week for a while. At least until everything gets settled – or this baby comes, whichever happens first." She is about my age, short and most-likely curvy when she's not enormously pregnant. She has long thick dark hair and a noticeable New York accent.

"Nice to meet you," I say, and I smile, because it is nice to meet her. It is nice to know that someone else in this building has the slightest clue about my life outside of handbags, and to meet a fellow member of the working-mother club. Although trying to come up to Boston from New York two days a week adds a layer of complexity to the whole thing that I can't begin to imagine.

"How old's your big one?" I ask.

"Oh, I've got two – a boy, Dylan, in kindergarten and my little girl, Madelyn, is two," she says.

"Mine are nearly three and seven months," I say. "How are the kids doing with you being up here?"

"Oh they're fine. My parents are right there and my husband has them the rest of the time. Honestly, a week apart from them seems like a vacation right now. Dylan is complaining, but he'll survive."

I laughs, and we both smile, and I turn to go back to my desk when she asks – "Hey, where is the pumping room? I don't remember seeing it."

Acknowledging the state of our pumping room/supply closet/dungeon would require me to say things that might disparage Katrina Aspinwall, which I have specifically resolved not to do, so I decide that I will just show Lauren the tiny room without comment. Perhaps this is the corporate standard for accommodations and not something to blame on Katrina at all (although I have certainly done my fair share of blaming while locked in the closet over the past month).

So I show her the supply room. My metal folding chair. The hanging light bulb. The way that my cord has to come under the door to plug into an outlet outside of the room. That it is still full of paper and toner so you have to worry about someone trying to open the door any minute. The lack of a lock on the door. She is silent and grim faced.

"Come with me," she says.

She takes me to Tom's office. Through the glass, we can see that Katrina is inside, but when Tom sees us outside his window, he holds his hand up to stop Katrina and calls Lauren into the office. I wait outside.

Several seconds later, Lauren leads him down the hall to my supply room, with Katrina in tow. Lauren is talking very seriously to Tom in a low tone. I hear something about safety code and morale and human resources, and I quite clearly hear her announce that there is no way, no how that she will be pumping in this dirty little shithole and that if Tom wants her to drive up from New York twice a week, something else needs to be figured out ASAP.

It is about now that I seriously consider peeling off. No one is paying attention to me, and perhaps it would be best if I just tiptoe away...

"Tess, have these always been the accommodations at Skyler Reed?" Tom asks. It's hard to read with his accent, but his voice sounds vaguely paternal.

"Well, no, but we never needed one before. It was just me, and I used my office, but then..." I leave out the part about Katrina stealing my office.

"And who chose the supply closet as a replacement?" Tom

says.

Tattling on my evil boss seems like a bad plan, so I say it was my idea.

"Surely, we can move this conversation to a more appropriate venue," Katrina interjects. "It does not seem comme il faut to speak about such matters in a business setting."

I curl my toes in my shoes. I have only known Lauren for 15 minutes, but I have a definite feeling that this is not going to sell well.

Sure enough – Lauren's head cocks to one side. I can see the full New York bubbling up, ready to unleash a torrent of words on the iceberg. Tom must see it too, because he puts his hand on Lauren's arm.

"It is enough to say that this is inadequate," he says. "Katrina and I will speak later today about working with the office staff to improve the situation. In the meantime, Tess, let me know the times of day when you need it, and you can use my office."

"Oh, no, I will be fine in the closet," I say. I almost say dungeon, which is what I've been calling it in my head.

"Times?" he asks again.

"11:00, 1:00 and 3:00," I say.

"Lauren, put that in my calendar for today," he says.

"But, Tom, your business is much too important," Katrina interjects. "It is so much time; so much time away and disconnected from the fast pace of our business. If we must displace Tess from the spot we have already so graciously accommodated, surely someone else's office, even my office, would be better used for..." She waves her hand in a manner that suggests such unspeakable things.

I can't tell if she's criticizing his offer of his office or the basic fact of my pumping.

"Oh, it will only be a day or two until you can get the room situation better worked out," he says. "It's not like I'm here every day. In fact, Tess, you are free to use my office on the days I'm not here for other things – phone calls and such. It must be strange to have moved from having an office to not having one. Make yourself at home in mine."

Katrina's lips tighten and she turns and stalks back to her office. I have a feeling that things are not going to get any easier for me. I don't think she even noticed my suit.

I do use Tom's office for the 11:00, and when I leave, Lauren meets me at the door.

"Wanna grab something to eat?"

I look toward Katrina's office. "I probably shouldn't. I've got a bunch of things to do."

"You gotta eat, right?" she says. "Besides, I saw her go out. She said something about a business lunch downtown. She can't be back until after 1:00, right? We'll just pick something up and eat it quick. I'll tell Tom on our way out, we can pick him something up – then we've got cover. Tom doesn't give a shit about face time."

It's not Tom I'm worried about, but we go together to grab

soup and sandwich.

As we eat, she asks me about how I get to work. I tell her that I take the train. It turns out that she does too. She asks me how I manage to lug the pump and everything else in with me.

I tell her about the Lands End bag.

And then I'm hit with a brainstorm.

"You know what would be perfect?" I say. "What if Medela partnered with a handbag designer to make a series of bags that could hold the motor and stuff? You could have enough of a selection that everyone wouldn't know exactly what you were carrying, and you could customize – make some that also have a compartment for a laptop, some that are small and delicate for people who don't need to carry so much other stuff. You could make a little purse that you could pull out for going to lunch or walking around the corner for a drink. If you think about how much people pay for handbags, and how much they pay for the pump itself, I bet it could really be a hit. Hell, you could even make it nice enough that someone could take out the pump itself and just carry the bag…"

"That's a great idea," she says. "All you would need is a corporation with enough experience and credibility to create a partnership like that."

"Yeah," I say. I can feel myself running out of steam as I think about it. "You would need to know the right people, and get in to see them. Probably there would be a lot of meetings. They're probably a multi-national corporation; I wouldn't even know how to get in the door."

Lauren is looking at me funny.

"Tess," she says. "You know that you work for a multi-national corporation, right? We do stuff like this all the time. I'll talk to Tom."

I think about Katrina. I think this is not going to go over well with Katrina at all.

"Maybe that's not such a great idea," I say. "Tom's got a lot on his mind. We shouldn't bother him with this…"

"Don't be a fricking idiot," she says. "Tom's going to need a million more good ideas if we are going to grow this company the way he's promised. Don't worry; he'll think it's great."

She's so confident. I don't have the guts to tell her I'm afraid of Katrina Aspinwall.

As soon as we get back to the office, we stop by Tom's office to drop off his lunch and I turn to go to my desk.

"Hey, Tom," Lauren says to my back, "you've got to get Tess to tell you about her great idea for partnering with breast pump manufacturers to make a kick ass mommy-bag. I'm sure it would sell through the roof."

Tom peeks his head out of the door.

"Tell me more," he says.

Crap. I turn around slowly. I consider stalling. I have not worked for Katrina long, but I know that she is going to want me to clear any big ideas with her before they get presented to Tom. However, he is the President of the company, and he just asked

Life, Motherhood & the Pursuit of the Perfect Handbag

me a direct question.

"So, there are only a couple of companies that make portable breast pumps, and they are all clearly not in the design business, and the carrying bags look terrible. So I thought it might be an opportunity to partner with one of those firms to make a series of bags that could hold a breast pump while also looking stylish."

"Is anyone else doing this?" he asks.

"Not that I know of, and believe me, I looked hard before agreeing to carry such a hideous thing."

"What are the firms?" he asks. His eyes sparkle and he looks as enthusiastic as I've seen him since he started here. "Have you done any research? Who should we talk to? Would they be interested in a partnership?"

"Whoa, whoa, Tom," Lauren says. "She just came up with the idea at lunch – give her a chance to breathe."

"Well, I think it's a great…"

Just then, I hear Katrina's shoes come tapping along the corridor. At first all she can see is Tom, so when I first spot her, she has the butter-melting smile that she reserves for him alone. Then she sees me. Her mouth flatlines.

When he sees her, Tom reaches out and brings her into our circle.

"Katrina, Tess has been telling us about the most wonderful idea for an expansion of the handbag business. I think it has great potential. You two should get right on finding ways to partner. Tess, work with Lauren to generate a list of the firms and the key decision makers. Get that to Katrina right away, and she and I will work on creating the partnerships. This is exactly the kind of creative thinking I like to see."

He turns and goes back into his office.

Katrina looks at me. Her anger is undisguised. She doesn't say anything, but I suspect there is a firestorm coming at me as soon as Tom and Lauren are safely back in New York.

I walk back to my cube wishing that I could learn to keep my mouth shut and wondering when I'm going to plan Jake's third birthday party for the weekend.

On the train home, I receive this email from Katrina:

Work on additional projects
It is very important that we all be responsive to the President. As such, please pursue the information that Tom requested. In the future, I would prefer that any communications with the President or his staff be routed first through me. Thus we avoid any confusion such as we saw this afternoon. I expect a memo from you on these matters by tomorrow morning. This must not delay any of your important work on the upcoming collection. I fear that we are not moving quickly enough to meet the schedules that I have established for the presentation of the new Skyler Reed.

15

It's Saturday after a brutal, brutal week of work. Somehow, I managed to get a memo with all the information about Medela to Katrina for Tuesday morning. I attended countless design and marketing meetings and made the drive down to New Bedford twice. At least with Tom and Lauren in the office all week, I avoided the dreaded tongue-lashing from Katrina.

However, now all the chickens have come home. Jake's birthday party is at 3:00 this afternoon and with working from home every evening and no Friday off, I am ridiculously behind where I should be organizationally. I broke open the Duncan Hines cake mix for cupcakes at 7 a.m., and now am madly trying to get everything cleaned and organized while they bake.

I decided to let Pete sleep in a little because he's post-call and he'll be on grill duty for the party. Without sleep there is a real chance of him falling asleep in front of the lighted grill. Leaving aside the possibility of physical injury, I can't stand the idea of listening to ten preschoolers whine about burned hot dogs.

Gracie must know there is something big planned for Jake today. She's just started crawling, and she's using her new abilities to follow him around and try to take things from him.

Right now they are in the dining room area that connects to our kitchen. Jake sits on the floor holding on tightly to his Power Rangers. He has two, one red and one blue. But Gracie isn't allowed to touch either of them. Gracie is supposed to be playing with her Little People garden set, but instead she's trying to get the Power Rangers from Jake.

"Noooooo," Jake screams. "The baby can't have it. She can't have it. It's mine."

He holds tight while she pulls on the red Power Ranger.

"Shhhhh, Jake," I say. "Daddy's sleeping. Can't you just give her the blue one?"

Gracie hits him hard on the head with a Little Person.

"Owww," Jake says, and puts his hands up to his head.

In his moment of inattention, Gracie grabs a Power Ranger and crawls rapidly towards the living room away from both me and Jake.

Of course, I'm much faster than a crawling baby.

I grab her, pry the Power Ranger from her chubby little fingers.

Then I drop the bomb.

"Time out, Gracie. No hitting brother. No hitting anyone for that matter."

I carry her to their room and put her into the crib.

I worry about Pete's sleeping, but I can't leave that hit unpunished, although I do secretly admire the sneakiness of it and how successfully it achieved her goal. The girl may have a future in business.

I close the door and she cries inconsolably – as though I had locked her up in the darkest dungeon instead of putting her into her crib with her stuffed animals.

She has one minute before I get her out.

Jake has followed me. He and I stand together outside the door.

"Mama, my baby is crying," Jake says.

"I know; we don't hit in our house."

"Mama, please get her out. She shouldn't be sad on my birthday."

I get her out when her time is up and then Jake gives her the blue Power Ranger unprompted.

That buys me ten minutes of peace to clean the kitchen before they find something else to fight over.

I stand in the kitchen thinking about what we have and what we may need. It won't be anything like Kerry's fancy birthday party for Madison, but it will hopefully be fun.

Then I realize: we don't have any cups or plates or napkins. I look in the cabinet. There are a few paper plates with Bob the Builder characters on them from his two-year-old party, but that's it. Using them would mean admitting that we didn't bother to get anything new for his next birthday – even if I could live with that, there are nowhere near enough. Other than those few plates, we have nothing to eat off of except our own dishes. The last thing that I want to do is carry my dishes down three flights of stairs before bringing them back up to wash them.

I call Kerry.

"Where did you get the cups and plates for Madison's party?" I ask. I seem to remember they were clear and not gender-specified.

"Let me guess, you didn't remember to buy plates," she says.

I sigh. "Just tell me where I need to go. And it'd better not be in New Hampshire, since it's already 8:00 and I still need to frost cupcakes and make burgers."

"Just come over here and get them. We have a million left over."

"Thank you, thank you, thank you," I say. "We'll be there in few minutes."

We are all the way downstairs before I remember that the cupcakes are still in the oven. I drag both kids back upstairs, take out the cupcakes and turn off the oven.

I think of taking the car, but then I think about how much I would hate to lose my parking space in front of our house. We take the double stroller instead.

When we come up to Kerry's house, we see the truck of the carpenter who has been working on the house since just before Madison's birthday. Jake spots him on a ladder and we all wave. As surprised as I am to see him there on a Saturday, I'm even more surprised to see that it's the same guy. Kevin would usually have found a reason to fire a contractor by now.

When we ring the doorbell, Kerry runs to open it and Madison and Jake do their super-cute little hugging, falling down together dance.

They immediately run to Madison's room to play with her toys.

Kerry's dressed casually in jeans and a button down shirt – I can tell by looking at her that these are not maternity jeans.

"Are you sure you are pregnant?" I ask. She's three months along with number two, she should be showing something by now.

She lifts up her shirt and shows that the top button of her pants is undone.

"I feel huge," she says.

"Please. I'd take your pregnant huge any day."

Gracie and I follow Kerry into the kitchen. I look around for any stray nails or circular saws before putting Gracie down on the floor to crawl around. By the time I'm in the pantry with Kerry, she's up on a step ladder before I can remind her that she's pregnant and shouldn't be climbing ladders. Just then, the phone rings.

The phone is on its jack all the way across the kitchen and Kerry is on the ladder with her arms full of paper plates.

"Hey, Tess, can you get that? Just take a message – It's probably a telemarketer, but Kevin's away at a conference, and I want to make sure it's not him calling."

I pick up the phone. "Gallagher's residence," I say.

There is a slight pause before a woman with a smooth, slightly British accented voice starts speaking.

"Oh, I'm sorry, I was expecting to leave a message," she says. "May I please speak to Mr. or Mrs. Gallagher?"

"I'm sorry, Mrs. Gallagher can't come to the phone, may I take a message?"

"Certainly. We tried to reach Mr. Gallagher by his cell phone, but it was not working or receiving messages – I was hoping he might check messages on his home phone before his arrival this evening. I am calling from the Cove Hotel and Villas. The Gallaghers are expected in the Honeymoon Villa this evening, but I regret to say that we have had something of a plumbing emergency, so we will temporarily replace the villa with one of our beautiful and luxurious suites. As soon as the situation is repaired, they may occupy the villa for the remainder of the week, if they so choose."

I am confused.

"I'm sorry, where are you calling from?" I say.

"The Cove Hotel and Villas," she says.

"Yes, and where exactly are you located?"

"The Bahamas," she says. "It is correct that Mr. and Mrs. Gallagher are planning to visit us this week, is it not?"

"Oh, of course, of course," I say. "I'll give her the message."

I hang up the phone and try to figure out how to tell Kerry what I just heard. I know that she isn't staying in the honeymoon villa in the Bahamas, because she's up a ladder in the kitchen. I know that Kevin is supposed to be at a biotech convention in San Diego for the weekend followed by a week long business trip to Ohio. I know this because Kerry told me how much she pitied him for having to hit both Cleveland and Columbus in one trip.

Maybe I shouldn't tell her. There might be some things it's better to not know. Then again, she is one of my best friends in the world, and if I hadn't been here, she would have been the one to take the call.

I decide to let her get down of the ladder before I tell her. What with her being three months pregnant and everything. Which reminds me, what a total asshole! Because I'm fairly sure that Kevin didn't rent the honeymoon villa in the Bahamas because he needs some time to himself.

"Um, hey Kerry, have you ever heard of the Cove Hotel and Villas in the Bahamas?"

"Sure, we went there on our honeymoon," she says. "Are you guys thinking of a vacation? That would be just the thing. As soon as you were looking at that beautiful view, smelling the sea air, this slow spot you're having would be gone right away."

"Who says we're in a slow spot?"

"Did you, or did you not tell me it had been three months since you'd had sex?"

"Almost four," I mumble.

"That's a season, Tess. A whole season! The last time you had sex it was spring. Just think about that for a minute."

"I'd rather not. But I didn't tell you that to give the impression that we were having any problems, I was just wondering if it was normal, that's all."

"Uh huh," she says.

Now we are very far away from where I was planning to take this conversation. I'm just going to look at it like a band-aid. The quicker you rip it off, the better...

"Kerry, that was the Cove calling to say that there is a problem with the villa that you and Kevin rented," I say.

Her face breaks into a huge smile.

"My God, I love that man – a vacation is just what I need right now. How sweet of him to surprise me. I wonder how he's going to get me on the plane? That's just like him. I hope he cleared it with my work. There's a lot going on lately, so I definitely can't take off with no notice... Has he already talked to my mom about taking care of Madison, I wonder? I'll have to call and ask her, in perfect secrecy, of course."

She practically dances over to the counter and picks up her cell phone.

I grab her hand before she can dial the phone.

"Kerry, the woman said the reservation is for tonight and all of this next week."

She sits down heavily on a bar stool.

"What does that mean?" she asks.

"That Kevin is headed to the Bahamas?" I ask, spectacularly unhelpfully I realize as soon as it leaves my mouth.

"Dammit, dammit, dammit," she says. Her shoulders sag and

Life, Motherhood & the Pursuit of the Perfect Handbag

she is crying and crying.

I hug her and almost start to cry too. Then I look up at the cups and plates on the counter. Jake's party! We still have so much to do for the party. This makes me think about Gracie, and it makes me realize that I haven't seen her in a few minutes.

"Um, honey, can you hold that thought? I think I've lost Gracie," I say.

"Oh, listen to me, just blubbering away and not even thinking of you, and Gracie, and Jake's party. Oh Tess, you have to get out of here. The party things are over there on the counter. You really should go."

"No, no, I can't go anywhere until I know that there will be someone here to take care of you," I call out as I search increasingly frantically for Gracie. I finally find her in the front hallway playing in the dog's water.

"Found her!" I yell when I come back into the kitchen holding my very wet baby.

Kerry is on the phone when I come in. She puts her hand over the mouthpiece and tells me, "You guys go ahead. My mom is on her way over. Don't worry; we'll be at the party this afternoon."

Her mom lives in a building two houses down, so we don't have to wait long.

It is torture to drag Jake away from Madison and out the front door.

I strap Gracie into the top seat and put the plates and cups into the rumble seat.

"Jake, honey, you are going to have to walk home," I say. "I don't have room for you to ride."

Generally Jake loves to walk, but not today.

I manage to drag him down Kerry's street, but when we get to Centre Street and the business district, he loses it. He wobbles his ankles and waves his arms around like a Star Wars Imperial Walker that's just been hit with a mass of rolling logs.

"Mommy, I can't walk," he says. "My legs don't work."

Then he sits down. On the sidewalk. On the disgusting, gum-stained, filthy, city sidewalk.

I grab his hand.

"No, no, no, buddy, you are not sitting down, not here. Come on, we just have to go home."

He doesn't budge. Then he looks me right in the face and yells, "I don't love you."

I don't love you? I don't love you? After I just did all this for his birthday?

I use my firmest librarian voice to tell him to come on.

Then he throws a sucker punch.

"I still don't love you, and you're not pretty."

Weren't you supposed to have to wait for junior high to get stuff like this?

"Stop acting like a baby," I say. "Stand up."

"Nooooooooooooooooooooooo." He actually lays down in the sidewalk and starts kicking his legs.

We are drawing a lot of looks.

One of the two older guys hanging out in front of the drug store says to the other one, "It's like we were back in the Sixties, man."

Then he yells at Jake, "Fight the power, dude, fight the power!"

It is at this point that I take Jake under my arm and firmly push our stroller toward home.

As we walk, I talk to Jake between gritted teeth. "If I have to carry you one more block, you are not getting any of your cupcakes. Not one birthday cupcake. Not today, not tomorrow, not the next day. If you can't tell me that you are sorry, you are not getting any cupcakes."

As we near the end of the appointed block, my message sinks in.

In a very small voice, he says, "I'm sorry, Mommy. I'll walk now."

I put him down and he walks at a normal speed, just like nothing just happened.

Right as we get to our door, he says, "I really do love you, Mommy. I was just saying that."

He doesn't apologize for saying that I'm not pretty. I remind myself that I am really not looking my best today.

When Jake was born, my dad said: 'he'll break your heart.' He wasn't lying.

I am not surprised when Kerry's mom brings Madison to the party. "She's hibernating," her mom says. "She told me, 'I'll think about it tomorrow.'"

I don't think Kerry has ever read *Gone with the Wind*, so her quote of Scarlet O'Hara's most famous line was probably unintentional. I, however, have fun imagining her as Scarlet O'Hara. A little Scarlet might be just what she needs in this situation.

Somehow we get through the birthday party unscathed, and Pete doesn't fall asleep in his chair until after he's grilled all the hot dogs.

16

Monday morning, Lauren and Tom are gone, and I have no protection from the wrath of Katrina.

I finally got the D&G jacket I wore at the beginning of this whole debacle cleaned, and I'm wearing it for luck today. Just to remind myself that it could be worse – that was an ambush, this is utterly predictable. I'm not sure if I'll ever be able to wear that cardigan again.

I actually manage to beat Katrina to the office for once and am just settling in with my coffee when she walks up to my desk.

"In my office. Now."

For a second, her mask slips, and she looks angrier than last week, brooding on my disloyalty has not helped the situation. In my most optimistic moments over the past week, I had hoped that my great memo and Tom's enthusiasm would let her own the project and gain me a little goodwill. Apparently not.

I take the walk of the condemned into Katrina's office.

When I come in, her face wears the brittle mask of politeness as she forcefully straightens the papers on her desk. I stand in front of her wishing I could sit down. This makes me feel very much like a schoolgirl who will soon be rapped across the knuckles with a ruler. I look at the tiny chair again and decide against it. I really don't want to break that chair today.

She doesn't look at me as she speaks.

"Please, do tell me, why it occurred to you to present an idea to the President of Skyler Reed? Who is also the Executive Vice President in charge not only of Skyler Reed, but of every single company in the OmniBrands universe, which, as you may or may not be aware, is a Fortune 500 company, currently traded on the New York Stock Exchange. In other words, Tom Finnigan is a very, very, busy and important person who reports only to the CEO. If every employee who had an idea presented it to Tom without first clearing it with his supervisor, what kind of company would this be? What sort of ship has every crewman running in to throw out his ideas about what to do to the captain? A drifting ship. A ship headed to calamity!"

"It's not what you think," I say.

"Oh, I know exactly what it is. You may have gotten used to just waltzing in and brainstorming with the President back in the haphazard, scatterbrained, scattershot Skyler Reed days. But that is not how it works in the real world. This is not a democracy. This is a hierarchy. It is very important that Tom see that any ideas that come to him from design have been considered from a business, marketing and tactical perspective. That means that you need to have the benefit and wisdom of my experience before presenting anything to the leadership of this company. If we are going to work together successfully, you are going to have to learn this lesson very quickly."

She looks like she might fire me on the spot. I have no shame at this point. No ego. I won't say anything about him liking the idea. I will not defend my right to speak to the President of the company if asked. Two weeks ago, I would have at least made an attempt at pushing back, but that was before my epiphany. I need this job. I don't have a Plan B. I will apologize, grovel if I have to.

"No, no, no," I say. "I just mentioned the idea to his assistant Lauren at lunch. I never intended to do anything without consulting you. Lauren told him herself – it wasn't me."

Her look softens.

"I understand. You should know that it's important not to get too close with Tom, his assistant, or any of the executive-level leadership. It can lead to perceptions of favoritism from others in the staff. I would recommend that you keep your social relationships with those from your same level and status."

Shell shocked, I return to my cube and my cold coffee.

Just as I'm considering whether to get another cup, Leo strolls into the office.

He has rolled up the sleeves to his suit jacket and he's wearing motorcycle boots again. Somehow he manages not to look ridiculous.

"Nice Dolce jacket," he says and he smiles that earth-moving smile. "If I'd known you had that one, I would have just gotten one Armani suit."

He's speaking in an intimate teasing tone, but I hope no one around can hear us.

"It's not a suit, though," I say. "I got it at a resale shop and they only had the jacket."

"You want to have lunch with me at the Taj today?" he says.

"We have meetings all day," I say. The Taj is famous for its languorous lunches, but they are not designed for working people – or at least not at my pay grade.

"Well how about Souper Salad then?"

"Sure – you know though – what is your social level and status? Because I'm supposed to keep my friendships at equivalent levels to my own."

"Well then, we can't have lunch – you're far too classy for me."

I laugh a little louder than I intend to, and I see Katrina's frosty glare as she sticks her head out of her office to locate the joy. And squash it.

I get my head back into the game, and barely look up from my desk for the next few hours. I grab soup and a salad with Leo and we talk design the whole way there and back. I eat lunch at my desk and am on the phone with New Bedford talking about some last minute design changes when I hear my cell ringing. I would generally leave it, but when I look at the number, it's Vanessa.

Vanessa is a fairly laid back baby-sitter, so I rarely get calls or questions unless it's important, so I apologize and hang up with

Life, Motherhood & the Pursuit of the Perfect Handbag

the factory.

When I pick up the phone, Vanessa sounds very upset.

"Gracie has a fever, and she is breathing funny, what should I do?" she asks. "She hasn't been very active all day, but now she really seems to be feeling bad."

Pete would get into a whole discussion about what kind of breathing and most likely recommend that she give some Tylenol and wait until we get home, but I am not so laid back about these things.

"Take her right to the doctor's office," I say. "I'll meet you there."

I call the doctor's office to tell them that Gracie is coming.

Now the hard part – telling Katrina that I'm cutting out at 2:00 in the afternoon just weeks before we show everything in New York. I don't like it either, but I don't see what else I can do. Pete certainly can't leave his patients to go to the Southern Jamaica Plain Health Center.

I knock lightly on her door and brace myself.

"You may come in," she says.

I take a deep breath and walk into her office.

"I am really sorry," I say. "An emergency has come up at home. I have to go to the doctor with Grace."

She narrows her eyes.

"Nothing serious, I hope."

"Just a high fever," I say. "It's probably nothing, but that kind of thing can be kind of a big deal for little kids."

She doesn't say yes.

"These next few weeks are of crucial importance for the future of the firm, and we are already handicapped by your inability to stay past 6:00. You must know that fashion is a 24-hour global business. It doesn't wait for our petty schedules."

I don't quite know what to say. The best I can come up with is – "Um, the nanny is taking her to the doctor right now, so I really do need to leave now to make it in time. I'll finish up and do my email and everything from home once we're done."

"If the nanny is already going to be there, I fail to see why it is important for you to attend. Can't the nanny can take her to the doctor? It is a simple thing really."

Words fail me.

"So I'll see you tomorrow," I say. I turn and leave.

I didn't hear her approval that I could go, but I am an adult and a professional, and really how seriously can I take someone who would suggest that I outsource doctor's visits?

When I get to the clinic, they've just called Gracie's name. Vanessa stays in the lobby with Jake while I go in with the baby.

It turns out that it's just the first ear infection of the season and the doctor prescribes amoxicillin. The wheezing was only a symptom of the summer cold that caused the ear infection. I keep my fingers crossed that there are not too many more of them.

17

Today is Thursday. Just two weeks before the New York fashion shows, and for once, I'm up at the office at 8:00 p.m., trying to get things done. I'm also hoping that I might get a little bit of extra credit from Katrina for the fact that I am staying so late. Even though I did go home early for the doctor's appointment on Monday, at least I'm not a slacker.

So I'm working, but I'm pissed off. I'm pissed off at Katrina for needing the face time, and I'm pissed of at Caitlin and any of Katrina's other secret minions for watching my comings and goings and reporting to Katrina. I'm pissed because me being here at all is just bullshit, all of this work could be done at home, she just doesn't trust that we are really working when we're 'working at home.' I'm pissed at Skyler for selling the company and making me put up with this crap. I'm pissed at Pete for having a job where I have to feel guilty about asking him to use one of his precious nights off to put the kids to bed. Most of all I'm angry at myself for caring what Katrina thinks about anything.

One of the most awful things about working for this evil bitch has been discovering that the pleaser/over-achiever in me still wants to win her over, even as it is abundantly clear that it is impossible. Between trying to please her and getting really angry and stewing about what she does, dealing with her takes up several hours of every week. And that doesn't include the time I have to spend clearing ideas with her and waiting for her response before I can send them to my team.

At 8:15, I decide that I am going home. Katrina is still in her office. It's clear that I'm not going to outlast her, and I decide that it is pathetic to try.

I pack my monstrous bag and head to the train.

One other time when I stayed late, I took a cab and expensed it (which was the way it always was back at the old Skyler Reed). Katrina raised holy hell about it. Tonight, I decide not to worry about it, I have enough grief with Katrina without adding an expense she won't sign off on. At the same time, I'm not spending $20 of my own money when I could ride for free on my MBTA pass.

It's not that late, and the way home is fully lighted. I look out the window. We still have a few more long summer days. It may even still be light outside when I get home. What could happen?

I have less of a good feeling about this when I get off the train at my station and it is pitch dark outside, except for the pools of light under the street lights. I call my sister Julia at the station and I have her on the Bluetooth as I walk the three-quarters of a mile back to our house.

A few people walk out of the station at the same time I do, but all turn off on other streets. By the time I make it up the hill, I'm alone.

I talk animatedly to Julia, telling her all about Katrina's reaction to the baby's ear infection. I hear a car pull up to the stop sign next to me.

The driver says, "Excuse me."

He's a young man driving a white Bronco. I don't notice much about him. He looks like a million kids I see every day, on the train, on the street, in the neighborhood. Nothing memorable.

"Can you tell me how to get to Jamaica Plain?" he asks.

This is a weird question. The whole neighborhood for miles around is Jamaica Plain. I can't quite figure out what he's asking.

"You're in Jamaica Plain," I say.

Next I see the barrel of the gun that he holds out the car window. This is memorable.

"Give me your fucking bag, bitch," he says.

I think of dropping my bag and running, but then I remember the pumped breast milk in my bag. No way is this punk getting my milk.

The street makes a T at the stop sign. To the left is the quickest way out of the neighborhood. To the right is my house. In a split second, it occurs to me that if I run in front of his car and to the right, he won't be able to shoot me without shooting out his own windshield. And most likely, if I start running, he's going to want to go left to get the hell out of the area as quickly as possible.

So without even thinking about it, I yell, "Fuck you, asshole!" and I start running. I run in front of his car and down the street toward my house.

As I run, I scream my head off. "Help! Help! Somebody call the police!"

I must be quite a sight – running, in heels, with my huge bag, screaming.

I hear his car turn to the left and he drives screeching out of the neighborhood.

I realize that Julia has heard everything and must be terrified.

"Someone just tried to rob me," I say, panting.

"Hang up and call the police!" she says.

"I'm hands-free, I can't find the hang-up button in the dark. You hang up on me and call Pete. Tell him to open the door so I can get in the house."

When I get home, Pete stands on the front porch waiting for me.

He swoops me into his arms and then hustles me into the building and up the stairs to our condo.

It takes me a long time to stop shaking.

Pete holds me tightly in his arms.

I have read before that if someone ever points a gun at you from a car, you are supposed to run. I have read that it is hard to hit a moving target. At the same time, I am pretty sure that the people who say this want you to throw your bag down and then run.

I'm not sure what made me do what I did – some mother instinct.

I wonder what the thief would have thought when he opened my bag of breast milk?

Pete and I have to go to the police station while our neighbors from downstairs watch the children.

I have to give a statement to the police, but mostly Pete and I do a lot of quiet waiting.

I wonder if it is time for us to move out of the city.

The policemen say that the guy went on to try the same thing in two suburbs to the south of us. If Dedham and Milton aren't safe, where is, I wonder?

I understand why people move to gated communities.

It is 1:00 in the morning before we get to bed.

I wake up knowing that there is no way that we can afford to move to a gated community. Hell, we can't even afford to move to the suburbs that he targeted.

I also realize after I wake up that the whole thing is funny as Hell.

"The Great Breast Milk Robbery."

Unfortunately, no one at work is going to find it funny.

If I tell Stacey, I'll get a lot of pity (which I'm already getting in spades from my family and my in-laws, all of whom were called by Julia, and all of whom left messages on my voicemail). If I tell Linette, I'll just get to hear her raft of mugging stories from when she was living in New York. Then I see the light on in Tom's office.

Yes, that means Lauren will be up from New York.

Lauren will think this is funny, or crazy, or both.

When I tell her, she does laugh, but then she says, "Why the hell didn't you take a cab? What were you doing on the train?"

Shit. Again I break the don't-complain-about-Katrina rule.

"Katrina says it's an unnecessary expense." I say as evenly as possible.

"What?!?" Lauren calls out loudly. People turn around to look at us. "It's company policy that if anyone stays after 7:00 they can take a cab home!"

I make a wry face.

"I'm telling Tom right now!" Lauren says. "This is outrageous."

"Oh, Lauren, don't bother him. Believe me, if I have to work late again, I'll just take a cab. I can pay for it, it's not a big deal…"

"Don't let me hear you talk like that – are you kidding? If you're staying late, we pay to get you home. Hell, I think Tom would say we want to pay for it. What would happen for OmniBrands if you'd been killed last night? It'd be all over the paper, and we'd have to find someone else to do your job. Sucks all around. Come with me."

"No, no, no," I say. "I can't. Talk to Tom if you have to, but leave me out of it."

No way I'm getting any more lectures from Katrina.

Sure I'd love to think that once she heard the whole story,

she'd feel bad about not paying for my cab, but I know it's not true. I'm sure she'll just lie to Tom about having denied it last time. If I'd been killed, I'm sure she'd find a reason to decide that I deserved it.

Soon afterward, Tom calls Katrina into his office.

She walks out 20 minutes later, looking sour.

When I get up to get coffee an hour later, she is in the break room talking with Caitlin and Therrien.

I overhear her.

"Really it seems to me like a desperate bid for attention… I mean really, if one chooses to live in a neighborhood in which such things happen, what can one really say?"

Therrien shoots me a look of apology, but I can't blame him – what can he do? We all work for her, and she's got him cornered. Caitlin is laughing – her I blame.

An email goes out from Tom at the end of the day, clarifying the company policy on taking taxis home if you must work late.

That night, at home, Pete looks up from his email to tell me that Gretchen will be arriving Saturday.

This would be Gretchen, my husband's kindred spirit… The one I kind of hate. The one who will be sleeping in this very room, which connects to the room I share with my husband.

I paste on a bright smile.

"Great! How long will she be staying?"

"Oh, I don't know, maybe a few weeks? It all depends on what happens. I think her visa should last a month or so."

18

Within 15 minutes of coming into our house, Gretchen throws away the chicken nuggets. She reads the ingredient list on the back of the box and nixes them.

"But they are from Trader Joe's," I whine, but she takes no notice.

I am of the opinion that if you bother to shop at a socially responsible seeming grocer (i.e. Trader Joe's, Whole Foods, your local co-op) you get a pass on reading labels. If it weren't healthy, why would they be selling it? Besides, my kids won't eat healthy food. Believe me, I've tried. I lose the argument when she gets the children to eat chickpeas for dinner.

She is exactly as I remembered her. Tall, outdoorsy, fabulously beautiful if you like that sort of thing. With her backpack, Vasque hiking boots, sweater and auburn hair in two braids, she seems to have stepped directly out of the REI catalog.

The children take to her immediately.

Yet another reason to hate her.

In the first hours with us, she manages to defuse several terrible situations without yelling, counting to three or putting anyone in time-out. Watching her, you would think that convincing a three-year-old to do what you want is a perfectly reasonable endeavor.

If I had an iota of self-respect (or energy) remaining, I would attempt to take back my children. As it is, I am grateful for the time she is giving them, as it gives me more time for work.

How sick is that?

I try not to think about it, and go into the office on Sunday to get a little bit of extra work done before Fashion Week.

When I let myself in the front door, I hear laughing voices coming from the back porch. It is a beautiful night and I try to remember the last time we just hung out on the porch and talked. I can't.

I stand in the pantry next to the window and, unseen in the darkness, listen to their voices.

It is Pete and Gretchen. The two of them lean on the railing, shoulders almost touching, as they look out at our back yard and the bright, clear early autumn sky.

"What do you mean you haven't been out here in months?" Gretchen says with a laugh. Her voice is husky and her tone intimate. "You have become quite the grind, if you can't see the beauty in your own backyard."

"There's just not time," Pete says.

"I hear that from you and Tess a lot," she says. "No time for an extra bedtime story or to let him get out of bed and check that you are really here; no time for a walk around the block to enjoy the beautiful night..."

"It's not like that, Gretch; you make it sound like we're neglecting them. We give them everything they need – and tonight, they needed to sleep... If you read them one more story, they'll want another, and another."

She laughs wryly. "And why not read it, and the next one, and the next one? Why are you living life, Peter, if there isn't time for the most important things? Do you think that they will be like this forever? You are missing everything, and for what? It's not as though you are back in the hospital in Nigeria, with people all around you dying of measles, yellow fever, cholera.

What do you have, managing chronic HIV and TB and endless ID consults? On the best day, maybe you get a real mess of a staph infection – not that it's nothing, but it's not worth neglecting your children... And Tess, handbags? Oh, wait, my children need me, but there is a huge issue with the strap placement on this purse... And the belts, we have to look at the belts..."

She breaks off, laughing.

"That's not fair," he says, but he's laughing too.

I drag myself to bed. I simply do not have the energy to deal with this today.

They look so comfortable out there, talking and laughing. When was the last time that Pete and I just stood outside and talked? When was the last time we sat together in companionable silence? Our jobs have taken a lot from us, but that has to be the biggest one. I know Gretchen doesn't think we do enough with the children, but at least we make time for them, we interact with them. But with each other, not so much. In fact, we both seem to view our time together as an opportunity to get more work done.

And with so much work and so little time, when we barely have the energy to talk, we certainly don't have the energy for sex. When was the last time? God, I don't know. Spring, it was spring. Once you've gone this long, how do you restart? I'm afraid to make the first move, afraid of what has grown between us. I am thankful for the gentleness he shows me: listening to me complain about work, holding me after the milk mugging, but our passion? Where did it go? Every time he comes close, I remember that he wishes he was somewhere else. And now we have Gretchen sleeping on the other side of the French doors, ensuring that I will not be in the mood. Before being a world savior was a dream he had, one I only vaguely understand from fund-raising letters and the National Geographic. Now we've got our own certified humanitarian hero sleeping in the next room. And she's hot too. I decide that I'm not going to fix it today. There isn't time. Fashion Week is only two weeks away and there is still so much to do.

SEPTEMBER

19

The next week is a blur of work as we frantically prepare for New York's spring fashion week, which starts September 6th. I always struggle to explain this to my mother – spring shows in the fall and fall shows in the spring.

Skyler and I had already laid out the theme for the season – travel and adventure with a focus on India, Skyler's idea of course. So it is a matter of combining what we already had with new designs – many of them abominations suggested by Katrina – and coordinating with Leo's clothes designs so that we can pres-

Life, Motherhood & the Pursuit of the Perfect Handbag

ent what Katrina calls "a unified vision" at fashion week.

It is in the middle of this that I get a call that Jake has finally gotten a coveted preschool spot. The only problem is that preschool starts on September 1. Fashion Week in New York starts on Saturday, September 6th. This is exactly five days after the first day of preschool.

We got on this waiting list the month that he was born, so there is no way we are not taking it.

The school is a fun-filled, happy-colored, natural-food, crunchy granola monument to our neighborhood's free-spirited hippiedom. It also has an 8:30 to 2:30 day, which means that I'll never be doing pick-up or drop-off.

For his first day, though, I think the child's own mother should drop him off instead of the nanny. I am especially proud of myself when I make that decision at the dinner table. Take that Miss "Tess has no time for her children" Gretchen.

Assuming that there is no drama, I can make that first drop off, run to the train and be into the office by 9:30. Maybe no one will even notice that I'm a little late. Now I know that this is blasphemy in the industry; in the days before fashion week, everyone is supposed to be a whirling dervish, flying around, acting like a crazy person, sacrificing everything including eating and sleeping to fashion. Nobody remembered to tell my little boy that he was on the chopping block, and I don't want to be that person who can't even take her kid to school on the first day.

I consider asking Katrina's permission, but I've realized that things go much better for us if I don't ever mention children in the office. If something happens to slow me down, I'll just have to blame it on the train. How much is really going to happen before 9:00 anyway?

So from the time I find out about Jake going to school, we talk about school. We pick out clothes. We buy a lunch box. He and Vanessa walk by the school and they look in the windows at the dark classroom.

At dinner Sunday night, he tells Pete, "Daddy, I'm a big boy. Did you know that I'm going to school? Mommy's taking me. Are you going too?"

"No, buddy, I'll be at work, but I sure am proud of you for being such a big boy," Pete says. Then they share a high-five. I feel so proud.

Monday morning, when Vanessa gets to our house, Jake is ready to go with his little lunch box in hand. I take his picture on the front porch. I can't believe my baby is going to school! I know, I know, it's just preschool, but still. He looks like such a little man.

I am dressed in the jacquard print Armani suit, which arrived from the tailors on Friday. I am aware that this may make an interesting impression on the other parents dropping their kids off out our preschool. I will make a fair guess that most everyone else will be dressed in some variation of mommy hipster casual (skirts or sundresses, silk-screened t-shirts, red Dansko clogs, long hair in a messy bun or twin braids, short hair pixie cut or looking like it was cut at home), or better yet, daddy hip-cat casual (t-shirt, jeans, All Stars or Keen shoes, heavy black rimmed glasses, often sporting some kind of hat). I'm sure they'll think I belong in the Back Bay, or better yet in the ritzier suburbs – I will have no time to explain that my boho-mama true self has been sent into exile by an evil dictator.

We walk over to school, and Jake keeps up his normal flow of chatter the whole way down the hill and into the turn. When we get closer to the school, I begin to see the first signs that this may not actually go so well.

First he stops talking, which is shocking in and of itself. Then he freezes on the doorstep.

I hold the door open and encourage him to go in.

Two families are in front of us, and a mom with a double stroller is behind.

I try to hold the door open for the mom with the stroller.

Her attempt to enter the building is stymied, however, by the fact that my kid stands squarely in the middle of the doorway and refuses to move.

I have to let go of the door, leaving her to her own defenses, and pick Jake up under my arm. Of course, this makes the Lands End bag fall off my other shoulder and hang as dead weight from my elbow. I wobble through the door, managing just barely to not fall in my heels.

I put Jake down and put the bag on the floor before it breaks my arm.

He lays prone and screaming in the middle of the hallway.

He thrashes when I pick him up and refuses to look into the door of the classroom when I show him all the things we've seen before.

We sit together on the bench outside his classroom and I try to get him to listen to me and tell me what is wrong. Finally I make out what he is saying.

"Gracie, snuffle, snuffle, where is my baby? Why isn't she here? I need her!" Then inconsolable sobs.

This never occurred to me. I didn't even mention the fact that Gracie wouldn't be coming to preschool. Of course she can't come to preschool – she can neither walk nor talk. That this would be a limit to the preschool experience is not obvious to the three-year-old mind, apparently.

As he hugs me and weeps onto my shoulder, I feel a certain callous hope that tear stains are a poetic metaphor and not something that can really happen to my incredibly expensive jacket.

Just then the teacher comes out of the classroom and sits down next to us.

She introduces herself to Jake, being careful to make eye contact without being intimidating. His crying slacks off a little.

"You think you're ready to come into the classroom?" she asks. "We're going to do a lot of fun stuff today."

And like that he's off. Barely even a 'bye, mom'.

Wow, I'm emotionally drained and the day hasn't even started.

I run into Mira by the bank of cubbies. Her son Amit is in

Jake's new class. Amit went to preschool last year, so they've done this before.

"Is it like that every day?" I ask.

"For a few weeks," she says.

"Wow, Vanessa is more of a softie than I am, I'm not sure she's going to be able to handle that."

She laughs.

"Speaking of Vanessa, can I have her phone number?"

"Sure, why?" In general, I would never, never give out our nanny's phone number for fear of poaching, but Mira and I have been best friends since freshman year. That guarantees that she wouldn't try to steal my nanny.

"I have a big shoot coming up and Raj has to travel for work. We just need someone to watch the boys over the weekend."

"Okay," I say. "You have arranged something during the days, right?"

"Kind of. Amit's here and stays for extended day until 6:00, and Ravi's at an in-home day care near our house. It's not perfect, but he is learning Spanish. It's just the nights and weekends that give us trouble."

That sounds innocent enough and it's up to Vanessa if she takes the work or not.

"Hey," I say. "Have you talked to Kerry? I hate to say it, but I've been so busy with work that I haven't even seen her."

"You should call her," Mira says.

I know, I know.

"She kicked Kevin out. He came home from the Bahamas to find all his Red Sox memorabilia on the sidewalk. Apparently, quite a few people thought it was being given away so a lot of it was already gone when he got there. He started yelling something about a Ted Williams rookie card and banging on the door. When he started kicking the door, the contractor who has been working on the house came around the corner and told him he ought to cool off and go away unless he wanted to make himself more trouble. The guy's bigger than Kevin and you know how Kevin feels about the real Irish. Apparently, the carpenter said he needed to get his head on straight if he was valuing a bunch of baseball cards over his wife. And, he said, 'and the next time you go to the Bahamas, you better damn well be taking that beautiful woman on a vacation, not whoring around with some slapper.'"

"What's a slapper?" I say.

She shrugs. "No idea. So anyway, that's the first Kevin hears that Kerry knows about the trip, and he starts crying and begging her to let him in to explain. Then the carpenter says, 'She ain't going to be listening to you today, friend. If I were you, I'd find another place to stand. You're making a spectacle of yourself, that's what you're doing.' So Kevin went back to his office with his bags, and from what Kerry says, he's been sleeping there."

"Or with the slapper," I say.

"Well, I didn't mention that possibility to Kerry, and you shouldn't either."

"What's the brave carpenter's name? Kevin's generally such

an ass, I'd be afraid he'd have beaten the guy up."

"Liam, she said his name is Liam."

"Well he's quite the knight in shining armor," I say. "I hope he's watching his back."

Then Mira introduces me to a few of the other parents, and it seems rude to not say hello and chat for a minute.

When I finally make it out of the building, it is already 9:45. So much for getting to work at 9:30.

It's only when I get to the train that I realize that my bag is still in the school building. Now I run in my heels back to the school, I have to knock to get someone to unlock the door, and when I see my bag on the bench, I have to crouch down walking past the classroom door so Jake doesn't see me.

It's 10:00 by the time I'm back on the train.

At least our big meeting doesn't start until noon.

20

I run into the office at 10:30 and I am met with ominous silence.

All the desks in my area are empty. The bank of offices is also silent and dark.

Crap.

I pull out my Blackberry and read my email.

There's an 8 a.m. email from Katrina rescheduling our noon meeting for 9:00. Perfect.

I kick myself for looking at a magazine on the train instead of checking email. Not that would have made the train move any faster, but at least I would have been mentally prepared.

I throw the huge bag under my desk and speed walk to the conference room.

I open the door slowly and attempt to sneak over to a seat. Basically everyone important at Skyler Reed is in the room and I am an hour and half late. This is the crucial meeting where we are finalizing the details on our presentation of the collection.

Leo smiles at me and motions to a seat near him.

Katrina stops speaking, and my hopes of being inconspicuous are dashed.

"Tess," she says. She flashes an icy smile. "So pleased that you could make the time for us in your schedule. Nothing important, I hope?"

She does not give me time to respond.

I squeeze past colleagues in the chairs around the edges of the room until I find my seat next to Leo at the conference table. He lifts his portfolio and it's clear that he's been holding the space for me.

"Nice suit," he whispers. "I saved you a seat."

"Thanks, preschool drop-off ran long. Why'd the meeting get moved up?"

He shrugs.

"She's almost done. You've got to hand it to her; she really knows how to organize one of these. The confirmed guest list is pretty amazing."

"That might have a little to do with you," I say.

"Well sure, the movie stars, but the big name editorial is her. Let's hope that we pull it off."

I feel like a naughty eighth grader talking to Leo while Katrina is speaking and I try to bring my attention back to the meeting.

My eyes glaze over as she talks with Tera about the menu.

I glance down at my notes and see a piece of paper that isn't mine atop my note pad. It's the beginning of a game of hangman.

Leo smiles.

I get the answer – it's Medusa.

I look at Katrina, a vision of tastefully arrayed corporate perfection. A lot of imagination is needed for the transformation to ancient Greek Gorgon – hair of snakes, chiton, chthonic atmosphere – the eyes, though, I'm sure the eyes were exactly the same.

For mine I do handbag. Easy, I know, but I'm trying to keep things on a more professional footing. Or as professional footing as you can have when you are playing hangman at a conference table during a very important meeting.

Leo is about to solve the puzzle when I hear Katrina say my name.

I pull my attention back to the meeting.

"Tess," she says. "We were going to do this earlier, but in your absence we delayed. Perhaps now you would be willing to share your thoughts about the display and presentation for the handbags?"

I stand and walk to the white board at the front of the room where I draw a quick schematic of the Asian exhibit halls at the Metropolitan Museum of Art in New York.

Unlike a fashion show where the clothes are sent out on the stage, what we are doing is more like a gallery opening. The handbags and other accessories will be displayed during an East/West themed lunchtime soiree in the exhibit halls at the Met.

How she pulled this off is something I don't understand. I don't have a clue about where you would even start in reserving the Met. Who do you talk to? How much does it cost? We always do a viewing of the new collection during Fashion Week (usually we get a suite at the Plaza) and we generally feed people, but nothing like this.

Our traditional audience is store buyers, stylists, the fashion press, and designers, but we never expect the designers to come to the viewing. They are far too busy putting on their own shows. We pull the designers in by meeting with them well in advance of Fashion Week to try to get them to show our shoes, bags and belts with their own collections. We have also had a good amount of celebrity exposure over the years, but that has been from targeting and marketing to stylists, not having the stars come themselves. There are a bunch of reasons for that, the single biggest is that it's expensive to have stars come to things – they expect special treatment and free stuff. We're happy to give away free stuff for exposure, but the celebrity fashion show circuit is a whole other story.

I start to explain the different ways that I had imagined displaying the handbags in the space. It is hard to know exactly how they will show, since all I have is maps and diagrams, and I haven't seen the Asian galleries at the Met in many, many years. I have already talked with Linette and Therrien, so we have the belts, shoes and handbags in pods that are related by color and theme. I have brought stacks of magnets from home to represent the different accessories and style groupings.

Leo comes forward to show me where he was planning to place the mannequins with the ten outfits he's designed. They are thematically tied to the handbags, so we will try to group them in ways that make sense. We move the magnets around the space, incorporating comments from the rest of the team.

After five minutes of this, Katrina interrupts us. "Frankly, I had expected a firm plan showing exactly where these things are to be placed. How can we be expected to work with the caterers to set up the stations if we don't know how the space will be used?"

I use a marker on the white board to try to show her that we have left space for the food stations, but are really just trying to decide the best way to show the merchandise.

She is unconvinced. I can see from her face that she is very uncomfortable with the level of collaboration in the room. People are throwing ideas around, upsetting the apple cart. It's anarchy.

"How can Caitlin be expected to set out the displays based on your doodling?" she asks.

"We will have tagged the items with a color, and I can certainly give her a firmer map, I just thought there might be some value in talking about it as a group before I made all the decisions. It wouldn't surprise me if between Leo, Linette and Therrien, it doesn't change a little bit once you get there anyway."

I say this in a way that is meant to be funny, but she doesn't crack a smile.

I see Tom lean forward.

"Excuse me," he says. "Why won't Tess be there to set up handbags?"

I look at the floor and try to make my face unreadable (which is one of those things that I seem to be constitutionally incapable of, but I really really try).

Katrina does her hand flick. The one that she uses any time something comes up that she feels is insignificant, barely worthy of consideration.

"We felt that it would not be necessary for Tess to inconvenience herself by attending Fashion Week."

"But won't the heads of the other product lines be there?" he asks.

"Certainly, but as handbags are our anchor line, I believed that it would be more than enough for me to attend as the representative of handbags as well as Creative Director."

Honestly, this is more than I've heard about it. It was clear from the very beginning of our planning for the Spring season that Katrina didn't expect me to be at Fashion Week. Although I found it upsetting that she wouldn't even consider me important enough to go, I actually haven't been for the past four years – between two pregnancies and the difficulties in managing childcare, it was something that I was happy to let Skyler manage without me.

Tom shakes his head.

"Tess was a founding member of Skyler Reed and her name is on as the leader of the handbag product line. It will look like we do not have confidence in the brand or its leadership if she isn't there. She should be there."

"Well, I suppose that we could arrange for her to take a commuter flight for the event on Saturday," Katrina says. "But to have her stay for the entire week with the rest of the team; well, the reservations have been made, everything has already been arranged. At this point, it is much too late to add another party to the group... Also, I'm sure that Tess has no desire to attend with her family obligations."

Tom turns his head and whispers something to Lauren sitting next to him.

"We will discuss the details at a later, more appropriate time," he says to Katrina. Then he looks at me, "I will say this, Tess, plan to attend Fashion Week in New York. I know that it may be logistically challenging, but it is important to me that you be there for as many days as you can."

It seems pointless to return to my diagram, so I go back to my chair and the meeting disperses for lunch.

As we leave the room, Tom stops me and Katrina at the door.

"Do you have a moment?" he asks.

Katrina hesitates before she delivers her full wattage smile. She wants to maintain her position as favorite, but she hasn't quite forgiven him for being nice to me.

"I was hoping for an update on the Medela collaboration initiative," he says.

Katrina looks confused.

"The breast pumps," I say. "In my memo I had identified some of the key staff, and you were going to explore any contacts or connections?"

"I have been quite busy," she says, her voice defensive.

"Oh, certainly," Tom says. "I know that it has been quite a matter to organize all of these different initiatives. I am afraid that we aren't the only people to have this idea, and would like to move forward on building those relationships. Perhaps we should have Tess contact the company and begin making the first inroads?"

"Oh, no, no, no," she says, and somehow she manages to rescue her tinkling laugh. "Tess is a designer – what does she know of marketing or corporate collaboration? As soon as Fashion Week is over, it will be my highest priority. It is at the very top of my list."

"I'm glad to hear that," he says. "Tess, Lauren will talk with you today about your reservations for New York."

With that, he leaves the room.

Katrina turns to me and in the moment that she turns, I catch a look of cold anger. She turns to leave without saying anything, but then turns back.

"Oh, Tess, I have been talking with Tera about our marketing efforts, and I think that the release of the new collections and the expanded brand would be a good time to change the character of our representation on the web. In the future, the 'From the Creative Desk' page will be penned by me as Creative Director."

Now she smiles and it is sick, because I can tell that she knew that it was important to me, and that she is very, very pleased with herself for having taken it away.

And I don't even have time to mourn or be angry, because I have to figure out what in the world I am going to do with my children during Fashion Week, which starts Wednesday. This Wednesday. Day after tomorrow. Shit. There's no way my mom could come in time.

Looks like I am going to have to eat some serious humble pie and beg Gretchen for help.

21

Imagine that you put on your best clothes and take the first express train from Boston to New York City. After arrival in Penn Station, you hop in a cab and arrive at your destination – one of the newest, most fashionable hotels in the city. The doorman who unloads your bags reminds you of a Weimaraner, both in the color of his coat and in his aloof but pleasant manner. He leads you into the lobby, where you are met by the concierge, a shockingly lovely young woman with a Russian accent, thin as a Borzoi. There is no reception desk – you are invited to have a seat, then another beautiful and smooth voiced young person brings you a drink (water, although he would be unfazed by a Bloody Mary), and asks you to wait for a moment, someone will help with your room.

Then you are met by the person who in any other hotel would be at the front desk, but here is a tall, curly headed blonde with a handheld computer (Standard Poodle, tastefully groomed).

She says that it will just take a moment to check you in.

Sitting in the beautiful and understated lobby – slate floors, cream colored suede chairs, teak plank ceiling – drinking your designer water, you feel like a very important person who has very important things to do.

But because the you is me, it is of course, too good to last.

There is no reservation in my name. How is that possible, I wonder? Lauren went into labor on Monday afternoon before she had been able to call the hotel, but Katrina promised me and Tom that she would have Caitlin take care of the reservation right away. I even volunteered to do it myself – but oh no, I was far too busy for such things.

I ask if there is a Katrina Aspinwall staying in the hotel. The poodle begins to look concerned and says that it is their policy to never give out the names of any guests.

Soon, the manager (Rhodesian Ridgeback) is standing at my side, his hand at my elbow, escorting me out the door. He's dreadfully sorry, but the hotel lobby is for guests and their companions only. I try to explain that I am supposed to have a room and that everyone else from my company is staying here. He says they will be happy to welcome me back when I am with someone who is actually staying at the hotel.

I did not pack expecting to walk. I even browbeat Pete into driving me to the train station on the way to work this morning. I have a huge rolling suitcase packed to bursting with high fashion, a laptop bag and my purse. I also dressed in a black long-sleeved dress and a trench coat expecting to be inside air conditioned hotels. I have folded my trench over the top of the roller bag. It is a lovely iridescent green Derek Lam that I hope does not get too rumpled. It is 9:30 in the morning and as I trudge down Columbus toward the upper West Side, the streets are still full of people going to work. They throw many dirty looks in my direction as I hog the sidewalk with my huge bag on my shoulder and my roller bag behind me. I am too downtrodden to even care.

I hope that by going in this direction, I can find somewhere to sit down, eat breakfast, have more coffee and improve my mood before I decide how bad my situation really is.

I remember a wonderful trip that Pete and I took before Jake was born. We stayed in a friend's studio apartment and spent all our money on restaurants: Cuban Chinese food, a great Dominican restaurant near our friend's apartment, a Tuscan restaurant on the Upper East Side. Most of all, I loved our leisurely brunches in sidewalk cafes near Central Park. I loved the people watching and the food. I loved imagining what our life would be like if we lived here. I wonder if there were any families trying to squeeze strollers into small restaurants on that trip? I wouldn't have noticed.

I manage ten blocks in my high heeled short boots before I realize that all the restaurants I had been imagining are actually only open for weekend brunch – and it's still only Thursday. I settle for an egg and cheese bagel and cup of coffee and I turn toward Central Park to try to find a place to sit down before I start making phone calls. I find an unoccupied park bench and after my coffee, I call Katrina.

"Oh, why Tess, have you arrived?" she asks. Her voice drips with false friendliness. "I hope you received my voicemail?"

"No, no voicemails – did you call my phone? I'm looking at it right now, and I don't see any messages or emails."

"Oh no, I called the phone at your desk – yes, yesterday afternoon at about 4:30? Surely you were there to see that I had called?"

Of course I wasn't there. Gretchen had interviews all day Tuesday, so I had to go a day behind the rest of the senior staff. So when I came to work yesterday and all the grownups were gone, I did what everyone else in the office did and cut out a little early. Not that any of this is her business, because I'm a damned handbag designer, so why does it matter whether I'm at my desk? Why in the world didn't she call my cell phone? I already know the answer. It is because she is an evil woman who lives to torture me.

"Nope, I must have missed it," I say, not conceding anything. "What was the message?"

"Only to say that Caitlin was unable to secure you a room at our hotel – they were all booked, it seems, for Fashion Week. After a great deal of effort on her part (and she really is under quite tremendous strain, with this being her first Fashion Week, and so much of the work that others really should be doing falling onto her shoulders) she was able to find you a room. I believe I have her note here – oh yes, it is the Holiday Inn Express off Canal Street in Chinatown."

I almost spill my coffee.

"In Chinatown? There was nothing in Midtown?"

"Really, Tess, I would think you would be more thankful; with Lauren's precipitous departure and Tom's last minute decision that you should attend, it really has been a great deal for Caitlin to juggle."

I give up.

"Where are we meeting?" I say. "I don't have a schedule."

"Oh, well the rest of us are headed to Badgley Mischka this afternoon and then a number of parties and events this evening. Unfortunately, given the late notice of your addition to our group, I was able to find no tickets for you to any of these events. It works out quite well, however, because we do need for someone to host our display suite at the hotel. As you know, we sent out many invitations to our long-time friends and the press to preview the collection at the hotel prior to the fête tomorrow evening. It would hardly do to have no one knowledgeable available to greet them."

"I thought that Caitlin was going to man the room."

"Certainly you don't expect that Caitlin, a woman with a bright future in our industry, should be relegated to room-watching while missing all the excitement of Fashion Week? Really, Tess, I thought you more of a mentor than that."

I can only answer with silence.

"So we will expect you back in the hotel by one o'clock at the latest. Oh and Tess, do be careful with your expenses – we are going to have to justify everything we do to corporate. I would encourage you to avoid cabs and take public transportation when you can. I will not be able to sign off on expenses that seem excessive, especially given the amount that your late addition has already added to our budget for this week."

And then she's gone.

I look at my watch. My 5:15 train put me into New York City at 9:00, but I have already sucked up the entire morning on this hotel business. There is no time to go all the way down to Chinatown and come back, especially if I'm lugging my bags on the subway. There's no reason to be early either, however, since it will just give me another opportunity for humiliation at the swanky hotel.

I am dragging my bag around Central Park when I see the unmistakable shape of the Rose Center for Earth and Space at the Museum of Natural History. I walk the extra blocks, then sit on a bench outside the museum, watching the families go into the museum. I feel maudlin.

I try not to remind myself of the stark disconnect between my last trip to New York, when I was with Skyler and we won a major award. That trip we stayed at the Plaza, where we have always hosted a suite to show the new season's bags. I love the Plaza. Katrina immediately nixed it – stodgy, conventional, so not Skyler Reed, she said. Skyler loved the Plaza too. Heavy curtains, velvet, high thread count sheets – she always said the Plaza made her feel like she was living in a movie.

After an hour of ogling other people's children and wallowing in my misery, I get up, turn around and hike back to the hotel.

The doorman cannot decide whether to smile at me or kick me out, so he looks the other way.

Thank God, Linette, Therrien and Caitlin are standing in the lobby when I walk in and I sidle up to them quickly before the poodle or ridgeback spots me.

"Hi guys," I say. "Can you sign me in or whatever, so I can get to our suite and put these bags down?"

Therrien clears his throat.

In a moment, the poodle is at his side.

Therrien explains our situation and the poodle graciously leads me to the suite. It is as though she has never seen me before. That makes things easier.

I don't see Katrina before they go. I resist the urge to say something nasty to Caitlin about my room. I know it is only Katrina's evilness that is making the poor girl choose between us. It does make me sad that our sweet little bunny of an intern would have chosen the Wicked Witch of the West over me. I do notice Caitlin's been straightening her hair and narrowing her eyes a lot more lately, so perhaps she thought she needed harder edges and sharper elbows to make it in fashion. Perhaps she's right.

I look perfunctorily at the display of handbags before settling into one of the butter soft grey suede sofas and opening my laptop.

Lately I've been reading Jake books of fairy tales from all over the world. The tales and illustrations are so rich and strange that I've been scanning images from them to pull together for a possible collection. With this spring's travel/East/West story told, it's time for the next one.

I open a new window and begin to compose a blog post. Then I remember – I don't have a blog anymore, Katrina took it away. I close the laptop and pace.

Why can't I start my own blog?

It's not like my name would have to be on it. I can keep it under the radar. It's not like anyone reads these things, right?

I open a blogging website and look at the instructions. It seems easy enough.

First I need a title… The first one I come up with is Going to Hell in a Handbag, but it seems a bit pessimistic. I need one that presumes the current struggles will eventually end. I need for it to be about my pursuit of happiness. Then it hits me –

Life, Motherhood and the Pursuit of the Perfect Handbag

I start typing.

www.lifemotherhoodhandbags.com/home

LIFE, MOTHERHOOD & THE PURSUIT OF THE PERFECT HANDBAG

September 6 – Does plaid deserve any attention...?

What is the craziest use of plaid you've seen – Sex Pistols punk tartan? Britney Spears? I've got a new one. We got a book of Celtic folktales, and it has the single weirdest plaid outfit I've ever seen. There's this two-headed giant named Gogmagog out tearing up the countryside. He's tall as a mountain and shirtless with super-tight, ripped tartan trousers. It looks like the Incredible Hulk meets the Edinburgh Military Tattoo. This has gotten me thinking about other unexpected uses for plaid... But then, do I really want to bring plaid back? Will the return of sexy schoolgirl skirts be my fault?

Comments (0):

About me

Since I was a little girl, I have dreamed about handbags... I am the lead handbag designer for a well-known firm. I am also married with a preschool son and a baby daughter. We were thinking of getting a gerbil, but are afraid it will be too much work.

22

After four interminable hours in the suite, I have seen no one, but I have a great start on my blog.

I ignore Katrina's advice about economizing and take a cab to Chinatown. If she gives me crap about that one, I'm calling Lauren on maternity leave and telling her about the Holiday Inn Express. Even Katrina should be terrified of a woman one week postpartum.

In front of the hotel, I check out a stand selling knock-off handbags. Sure enough, they have some Skyler Reed stuff. The shapes are the same, labels identical, but the workmanship and materials? Yuck.

I don't begrudge women for buying these – most people can't afford a $2,000 handbag, I know that. At the same time, these disposable bags are so far from what I want to do. I want my bags to be heirlooms, not landfill fodder.

On that happy note, I schlep into the Holiday Inn.

Couldn't be more different than the palace of luxury. But

at least I know what to expect; a Holiday Inn is a Holiday Inn. There's a front desk, an elevator, and no one kicks me out of the lobby.

I get some pretzels from the vending machine and go up to my room. Once I'm there, I kick off my boots, change into my PJs and call my kids. I don't tell Pete about the disastrous trip. Everyone is juggling so I can do this; no reason for them to know that it's for no reason.

I fall asleep watching a rerun of Sex in the City.

At 10:00 my phone rings.

I manage to answer it, but am not awake enough to lie when Leo's voice comes on asking where I am.

"The Holiday Inn in Chinatown?" he says. "What in the Hell are you doing in Chinatown?"

"It's complicated," I say.

"Well get dressed, I'm sending a car to get you. I'm at the party at Club Ganymede. You'll like it."

He hangs up before I can tell him that I don't go to parties that have me leaving my room after my official bedtime.

I have no idea what Club Ganymede is and thus no idea what to wear, so I end up going with something inconspicuous – shiny black pants and fitted jacket with a black shirt. Fabulous silver snakeskin high heeled sandals and tiny bag, though.

I go down into the city at night, and I'm glad to be out. I love New York City. Cabs fly down the street, and I look for Leo's car.

Black, shining and beautiful, it waits at the curb.

I feel like I'm headed to my prom. But by myself. And dressed like a chaperone.

When we pull up to the West Village brownstone where the party is going on, I begin to wonder what I've gotten myself into.

A crowd is lined up on the stairs and coming down the sidewalk. This line is trying to get into this party. There is no way I'm getting in.

The driver pushes some buttons on his phone and tells me that Leo will be right out.

I step out of the car, and I feel all eyes on me for just a second. I must not register as someone worth looking at, because the attention quickly turns to the next car.

Then Leo's beautiful face peeks out of the open door and he waves me in.

Leo is known by this crowd. I feel a slight surge forward in the group as everyone hopes for a minute that he's waving at them. I run up the stairs and squeeze in the door. I can feel them looking at me now. Clearly they have misjudged my importance, but it's too late to correct the error, because the door is closed again very quickly.

The Ganymede Club is a gorgeous old home that has been converted into an ersatz British private club. The furnishings have the shabby chic look of an old money family; although there is less art, and more bartenders selling drinks than in the authentic version.

There are also far, far, far more people. I feel a bit like I'm in a

Life, Motherhood & the Pursuit of the Perfect Handbag

beehive. A beehive full of sweaty people, half of whom are dancing to loud pulsing music while the other half shout at one another. It's very fashionable: one of those parties where head-to-toe high fashion mingles with thrift-store fabulous. I am alone in wearing a black suit. I feel like I've been airflighted in from a PTA fundraiser on Long Island.

Leo leans in and asks me if I'd like a drink.

"Yes, yes, yes. Gin, tonic, lime. Please."

Leo raises his hand, and in a second a young hipster is at his side to take my order. This guy does not work for the club. This is a minion. In fact, Leo is surrounded by them. I only know Leo from Boston, but suddenly I understand. Leo is somebody important. In his real life, he is a man with an entourage. That requires some recalibration.

He takes my elbow and pulls me forward.

"There's someone you have to meet – this is James, my partner. James, this is Tess Holland, from Skyler Reed."

James is a portly man of about 45 in a tweed suit with heavy tortoiseshell glasses and floppy brown hair.

"Delighted to meet you," James said. And it's true, he is British. Everything else, however, is not exactly as I had pictured.

"We have to help Tess," Leo says. "Katrina Aspinwall has done everything but put out a fatwa against her."

"Pardon?"

"You know, the ayatollahs. Actually, it's more like one of those things in the Japanese companies, where you can't fire people – you come to work and your chair's gone – she's trying to get Tess to commit hari kari."

I protest – "That's a little strong!"

"She got your hotel reservations in Chinatown!"

"It was an accident," I say weakly.

"If she'd put you up in Staten Island, you'd be talking about the lovely boat ride over to Manhattan," he says. "She's a bitch, Tess, and she's trying to make you quit."

"It does sound that way," James says.

I gulp my drink.

"But I can't quit," I say. I don't tell him all of my reasoning – finances, Boston, wanting my old life back. "It'll get better…"

Leo raises his eyebrow.

"Can we save Tess?" Leo asks James.

"As in, can you, Leo, and me, James, try to look out for Tess to the best of our abilities? Absolutely. But if you mean can Leo Magnusson Inc. do anything to help Tess – well, sorry to say, Tess, but there it gets more complicated – we are partnered with OmniBrands and OmniBrands has decided to employ the bitch. Therefore, we are partnered with the bitch. As you well know, it's just…"

Before he can finish, Leo chimes in with "business."

Leo turns to me. "Before I hooked up with James, I never could manage to keep any money. I was always giving clothes away, giving parties instead of attending parties. I didn't even know that you could charge people for going to their parties…

The things I've learned from James."

"You get paid to go to parties?" I ask.

"Sure, attendance fees. It's crazy, right? Well that's why I need a business partner; I mean I would just be going to parties anyway. James is the one who figured out how to turn it into a revenue stream."

James clears his throat.

"I know, I know," Leo says. "My contract says that I have to circulate."

He points at my empty glass. "Can Gunther get you another drink?"

I nod and wait for Gunther as Leo moves off to work the room.

Business partner? I may have made a massive miscalculation.

It is on my third gin and tonic that I remember that I only had pretzels for dinner. I look for a place to sit down and I realize that all of the couches are taken over by couples in various stages of passion.

Since speaking with Leo, I have not shared a word with a human being other than asking a very drunk fashion model where I could find the ladies room. As an unknown in a conservative black suit, I am invisible at this party.

I am drunk enough to know that I am drunk without being nearly drunk enough to start dancing. I decide that it is probably time for me to head back to Chinatown.

I go upstairs to find Leo and tell him that I'll see him tomorrow at the Skyler Reed party.

I bump through the crowded room like a ball in a pinball machine. Finally I spot Leo's golden hair glistening above the crowd. He stands next to the opposite wall, and I head in his direction. I push my way through his entourage, waving at James as I pass. I am about to touch Leo's shoulder from behind when I realize what is going on.

He is talking one-on-one with a world-famous Brazilian model. She stands with her back to the wall, looking up at him. He has his arm on the wall behind her and is doing the classic lean-in, used by boys the world over starting sometime around Junior High School. Before I can turn away, he kisses her on the mouth and she responds with enthusiasm.

I decide not to bother him.

I guess that really was one hell of a miscalculation.

I feel unaccountably sad in the cab on the way back to the hotel. I really am quite fond of Leo, and it was nice to have him as a safe gay friend. I look down at myself in the suit and remember the Brazilian model. What am I worried about? He's going to be a safe straight friend too. I mean really – if he can have that, he's not going to be any threat to Pete.

23

Although I'm a little hungover, I don't feel too terrible, because I remember that I don't have to sit in the suite today. Instead, today is our fabulous soirée, so I get to spend the day styling bags, shoes, belts and clothes and eating take-out. With a blissful smile on my face as I leave the Holiday Inn, there is no fear of me being mistaken for a native New Yorker.

I am dressed in jeans and flats, but I packed my dress for the evening (a bright blue, knee-length, flowing Derek Lam one-shoulder number with a black leather belt and gloves – Aphrodite meets the Marquis de Sade), so I won't have to schlep back across town. I wish I had a bandana to tie over my hair I Love Lucy style; it just seems like that kind of day.

I meet the team in front of the Metropolitan Museum and we must look like a strange mob carrying bags and mannequins up the monumental staircase. Caitlin and several young assistants are halted at the bottom of the stairs with two rolling racks of clothes.

"Well," Katrina says to them, expectantly. "Aren't you going to bring them in?"

These tiny young women now struggle to carry the rolling racks up the staircase.

"Do you think there's probably a cargo entrance?" I ask Therrien.

"Do you want to tell her?"

I remain silent.

Katrina is her commanding self as she leads us into the lobby and demands to see the event manager. The manager seems to be well-versed in dealing with the high strung (it must be an important job component) and gets us up to the Asian galleries without too much difficulty. She does point the girls toward an elevator.

The whole project is controlled chaos as we set up the clothes and accessories and work with the caterers, all while trying to be unobtrusive, since there are people who are actually here to enjoy the Museum and we don't officially get the space until 4:00.

Blissfully, we have several hours for set up without Katrina's presence – soon after lunch, she disappears for an appointment. I didn't ask.

Looking around the room, I am happy with the collection. Given the number of different voices involved, I'm amazed that it looks coherent at all. The pieces that Skyler led are fabulous and heavy with gold, shimmering fabrics and beading. I can imagine the jingling sound that a woman wearing them would make, and it makes me smile and think of Skyler.

Life, Motherhood & the Pursuit of the Perfect Handbag

I am very proud of mine this time. They reference travel as well, but of packages and letters rather than people. They are based on basic envelope shapes including an evening clutch in watered silk that looks like a party invitation, an everyday bag in a range of colors and fabrics with the dimensions of a #10 letter, and a brown suede day-time bag shaped like a manila envelope with a metal latch. But my favorite of the season is in crocodile and it borrows its shape from an accordion file folder. It was quite a pain to figure out how to construct it, but finished and next to one of Leo's lovely daytime dresses, it looks perfect – beautiful but quirky too, and large enough to carry documents to a meeting.

Katrina's designs are all serviceable and fine; not much different than what you'd see on the floor at Macy's.

Then we hear the click of Katrina's shoes and her voice echoing through the gallery. Everyone looks doubly busy out of fear that she will call us out.

She lights on Caitlin first. Caitlin is telling the caterers to set up a table in the balcony area outside the gallery.

"What is this service station doing here?" Katrina asks. "I understood that it was to be in the center of the room?"

Caitlin is clearly flustered, but she gives it a try. "Um, well, you know, the museum people told us to put it out here – they said the food might like mess up the art or something."

"That is preposterous! I cannot believe that you agreed to such a thing without asking me first. It is simply unacceptable."

"But, you weren't here, and the caterers came, and they needed to set up..." Caitlin manages lamely, but Katrina is already gone, rounding on Linette who is styling a mannequin with one of my bags in the Far Eastern gallery.

"Why on earth is this belt paired with this dress? We never discussed this. It ruins the proportions. Take it off immediately. And this can't be the bag that we were planning to show with that one. Did you decide to do this independently?"

She spits out the word independently as though it is a curse.

Just then Leo lopes up the stairs and to Linette's rescue. He too has been in and out all day, and arrived in the nick of time.

"The belt and bag were my idea, Katrina. I like it."

Leo is a famous fashion designer and a man. Therefore, Leo's word is gold. She does not apologize to Linette, but at least she turns away. Linette goes back to belting the mannequin.

Katrina strides back into the South Asian gallery, where she sees Caitlin moving the table into the gallery with the help of the caterers.

"What are you doing?" Katrina demands.

"Moving the table back to the gallery where you wanted it."

"Absolutely not, the Metropolitan Museum is our host – if they want us to set up in the balcony, that is of course what we must do. Really Caitlin what can you have been thinking?"

It is that way for the next hour –

"Why is this here, I wanted it next to the statue."

"Who ordered satay? Has anyone tasted the satay? We really must be careful about peanuts."

"Is no one trained in service any more?"

"That can't possibly be what you are wearing."

We scurry around answering her demands, and I am delighted when the pencils-down moment comes and we all have to get ready for the arrival of real guests.

Once the party starts, I am surprised to find myself having a nice time. Unlike last night, a few of the people in the room were actually active in the fashion industry five years ago, so I find a few people that I know to talk with. I also get some pleasure out of celebrity gawking – especially when I see several famous actresses carrying my bags. That never gets old.

I fill a little plate with satay and head back toward the South Asian gallery when I hear my name. I stand a little behind the entrance where I am out of sight, but I can hear – it's Katrina's drawl.

"I am so glad that we are represented by the remainder of Skyler's work and my own contributions. How terrible it would have been had Skyler not left the bones of a collection. Clearly some people are simply not up to the challenge. I mean really – office supplies… As though we were a Staples. Honestly, I have only allowed these bags to be included in the collection to demonstrate that some of us truly understand fashion, while others…" Her cocktail party laughter tinkles, and I can imagine her hand waving me and my bags away like bothersome mosquitoes.

I take a breath and round the corner to see Katrina talking to Caitlin, Therrien, Linette, and two department store buyers who I met earlier in the evening. They are all standing together laughing. My co-workers aren't busting a gut or anything, but they are laughing politely.

Oh God, I hired all of them. Would Stacey have laughed?

Does she talk about me like this all the time, or just when she has a few glasses of wine in her? Doesn't she want these people to buy our handbags? And then it occurs to me – the collection will be assessed on which particular bags sold well or didn't. If she can make sure mine don't, she'll have yet another thing on me.

I try to put it out of my mind, and walk past as though I had not noticed them.

After a few more coconut shrimp, I decide to make one final round of the room before heading back to Chinatown.

As I pass Katrina, I see her talking with Hilda Adams, the fashion writer who first discovered Skyler Reed so many years ago. Hilda is stumpy, plump, and famously blunt in her fashion judgments. Over the years she has been a big supporter of Skyler Reed, and Katrina needs to win her over if this acquisition is going to be successful.

Hilda reaches her hand out and grabs my arm as I pass, so I find myself drawn against my will into conversation with Katrina.

"Tess, dear," Hilda says. "I was just telling Katrina how interesting I found this season's collection. I had feared that Skyler Reed would be commoditized, marginalized and anesthetized with this acquisition, but I was wrong – the spirit of Skyler Reed survives. True, there are false starts, boring shapes and been-done ideas, but also such creativity and sass. I love, love, love the envelopes. Envelopes! A conceit, I know, but with the strength of the craftsmanship and the beautiful materials – it works! And the file folder! I am crazy for the file folder."

"Well," Katrina says. "When I first had the idea, there were a great many questions, doubts even – how could we possibly make it work? But really the handbag team has done an amazing job in executing the creative vision that I brought to the table. Skyler Reed has always been the brand of the working woman, and I just thought, why not bring some whimsy to the world of work?"

I feel my face flush. She hated the idea. She hated the idea from the very first day. If Leo had not pushed the idea, it never would have gotten off the ground. In fact, none of the envelopes would have made it past the concept stage based on her opinions. If she'd had her way, the whole thing would look just like something from Liz Claiborne.

There is no way to fight this. If I start saying it's really my idea, it will just look like sour grapes, or like I am insane.

I smile politely instead, but suddenly I know, I cannot work with this woman. I must defeat her.

I go back to Chinatown, ready to read the Art of War.

Thankfully a package of tickets for all the remaining events is waiting for me at the hotel (courtesy of Leo), and I try to enjoy the rest of the trip as best I can.

The seats are good ones, near the front, but I don't know anyone, and I feel Katrina's eyes on me from across the room, wondering how I got them.

It is great to see what everyone is doing, and I am reminded that I actually do work in the fashion industry.

After one of the evening shows, I see something that makes me truly happy.

One of the models rides her bicycle home through a rain shower. She wears a yellow raincoat with the hood up, and the streets are black and slick. The reflection of the streetlights on the shiny black asphalt smears like a watercolor that's been left out in the rain. I think about a bag for that girl. She needs a better bag. I wonder if any of our bags would work riding a bike. I resolve to design one.

That night, I have a voicemail from the kids – they've been to Centre Street Café with Pete and Gretchen – I can hear her laughing in the background as Jake yells that he loves me.

When I leave the hotel four days later, I look again at the handbag stand. They already have a copy of the accordion folder bag. It's in pleather.

OCTOBER

24

It has been almost a month since Fashion Week, and I still haven't figured out how to defeat Katrina Aspinwall. Instead, I drag myself between work and home, feeling like I'm never doing quite enough in either place.

At least it's October and the leaves are changing. Nothing like fall in New England.

Today is the day that Mega Stores is finally going to launch our little line. They've decided to hold an event in Boston, to honor the home of Skyler Reed+Boston. Unfortunately, the closest

Mega Store is the anchor box store for a shopping center along Route 128, the belt highway that circles the city. I've heard they will be serving clam chowder, so I'm sure no one will notice the difference between Beacon Hill and a four-acre store sitting in the middle of a huge parking lot.

I need to look nice, but I don't want to look too nice – the Armani would leave me looking like a true asshole in the middle of a gigantic Mega Store. So I decide to wear the same outfit of black shirtdress and iridescent raincoat that I wore on the first day of Fashion Week – not like anyone got to see it while I was trapped in the hotel suite.

A group of us go out midafternoon, and I ride in the back seat of Therrien's Acura with Linette on one side and Stacey on the other.

Although it's not that late, we hit rush hour traffic, and it's a long ride over, and we struggle a little for conversation. Before, that would never have been a problem, but the acquisition has complicated our relationships.

"Hey," Therrien asks after a long silence, "did you guys ever drink that wine that Katrina gave us at Fashion Week? We broke it out this weekend – it was really good."

"No," Stacy says. "I haven't opened mine yet."

"Wine?" I ask.

The car goes quiet. It is an awkward silence.

"Yeah, she gave it to us that first night, when you weren't there," Therrien says. "She must have forgotten."

Life, Motherhood & the Pursuit of the Perfect Handbag

"Sure," I say.

Stacey wasn't even there, as there is no stationery component to Fashion Week, and she got a bottle of wine. Not that I want the nasty woman's wine, but really.

I work to maintain my bright smile when we pull into the massive parking lot.

This is, after all, a big honor; the culmination of months of work. It is also the first time we will see the actual bags, belts and shoes that they produced in Guam or wherever. We've seen prototypes, but not the real things.

When we arrive and walk into the store, all the muckety-mucks are there. Jim and Tom and Katrina stand together talking with the project managers from Mega Stores.

A table with food and drink has been set up in front of the women's wear section where Skyler Reed + Boston for Mega Stores ™ has a prominent display. It is a large folding table, draped with a bright orange cloth, but it looks small and forlorn within the vast space. I am sorry to see that the organizers scrapped the chowder. There are oyster crackers, though.

We have a big table with free food at the entrance area of a big box store, so of course a parade of shoppers stops to sample the snacks. These are Mega Stores shoppers. They wear big T-shirts and jeans, track suits, all the messy things that anyone throws on just to rush out to a Mega Store. They push carts holding grubby screaming children.

Katrina wears her look of profound indigestion and her contempt is not disguised. She clearly does not think much of the track-suited masses. I wonder if before today, she has ever actually been inside a Mega Store.

I, however, have been to Mega Stores on many occasions, there being no better place to buy bulk diapers. Therefore, I am very familiar with the average Mega Stores shopper. It is for that reason that I am very surprised to see a small but growing group of very fashionable young women, all whippet thin and tottering on high heels. They crowd around the table. They are fashionable, so they don't eat any of the food that we have on offer.

They are looking at each of us, and I wonder if they know who we all are.

Tom says a few words, and then the Mega project managers talk.

Then the woman project manager begs Katrina to say a few words.

She acts for all the world as though she has won a design award. Now that she's before an audience, she shows no sign of the fact that she's standing behind a folding table near the office supplies section of a ginormous store in Stoneham. Her dyspeptic look is erased and replaced with an attractive, if condescending, smile.

"Thank you so much, everyone," she says. "This has been a wonderful opportunity for us at Skyler Reed to open our brand to the world. I cannot thank you at Mega Stores enough for giving me the opportunity to partner with you in creating this small collection."

How many things can I find wrong with this statement? First, the original partnership was with Skyler, before this nasty bitch even came on board; second, she didn't design any of it – my team and I did. I know enough to expect no thanks for her. It is true that she had to school us in the dark arts of using off-shore labor to produce what had previously been hand-made with love, and I'll be happy to give her all the credit for that.

She's still talking…

"In the past, we may have been small, parochial, hidebound, but now – Skyler Reed+Boston is opening to the wider world. That is why I am pleased to use this opportunity to announce that we are officially dropping the Boston from our name. Boston will, of course, always be the first home of our brand, but in this global world, Skyler Reed cannot be bound by one place or one identity."

Why drop the Boston? People like Boston. I guess now at least you could call it truth in advertising… If she didn't drop it, they'd have to change the name to Skyler Reed+Guam or Malaysia or wherever these things were actually made.

Finally she finishes.

The young fashion mavens have been hanging on her every word.

I look at Caitlin, standing behind Katrina's shoulder. Caitlin needs a palm frond for fanning Katrina should she get hot. I imagine a generation of handbag designers trained by this woman – I imagine how different it would have been under Skyler. I weep for the future.

I am glad that they didn't ask me to talk. I'm not sure I could have brought myself to say anything.

I walk over to check out the bags. I actually have to push through a crowd.

The proportions are right. The labels are right. The fabric is cheap but not terrible. They actually look pretty good up there on display.

Then I pull down one of the tinies in fake snake skin and really look at it. The lining is polyester and has a small run. The stitching is not perfect and looks like it will unravel within a few months of buying one of the bags. Honestly, they look just like the ones I saw in Chinatown.

Hell, maybe they were made in the same factory.

Everyone is so happy, patting each other on the back about how great it all looks. I feel like a spoilsport.

And the shoppers. The young women are now starting to push forward and grab things off the racks. It turns out that a fashion blog posted about the opening and a bunch of committed fashionistas have made their way to the suburbs for cheap Skyler Reed.

One of them, a girl in her twenties wearing a dress, scarf in her hair, fabulous Skyler Reed shoes from three seasons ago, and carrying four of the new bags, touches my arm.

"Excuse me," she says. "I saw you standing at the front. Do you work for Skyler Reed?"

Life, Motherhood & the Pursuit of the Perfect Handbag

"Yes," I say. "I'm Tess Holland."

"The Tess Holland?"

That's a first.

"Yes."

"You used to write the 'From the Creative Desk' feature on the web site!"

"Yes, that was me," I say.

"I love that!" she says.

Wow, flattery is actually kind of nice.

"Why aren't you doing it anymore?"

I almost say – because I'm not Creative Director anymore, but I stop myself.

I don't really know what to say. I don't want to say that I stopped doing it, because I'm doing the new blog. I don't want to say that it got pulled from me, because that sounds petty. Also, Katrina may like putting me down in front of our customers and buyers to make herself feel better, but that's so not me. On the other hand, this girl did like the old feature. What would be the harm of telling her about the new one? It's not like I'm saying anything bad about Skyler Reed.

"I have a new blog," I say. "It's pretty similar to what I was doing."

"What's it called?" she asks.

"Life, Motherhood and the Pursuit of the Perfect Handbag."

"Cool," she says. "I'll check it out."

Okay, maybe that wasn't such a great idea. I had envisioned

keeping myself fairly anonymous… I'm sure telling just one person won't be any big deal.

After that, I circle the room, talking to people and making nice. I have a genuine smile for Tom. I have no ill feelings toward the man – except for the whole hiring Katrina Aspinwall thing, and I am dying for news about Lauren and the baby.

"How's she doing?" I ask.

"I talked to her last Friday," he says. "Things are going well. She told me that I need to get a fire under you about the Medela partnership. Something about needing a nicer bag when she comes back in January. Where do we stand with that?"

I look at my shoes. Then I clear my throat. "I am still waiting for Katrina to get back with me about her connections on the pump side of things."

He leans forward and speaks confidentially. "I'll tell you the truth; I don't think that Katrina is that interested in the project. Why don't you just move forward on it, and we can just keep it under her radar. If she gives you any trouble, you can blame me."

He smiles his crinkling smile, and I really do like him.

I wish he hadn't just put me in another awkward position with respect to Katrina, but it's hard to imagine that it could make things worse…

I have lured Kerry and Mira to come with the promise of a trip to the North Shore for dinner after, so I eye the door for their arrival.

As soon as they show up, we leave for dinner. I decide that I won't say a word about handbags. Or Katrina. Or bottles of wine. I take that back, I'll say plenty about a bottle of wine, just not one that I didn't get from Katrina.

As soon as we get settled in at our table with a view of the water, Mira and I start to quiz Kerry. What's going on? Has Kevin come home? Has he explained anything? We don't ask, but we both are desperate to know if they are divorcing.

Kerry has always been very clear about certain things – a woman should never leave the house without makeup, beer is not to be drunk from the bottle, and that she would never, never, never get divorced. Appearance is very important to her, and with Kevin's position and their social prominence (I mean Boston Magazine came to their kid's birthday party) a divorce could be very damaging socially and professionally.

Kerry sips her water then rests her hands on her now obviously pregnant belly.

"It's up to him," she says.

"I thought that he said he wanted to get back together and that he was coming home," Mira says.

Mira has been much more on top of the whole Kerry/Kevin situation than I have – I have honestly not been much of a friend lately. So I didn't even know that she was considering letting Kevin come home.

"I thought so too," she says. Then she pulls out her blackberry and opens up a picture.

"His secretary just sent me this," she says.

She shows a picture of Kevin in bike clothes with his arm around a beautiful red-head who looks strikingly like Kerry, only about ten years younger and dressed for a ride.

"His secretary sent this?" I ask.

"Yes, she's so mad at him!" she laughs. "It was just taken last weekend, when he said that he couldn't come see Madison because he had an important meeting for work. I think she downloaded it from his phone."

"Who is the girl?" Mira asks.

"Junior corporate counsel…"

"A lawyer?" I say. "A lawyer who looks just like you? That's sick."

"I know, I know. But no kids and not fat," she says.

"You're not fat," Mira says, too loudly. "You're pregnant."

Kerry looks like she might cry, but she brightens. "On the good news front, with Kevin gone, work is going really well on the house. It looks like it might actually get finished before the end of the year."

"That's great," I say. "I did notice that Liam looked like he's been working there a lot. Every time we walk by, Jake notices the van."

Kerry blushes.

"Wait a minute," Mira says. "Is something going on?"

Kerry blushes deeper.

"Really? The carpenter?" I say.

She melts.

"He's just so handsome and so thoughtful... But the way he looks at me. Like I'm unbearably precious to him."

This is shocking. Shocking. I've known Kerry since she was 18 and hot carpenters are not exactly her type – she's more of a president of the fraternity, business school grad type of girl.

"Are you, you know?" Mira asks.

Kerry jumps. "No, nothing like that – I mean Kevin and I are still married. I can't do something like that... No, it was just one kiss... But what a kiss, it definitely makes me feel how long the dry spell has been, nothing like Tess and Pete, but still a long time..."

"Hey, wait a minute," I say.

Mira looks at me.

"You mean that you guys still haven't figured things out?" she says.

"I thought we were talking about Kerry here."

"We were, but now we're done," Mira says. "Now we're talking about you. Have you tried lingerie? Candlelight? Don't let it go too long; my sister and her husband couldn't have sex because of having a baby in the bed, and the next thing you know, it had been three years and he ended up running off with his massage therapist."

"Thanks," I say. "It's nothing like that, it's just that we're just so busy."

"Never too busy for that," Mira says.

"Are you saying you and Raj?"

"Every other night, except when one of us is out of town," she says.

I see a hole in her argument. "And how often is Raj out of town now with the new job?"

She looks at the tablecloth. "Almost every week..."

"See, it's hard," I say.

"But worth it," Kerry says with a big smile.

I was planning to tell them about Leo not being gay, but in the context of the conversation it seems an awkward thing to bring up.

When I get home, I open the blog to make a small post about the event.

I get a shocking surprise.

The hit counter in the far corner of the page has seen a radical transformation.

When I last posted yesterday, it was at about 30 hits – that would be my friends and immediate family, each visiting multiple times.

Tonight, the hit counter is at 900. What happened?

I go to the comments area for one of my recent posts. There I see dozens of comments. Buzzing through them, I realize that they are all thanking someone named Cordelia for showing them the way.

I Google Cordelia and fashion.

I find handbagmaven.com, which is a blog all about handbags, written by one Cordelia. I look at her profile picture. It's the girl I talked to at the event.

I go to her most recent post. It says:

A little Skyler Reed serendipity – I was just at the Mega Stores/Skyler Reed opening here in the Boston area! Not every day that something like that shows up in my back yard! Standing there talking to a sharp-dressed lady in a fabulous raincoat – I knew she must work at Skyler Reed, so I struck up a conversation. It turns out that it was Tess Holland! For those in the know, Tess was the Creative Director for Skyler Reed before the ominous acquisition. Anyway, I told her I missed her blog on the website (I don't know if any of you checked it out, but it was a very cool insight into the designer's mind). Anyway, she told me that she has a new one – Life, Motherhood and the Pursuit of the Perfect Handbag at LifeMotherhoodHandbags.com! So check it out.

That explains the hits, but now I'm terrified. I suspect I need Corporate approval before I start a blog. It seems late to ask now. I have to hope that they won't find out… Given that Katrina hates reading email, I hardly think I have to worry about her Googling me.

25

"A grape?"

"No."

"A bunch of grapes?"

"No."

"Watermelon?"

"No."

"What about a vegetable? You could be a pickle."

"No, no, no. I want to be a fireman. I want to wear my fireman boots and my fireman coat and my fireman hat."

I look up from sewing the last few stitches attaching the leaves to the hat of Gracie's strawberry costume.

She has the rest of the costume on right now, and she is toddling around the living room – a little blonde berry. Since she'll be riding in the stroller on Halloween and may end up having a coat on, the hat is the crucial element of the costume. I hope she'll keep it on.

Jake, however, wants nothing to do with being a fruit or

vegetable.

He wants to wear his fireman raincoat and galoshes and the cheap plastic fire hat he got on a tour of our fire station.

This seems inutterably boring - but this holiday is supposed to be about him.

As a kid, when I dreamed of making costumes for my own kids, I didn't know that they would have actual opinions...

I used to love Halloween. I always designed my own costumes, and continued wearing homemade costumes for years after everyone else had graduated to polyester superheroes from the supermarket. I planned and dreamed about the Halloweens I would spend with my own children someday.

Nobody told me that Halloween is the nightmare holiday for working parents.

Perhaps that was deemed inappropriate information for a pre-teen.

It goes something like this – if you want to take your very small children trick-or-treating, it starts at about 5:00 (in our case, the neighborhood merchants offer candy at from 5:00 until 6:30 or so), then, maybe you live somewhere where there is a big Halloween event, a festival or some such (in our neighborhood, it's a Lantern Parade where people carry elaborate homemade lanterns on a walking track around Jamaica Pond). For all this to work, a parent who wishes to take his or her child to these events will need to be home by 4:15 at the latest, so that everyone can be dressed and out of the house before all the candy is gone. This also assumes that you've actually organized the costume and the lantern making, which is a whole other issue.

That would mean that I need to leave work at 3:45. I am given constant grief over leaving at 5:30 or 6:00, so am fairly certain that Katrina is not going to recognize All Hallows Eve as a valid excuse for me to leave early.

This is proven a few weeks before the holiday, when I get an email from Katrina calling a crucial meeting for 2:00 p.m. on October 31st. No way I can miss that.

Now I have to ask our nanny to take the kids trick-or-treating and hope that Pete makes it home in time to take them to the Lantern Parade. If he doesn't, the dreaded Gretchen will have to take them. Or maybe Gretchen and Pete will take them together and I can just go live where they send bad mommies…

I lay out the costumes on Tuesday night and head into the office the next morning with a black cloud over my head.

I spend some of the morning emailing back and forth with Medela. The day after our Mega Stores event, I started calling names on the list, and things moved pretty quickly from there. It turned out that they were thrilled at the idea of partnering with a high-fashion brand. There are some pretty rigorous specifications for the pump, but the constraints have definitely sparked my creative energy, and I have three or four strong designs.

I also meet with my team in the morning to prepare for the afternoon meeting with Katrina, where I'll present our preliminary ideas for the fall collection, which will be shown in February. I showed them a picture of a Celtic Giant in plaid as well as some other ideas I'd picked up from fairy tales, and it turned out to spark a really creative meeting. Now we've been trying to figure out how to get the designs into a shape that Katrina won't reject them out of hand. We've been playing around with metamorphoses and connections between made things and the natural world. We have a handbag that looks like vines are coming out of one side of it and engulfing it, and a very structured and ladylike bag where one small corner is made of a different, natural material, like bamboo. Also, I have about twenty sketches of crazy things in distressed plaid.

When we walk into the conference room at two, the table is covered in sunglasses, belts, shoes, jewelry, handbags and a wide variety of household knickknacks like candle holders and napkin rings. All have the Skyler Reed label, and I know for sure that we didn't make any of them.

It's a pretty small meeting – Tom and Katrina; Linda, the corporate marketing director from New York; Tera, Leo, Linette, Therrien and me. Caitlin is there to run the projector. I look at the goods. Most of them look okay – nothing spectacular, but stylish in a mid-century modern way that is a good complement to our work. The handbags, shoes and bags all look like the things we saw at Mega Stores – inexpensively made and stylistically safe.

Therrien picks up a belt and Linette a shoe, while I examine a handbag. These are not our designs; they were not made in our factory; and yet they have our name on them. None of us are smiling.

Katrina stands at the head of the table, beaming.

Once we are all seated, she tells us that she has exciting news. These are the samples that she has received from the licensing partners that she has arranged for us. The sunglasses are shipping to stores next week – at a price of $300 each – while the other things all have their own timetables.

I look at Linette and Therrien. I know that we all have serious problems with licensing out the core brand items. Sunglasses and tchotchkes are one thing, but not our bread and butter. I don't know how we are supposed to register a protest.

Clearly not at this meeting, because when she finishes her statement, she asks us to move forward with our presentations.

Linette starts. She is flustered, but she manages. Katrina lets her go with minimal questioning.

Katrina beams during Therrien's presentation. Belts can do no wrong.

I go next.

I put together a Power Point presentation, so I move over to stand in front of the screen while Caitlin runs the computer.

I show the picture of the two-headed giant, which gets a laugh, and then I show our ideas. I explain about metamorphoses, fairies and monsters, and connections with the natural world. This is the way we've always done design at Skyler Reed – you get an idea, the more outlandish the better, and you go crazy for two months; then you use November and a December to figure out how to make it and sell it. January is for manufacturing and marketing, and then it all goes to show in February. If you don't start with crazy, you'll just end up copying everyone else's ideas.

Besides, crazy has done pretty well for us over the years – the accordion file folder is currently our best selling bag.

I try not to look at Katrina while I'm presenting, but when I do, her habitual frown has deepened to a scowl.

"Fairy tales?" she says. "Monsters? Really?"

"That's just where the ideas come from," I say. "What do you think of the bags?"

She narrows her eyes, and her tone is short.

"You have had nearly two months, and this is the best that you could do? Really, Tess, everyone here makes a lot of sacrifices to make up for the hours when you are not here…"

She pauses dramatically.

"This season is of the utmost importance for Skyler Reed, now is the time to show that we can meet our promises… We all need to know that you will be giving 100 percent."

That's it. I've had enough.

I am standing at the other end of the long conference table from her. I lean forward and look directly into her face. This is the first time in months that I have looked into her eyes without dropping my gaze.

I speak very slowly and enunciate. No way she is missing what I have to say.

"I have never given less than 100 percent. This is what I do. I have done it for years, and I am considered by most people to be quite good at it. It is clear, however, that you don't feel that way. Based on that, it probably would be best for you to find someone else to fill my position."

Mouths are open around the room.

I look at Linette – her eyes are on me with fascination. She can't believe I'm saying this. Therrien is looking at the papers in front of him. I know he agrees with me – I know he can't like how things have been going; but he has to look after his own ass, he certainly isn't going to put it on the line for me.

Leo is wearing a small grin, while he leans back to watch the show.

Nobody else in this room is going to have the balls to tell her how they really feel. Everyone else is too afraid. Well, I just quit, what the hell do I have to be afraid of?

I don't walk out.

I have had things to say for months, and I'm not going to leave them unsaid just because I'm mad as hell.

"I will say, however, that from what I have seen of these mediocre handbags on display here today and the disposable fashion that your friends at Mega Stores created, I firmly believe you are taking Skyler Reed in exactly the wrong direction."

Therrien nods. It's almost imperceptible and probably unconscious, but it keeps me going. I'm not the only person who has noticed.

"People don't buy Skyler Reed because of our name, and

not even necessarily because of the look of our bags. They buy us because of our quality. If they wanted substandard merchandise that looks like Skyler Reed and has our name on it, they don't have to buy it from us for two grand. They can go to Chinatown or eBay and pick up a knockoff. They buy our bags because they can trust us. And you are betraying that trust."

I pick up my things and leave the room.

Poor Leo. He was supposed to talk next. I wonder if he'll present like nothing happened. He was pretty excited about the ripped plaid. Then again, he loves a show and he was watching this one with clear enjoyment.

I feel a few stray tears running down my cheeks as I pack up my laptop and put the pictures of the kids into the big red bag. I'm hoping that they will mail everything else to me, but those pictures are precious (and they were expensive); no way I trust the packing abilities of a 24-year-old design assistant.

At least I'll be home in time for trick-or-treating.

I'm walking down Boylston Street when I hear my phone ring.

It's the office.

I pick it up.

It's Tom.

"Tess," he says. "Would you let me buy you a cup of tea?"

I guess I won't be trick-or-treating.

We meet at Tealuxe on Newbury Street.

We are settled in at an outdoor table before he says anything about the meeting.

"Feeling better?" he asks after I've had a sip of my steaming hot tea.

I think about that.

"Yes, yes, I am."

"Any chance you'd come back?"

"To that? No."

"I saw those emails from Medela. I'm really impressed by how much progress you have made on that project – especially in the midst of planning for Fall."

I shrug. "Thanks. I guess we should figure out who to hand it off to. Nobody else knows much about breast pumps."

He leans forward. I can tell that he wants to touch my hand, but doesn't because of corporate correctness.

"Tess, I don't want you to go anywhere. Will you come back if I promise that Katrina will only be in charge of the operational elements of the brand? What if I say that you and your creative team will have total freedom and creative control over the traditional elements of the Skyler Reed brand? Katrina can manage outsourcing, licensing, as well as our marketing and outreach efforts worldwide, but the rest of it I give to you."

I think about it.

"What about Creative Director?"

"It's yours."

"No licensing of core brand items?"

"How about no licensing without approval from the Creative

Director?" he says.

"Salary commensurate with the position?"

He narrows his eyes.

"How will that be determined?" he asks.

"Easy, pay me whatever you were paying her."

"I'll have to think about that one," he says.

"Well then, I'll have to think about coming back…"

"Okay, okay, Katrina salary."

"That's great," I say, and I mean it. "May I have an office?"

"Would you take the small conference room if we put up blinds on the glass window?"

"Yes," I say, without hesitation. "I'll do it."

"Will you come back to the office with me? I'm done with my tea."

We stand and walk back together.

When I get into the office, no one looks directly at me. The word of my departure must have spread rapidly after our meeting.

Then Tom goes into Katrina's office and closes the door.

Therrien shoots me a big grin and a thumbs-up.

I think of him laughing as Katrina put me down, and I decide to forgive him and Linette too. After all, as Leo's partner said – it's just business.

Pete calls to say he'll be able to make it to the Lantern Parade, so I don't rush home. I want desperately to tell him about everything that has happened today, but I can't talk in my cube.

I stay long enough to see Tom leave Katrina's office, and a while later, Katrina stride out with her coat on and leave the building, not looking at anyone.

It's well after 7:00 when I get home to find Pete half-asleep on the sofa with a sleeping trick-or-treater on either side of him. Gretchen is cleaning up in the kitchen.

I kick off my shoes, scoot Gracie over a little and snuggle in next to him.

"I quit my job today," I say.

That wakes him up.

"What happened?"

"I should have done it months ago. Tom gave me back Creative Director and moved Katrina to purely business side."

He turns to put his arms around me and kiss me. His move wakes Jake up just enough to get him talking.

"Daddy, did you know they give you candy at every place you stop? You just have to say those words... But Gracie, she couldn't say the words, but they gave her the candy anyway. I said her words for her, Daddy, but it was so she could get her candy. I love candy..."

He drifts off again.

Pete's kiss deepens.

He takes me by the hand and pulls me up off the sofa.

Jake and Gracie both slump over and barely avoid bumping heads.

"You're coming with me," Pete says, and pushes me on the

lower back.

"But what about the kids?" I say. It must be dangerous to leave them on the sofa like this.

"They aren't going anywhere, Tess, and I'm not taking any chances."

"What about Gretchen?" I whisper, nodding toward the kitchen.

"She's a grown-up, Tess…"

With that, he leads me to our bedroom.

And finally, the dry spell is over.

www.lifemotherhoodhandbags.com/home

LIFE, MOTHERHOOD & THE PURSUIT OF THE PERFECT HANDBAG

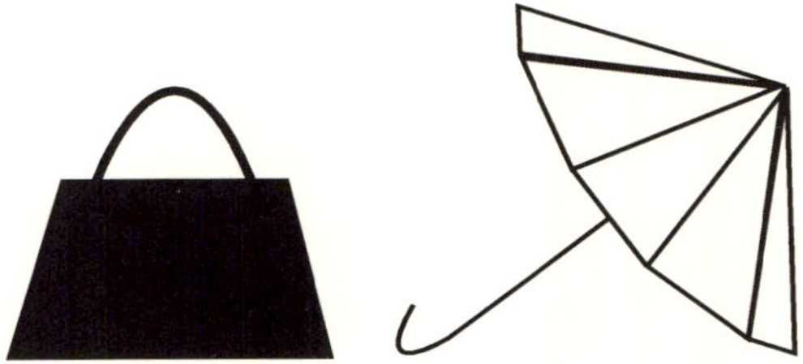

October 15 - The trouble with raincoats

Fall is here and I'm again reminded of the trouble with raincoats. My husband's raincoat is from REI and it laughs at the raindrops that dare to penetrate its high-tech fabric. It is also, in my opinion, unforgivably ugly – fine for a hike in the wilderness, but disastrous when worn over anything else. My raincoat is quite stylish, but it is useless in the rain. What I want is stylish raincoats in fabrics that work. And don't get me started on the umbrellas.
Comments (17):

About me

Since I was a little girl, I have dreamed about handbags... I am the lead handbag designer for a well-known firm. I am also married with a preschool son and a baby daughter. I am lobbying for us to get a fish.

NOVEMBER

26

I walk into Jake's preschool Harvest Assembly five minutes late and hope that I haven't missed anything. Given that 40 minutes ago I didn't even remember that he had a Harvest Assembly, I'm lucky to be here at all. Thankfully, after remembering the assembly, I also remembered that we were supposed to bring snacks, so I at least managed to pick up a box of Munchkins in the Dunkin' Donuts in Back Bay Station and am not walking in empty handed.

Going back to Creative Director has been great – people listen to me, my ideas get implemented, Katrina can't beat me up to my face, I get to wear my own clothes – but with this brand expansion for bags, shoes and belts, as well as a full line of clothes for New York fashion week, I'm having a little trouble balancing everything. Thus, I knew this morning that there was an assembly at 1 p.m., but had completely forgotten about it four hours later. Thank God for cell phone alarms.

Vanessa is waiting for me by the door. She hands me Gracie and says brusquely, "I'm going to lunch."

I wonder what has gotten into Vanessa.

If I really give myself time to think about it, I know exactly what has gotten into her: the combination of my coming home late and working every Friday is dragging her down. Hell, it's dragging me down, when I have time to think about it.

I'll have to do something to make it up to her. Perhaps a card? If I had the time to find a card… A handbag? I imagine crunchy patchouli Vanessa with a Skyler Reed handbag and almost laugh. Perhaps I should offer her a bit more money. I'll have to think about it tomorrow.

I put down my Munchkins at a snack table and notice that all of the snacks look very home-made and healthy: whole grain muffins, carrot sticks, hummus. I guess I'm the bad-influence donut mom.

The class is up on the stage. I look hard, trying to spot my little man… But Jake is not on the stage.

Finally I spot him standing on the stairs at the side of the stage, frozen in place, looking terrified. I know exactly what has happened. Jake doesn't like to be stared at. He has asked me more than once to cut his pretty blond hair so that people don't complement him on it, and now here are 100 parents all starting at the children. We had talked about the songs and hand movements, but it hadn't occurred to me that he wouldn't know about the audience. He must be so scared.

His teachers are so busy getting everyone lined up that they haven't noticed.

He looks like he doesn't know where to go.

I am ready to jump from my seat with Gracie and run forward to help him, when I see Raj stand up from the front row. He walks over to Jake and whispers in his ear. Raj points to Amit on the stage, who waves at Jake.

At that, Jake runs out and stands next to his friend.

He then sings happily about grey squirrels, the harvest, pumpkins and teapots.

I'm thankful to my friend while also wishing I could have managed to get here a little earlier. What kind of mom forgets about the assembly?

I look around the room to see who else is there, and I am shocked to see Kerry and Kevin sitting together, both loudly cheering for Madison. In fact, it is suspiciously loud. After the Grey Squirrel song, Kerry claps enthusiastically and yells, "Go Madison!" Kevin hoots, "that's my girl!" By the time she sings about the teapot, they are both giving her a standing ovation.

Soon afterward, every one else stands, because the show is over, but for one enormously uncomfortable moment, Kevin and Kerry are the only ones standing. They seem not to notice.

I wonder what is going on. I know that I have been out of the loop since getting promoted, but I hadn't realized that this was on the horizon. I make a note to ask Mira about it.

After the assembly, there is a reception – with snacks and conversation.

Jake is very excited to see me and wants me to meet his friends. I also meet the parents, many of them for the first time. They all seem to know one another – this is likely a function of talking to each other at pick-up and drop-off. I never do pick-up or drop-off, since I am have gone to work before Jake goes to school and I get home after he comes back. I make a note to try to take him to preschool a few times. How hard could it be, really? The first day was a nightmare, but there's no reason every day has to be. I'll take him soon. That should make Vanessa feel better.

I try to make conversation while also looking for the families I do know. I need to thank Raj for helping Jake and to ask Mira about Kerry and Kevin.

Finally I spot Raj. He looks good, but tired. He's lost some of the weight that he'd put on, and he's dressed casually, but business casual – nothing like the Cuban shirts he'd been favoring before going back to work. He looks like a consultant on casual Friday. Which is what he is now, I guess. I miss Mr. Mom.

"Where's Mira?" I ask.

Life, Motherhood & the Pursuit of the Perfect Handbag

"She's on a shoot – it's just me today."

"How did you manage to get off? I thought you traveled three or four days a week?"

"I asked to work from Boston today, they let me do it – don't worry, I'll pay for it later." He sounds like me.

"How do you like it?"

"Work's great, but the logistics are a pain in the ass. Trying to make everything work is just complicated – especially with my travel and Mira working on the weekends. We're thinking of getting an au pair, to cover the evenings and weekends."

I want to ask if he misses seeing the kids, but then I'd have to think about missing my kids and I'd rather not cry at the Harvest Assembly.

During this conversation, we have been trailing our children, who are playing together. I look at Gracie toddling after Ravi, who is slightly older, and I notice something funny about how she is walking.

Her diaper has disconnected on one side and is slowly sliding down her leg. Her pink overalls are soaked.

I look for the diaper bag and realize that Vanessa must have taken it with her.

How can her diaper have gotten so overfilled that it has come free and is hanging around her ankles? Did Vanessa change her at all today?

I borrow a diaper from Raj and lead my kids out of the auditorium to the bathroom and cubbies.

Gracie's clothes are soaked, and I don't have a change, so I grab some of Jake's clothes from his cubby. They are, of course, huge on her and boy's clothes, but they will have to do. They are also awful – grey sweat pants and a red and yellow monster truck shirt – since I put the ugliest of his things in the school cubby.

I change her and then we head back into the auditorium.

Jake refills his plate with Munchkins (ignoring all healthy snacks), and I give Gracie a munchkin and put her down.

Just then Kerry and Kevin walk by, each holding one of Madison's hands.

I find Raj again.

"What is going on with that?" I point at Kerry and Kevin.

"Apparently, they are giving it another try, Mira tells me. For Madison and the new baby."

"What about his girlfriend?"

Raj shrugs.

I don't know how much Raj knows about Kerry's relationship with the contractor, so I just ask. "Did all the work get wrapped up on their house?"

He winks at me.

"Yes, Mira says that Liam has gone on to the next job –she says she's committed to her marriage…"

We both just shake our heads – in our long Fridays, we had found that we have similarly negative feelings about Kevin.

I have Gracie in sight but she is twenty feet away from me playing on the floor with Ravi, when I see one of the teachers looking at her fearfully. Before I can get there, the teacher has picked Gracie up and is talking to the surrounding parents with a worried look on her face.

I rush over soon enough to hear, "Do you know who this little boy belongs to? Does anyone know who his parents are?"

She has apparently asked several people, because parents are starting to gather with helpful looks on their faces.

I step up, blushing. "Oh, don't worry, he's mine – I mean she's mine. She's Jake's little sister."

The teacher looks at me suspiciously. "This is Gracie?"

She has likely only seen her with Vanessa, and dressed very smartly in shades of pink.

I mumble something about an accident and take her back.

I am thankful to see Vanessa waiting as we gather Jake and approach the door.

"She had a diaper failure," I say, passing her back to Vanessa.

"Do you think you'll be home by 6:00 tonight? I really have somewhere I need to be."

"Yes, yes, I'm sorry I've been so late the last few weeks."

Her face shows that I'm not forgiven.

I rush back to work.

27

The morning after Thanksgiving, Jake crawls into bed next to me. Gracie is snuggled in at my side and I still have the pleasantly full feeling from our delicious traditional New England Thanksgiving dinner at the home of one of Pete's attendings. I smile lazily at Jake.

He holds the little toy Beanie Baby Christmas moose that he's had since he was a baby. He brings the moose up to his ear. Then he holds its ear to his mouth.

"Is Moosie telling you a story?" I ask.

"Yeah, a story about bean bags."

"Why?"

"Because he's a bean bag!"

He leans over and sniffs Pete's pillow.

"Mmmm," Jake says. "I smell that Daddy smell. Is he staying home today?"

"I'm here all day, buddy," Pete calls from the bathroom.

"You guys should look out the window," Pete says.

The three of us get out of bed and hurry to the front window – the world outside has been transformed by over a foot of snow that fell in the night.

"It snowed, mommy, it snowed. Are we allowed to touch it?" Jake says.

I realize that he doesn't remember the snow from last year.

"Hey," I say. "Let's all go sledding at the Arboretum today."

"Yay!" Jake calls.

Amazingly Pete doesn't beg off even though he has to go to work tomorrow and Sunday. Gretchen has gone to visit friends in Maine for the long weekend, so we have a blissful day to ourselves.

In record time, I feed the children and bundle them in their snow suits. Pete goes down to the basement to find our sleds. It turns out that we have a great sled for Jake, but nothing that is specifically designed for babies. I hope that Gracie isn't too upset.

We walk together to the Arboretum. Jake holds Pete's hand.

It is slow-going, with Gracie strapped to my back in the Ergo carrier and Jake traveling at his own (very slow) pace. He is further slowed by the stick that he drags through the snow bank beside him as he walks.

It doesn't matter – we are in no hurry.

Our neighborhood has been transformed.

The plows have built snow banks along the sidewalks, and as we walk together, I feel like I'm experiencing our old neighborhood in an earlier time. I almost hear the voices of the wealthy

Victorian children and their nannies coming out of their pondside mansions; and the calls and screeches of the kids from the triple-deckers like ours, shouting as they run to skate on Jamaica Pond. The city is silent, muffled by the snow, and I pretend that we have it all to ourselves. It is our private frozen fairyland.

Since it is not yet nine in the morning, we do have the Arboretum mostly to ourselves, a few solitary dogwalkers, snowshoers and cross-country skiers pass us, but they are all older and are disinclined to break the silence.

I hope they don't mind us too much, because Jake shrieks with joy as he stumbles and bumbles up the hill with Pete for his first time sledding.

Gracie and I stand at the bottom of the small hill watching Pete and Jake slide down again and again.

Finally, I take Gracie out of the Ergo and put her down in the snow. She is really walking on her own now, and I wonder how she'll do in the snow.

Initially, she walks like a cat in snow, trying to shake the snow off her foot with each step. She takes off her mitten and touches it, then cries when she feels that it is cold.

Soon afterward, more families begin arriving.

We see Raj and Mira with the kids and her parents. Raj takes the boys to sled with Pete and Jake.

Mira walks over to say hello.

"How's everything?" I ask.

"Great, except I'm freaked out about Christmas," Mira says.

"Why?"

"Preschool is closed for two weeks, and our baby-sitter is going out of town, and there's no way that we can take off. If you had told me in college that childcare arrangements would take up so much of my mental energy, I never would have believed you…"

"You can call Vanessa, if you like," I say. They have been using Vanessa for evenings and weekends (so I can't take the whole responsibility for her feeling overworked). I don't mind her working for them when we don't need her, and since I'll be paying her vacation pay while we're away, she'll probably be glad for the extra money.

"Really? Won't you be needing her?" Mira asks. "I thought you told me that the week after Christmas was going to be insane for you."

"Unbelievably, for the first time in five years, Pete has two weeks off around Christmas and New Year's, and we are going home to Memphis. In fact, I'll be coming back to work before Pete does. I come back here for work the day after Christmas, but he's going to spend the New Year's week in Memphis with the children and his parents. His mother is ecstatic. We are trying to talk her out of hiring a brass band and inviting everyone he's ever met to have a Christmas parade."

She smiles at me gratefully.

At this point, I realize that Gracie has toddled over to a small child on a sled and is looking at him with malicious intent.

I rush away.

He is so cute in his little snowsuit – not quite two and sitting on top of his long green plastic sled, believing himself to be doing something. And then, like a wolf on the fold, my little pink and white demon descends on him and pushes him off the sled.

"Gracie!" I say loudly. Then I lower my voice a little when I realize that his mother has turned away to help her older child and has missed this dreadful little display. The little boy picks himself up, toddles over to Gracie, who is now perched atop his sled, and pushes her.

His mother sees this and runs over to him.

"Ewan, how could you!" she says. "Apologize to the little girl!"

Gracie sits there, the picture of wounded innocence.

I try to explain that it is not his fault, but his mother carries him off for a time out and leaves my little hellion in possession of the sled. I know that I should punish her, but I'm not sure how to do it. I don't have the stroller, only an Ergo carrier, and I don't really want to have my back be the location of a time-out.

Just then, Kerry walks up with Madison.

Kerry looks tired.

"What are you doing out here? You know you can't sled with her," I say.

"I know, I know, it was just too pretty to miss, I felt terrible keeping Madison inside. I was hoping that someone else might be able to take her down."

I send Madison off to sled with Pete and Jake.

I look at Kerry with narrowed eyes.

"You should be at home with your feet up."

"I know, I know. Kev had to go into the office..." She shrugs.

"On the day after Thanksgiving?"

"It's a big project," she says.

I wonder if she believes that.

Hours later, we trudge home from the Arboretum. Gracie is asleep on my back, and Pete holds Jake in his arms while I pull the sled.

What a great day.

We are close to our house when Pete grabs my hand. Jake is asleep on his shoulder.

"I have to tell you something, but you are not going to like it," he says.

That's promising.

I wait to hear what it could be, and I try not to worry too much – he's changed his mind about being a doctor and wants to go back to school and become a paleontologist? He's decided he wants Gretchen to sleep on our side of the French doors? He despises handbags?

We walk along as I wait to hear what he's got to tell me.

"On Wednesday, Dr. van de Berg pulled me aside and said that he would like to have me come on his next trip to Mali."

Is that all? It's important to Pete, and we will work it out – I'm practically a single mother anyway – what is a week or so in

Africa?

"That's great," I say. "I mean I know what a big deal it is for you. Don't worry, I'm not mad… We can see if your mom can come and stay, but it's not like you are that big of an issue for childcare anyway…"

"It's not that – the trip is during my December break…"

I stop dead.

"You mean at Christmastime?"

He nods.

"Your first Christmas off in five years?"

He nods again.

"The first Christmas that you will actually be able to spend with your children? The Christmas when you are supposed to bringing them back on the plane by yourself while I'm back here working?"

"Now, Tess, don't get mad," he says.

"I can't stay, Pete, work doesn't even want me to go away for the days around Christmas."

"That's okay, honey."

"No, it's not, how are you planning to get your children back to Boston? They can hardly fly back by themselves? I'm sure the stewardesses would love that…"

"Flight attendants," he says. He is using his jokey tone, trying to get me to lighten up.

I refused to be leavened. I say nothing.

"My mom can bring them on my ticket – we can just get her a

one-way ticket back to Memphis."

"How are you going to explain it to them, Pete? They have been talking for weeks about having Christmas with Daddy this year."

He pats Jake's sleeping back. "They are so little, they won't remember… Do you remember anything from before you were five? I don't."

"I would remember my dad missing Christmas for an African vacation."

"Tess, it's not like that – Listen, it's really a big deal. It could lead to really great things for us… I heard someone saying last week that one of the lead doctors in the group in Mali is leaving – this could really be my shot to prove myself. He never invites fellows, Tess. I can't say no."

Does this mean that he is considering taking a job in Mali? I'm not even entirely sure where Mali is.

I nod in acquiescence. What else can I do?

I can't say no.

www.lifemotherhoodhandbags.com/home

LIFE, MOTHERHOOD & THE PURSUIT OF THE PERFECT HANDBAG

November 23 - Snow!!!

It snowed! I know by March I'll be cursing the dirty, crusty piles of it, but for now, how beautiful. What bag for playing in the snow? I don't want a tiny bag, but no big backpacks either. Next assignment –a beautiful bag that's useful when you need free hands… Enough handbags, we're going sledding!

Comments (4):

November 23 - Bah humbug…

The holidays are too soon and there's too much to do. Let's skip X-mas
Comments (25):

About me

Since I was a little girl, I have dreamed about handbags… I am the lead handbag designer for a well-known firm. I am also married with a preschool son and a baby daughter.. Fish don't seem to have much personality – we have returned to considering getting the gerbil, or perhaps a guinea pig.

DECEMBER

28

Speaking of the inability to say no – I am now in my 20th straight day of work. Now I've had a few hours off here and there – a Saturday morning with the kids before dropping them off with Raj and Mira, a glass of wine one evening after midnight, all day for two Sundays if you don't count the time I dropped them off in Sunday school and lurked in the vestibule with my laptop.

That is why I have had no time for Christmas shopping, no time for Christmas light viewing, no time for a single moment of holiday cheer. Our flight to Memphis is only five days away, and

I still have a million things to review and sign off on before I go. I have deputized my mother to be Santa. I expect to return with a suitcase full of toys that are culturally inappropriate for Jamaica Plain – bee bee guns, water guns, light sabers, small video games, action movie DVDs, Barbies, maybe even a Bratz doll or two, little girl make-up, perhaps some plastic high heels and a princess gown. This is the chance I will have to take.

It is safe to say that this work is orders of magnitude different from anything that I've ever done before. There are so many more moving parts; so many more people for me to supervise and keep on task; so many more schedules; so many, many, many more superiors to keep informed of my every move through endless meetings, video conferences and memos. Life in a huge corporation is vastly different than little old Skyler Reed. We had one boss, Skyler, and if we lost money, Skyler would be pissed and we might have to lay somebody off, but nothing like this. As I hear on a daily basis, we have a CEO, we have a Board of Directors, and most frighteningly of all, we have shareholders – and shareholders have stock, and if they think we are in trouble, they will unload their stock, and all of the rest of us will fall with them.

And believe me, I like Tom as well as the next person, but when I look around the conference room I know in my bones that if something goes really wrong with this Skyler Reed expansion, my head is going to be the one to roll. I'm the only person who doesn't have a constituency. Even evil Katrina has people who are looking out for her. There is no room for failure for me.

And they would be right – this is my deal. We're running with my ideas for the season, I'm okaying every design decision for the core brand items, the width of every belt, height of every heel and embellishment on every handbag.

I am proud to say that at least I present an image of clear competent confidence at work. Katrina's eyes following my every move, ticking off every misstep, assures that. All the chaos is hidden behind a curtain, and at least I don't have any time to worry about my marriage.

I sit down in my office with my third cup of coffee and listen to my messages. There is one from my mother.

"Tess, honey, I think you might be too busy – did you really say that the children would need stockings, gingerbread houses and bubble bath? I don't quite understand…"

I don't even remember leaving my mother a message about bubble bath. What can I have been thinking?

Just then, Leo comes in.

"Do you have a few minutes to get lunch? I'd like to talk to you about something."

No, I do not have time for lunch. I have a million things to do before I leave town for six days only weeks before my first major fashion show as the Creative Director for the new Skyler Reed.

Leo looks serious.

I say yes.

He takes me to lunch at the Taj. The Taj is not a place to eat if you are in a hurry.

The waiters know him and escort us to his favorite table.

I decide to sit back and enjoy it and not worry about the clock. I may as well, because there is no way we are getting out of here in under two hours.

The dining room is beautiful and full of light. The dominant color is ecru. The tables are laid with china and crystal and set well apart so conversations cannot be overheard by the next table. The average age is closer to 80 than 30, and the clothes are tasteful, well made and frightfully expensive.

The starched upper crust Bostonian spirit of the hotel and restaurant would seem a poor fit for Leo's laid-back California vibe, but the staff has clearly embraced him. People just can't help loving him.

Leo's favorite bottled water is already on the table when we get there. Leo gives me a few minutes to look at the menu, but he orders without looking at it.

After I've ordered, he rubs his hand across his face, then through his hair.

"Tess, I need your help."

I've ordered a glass of wine, so I take a sip.

"Sure."

"Well, really, I need your advice. How do you know when you are ready to settle down? I'm nearly 40, and I have this cool thing with Gabriela…"

"Wait, Leo, you're a year younger than I am – 34 is not nearly 40…"

I don't know who Gabriela is – is she someone he has mentioned before? The name sounds familiar. Then it hits me – world-famous Brazilian supermodel, the sort of person who is known by only one name. She's the one I saw him flirting with during fashion week. Of all the places I would have imagined myself in my life, sitting across the table from the most beautiful man I've ever seen in person, discussing his relationship with the world's most famous Brazilian supermodel is very low on the list.

"I mean it's fun and all," he says. "And of course, she's gorgeous, but I'm just not sure where it's going."

"What do you mean?"

"Well, she just wants to go out every night and travel, and shop, and have sex. I'm not sure what to do."

"So what exactly is the problem?" I ask. This sounds like every man's dream if you take away the shopping – and Leo actually loves shopping.

"I don't know, I look at your kids, or my brothers' families out in California, and I know that I really want that, someday… To be somebody's dad and I don't want to be so old that I can't pick them up. She doesn't even want to talk about our future."

"Leo, she is 20 or something, isn't she?"

"19."

"Well, there you go… If you want a mature relationship, you need to date someone who is a little more mature."

"Where am I supposed to meet someone like that?"

I shrug. "I don't know, Leo. Match.com?"

He laughs loudly.

I get serious. "Look, I don't know enough to tell you what to do with Gabriela, but I will tell you, from experience – if someone isn't sure that they want what you want, don't do it. It'll just be 10 years later, and you still want to go in different directions."

"Is that the voice of experience?"

I am non-committal. I would rather not talk to Leo about my marriage.

"Let's just say that balancing two demanding careers is a challenge."

"So I should just give up on having a life with someone who will have her own pursuits and choose someone who just wants to be my wife? That goes against the strong advice of my business partner and accountants…"

"I'm sorry," I say. "I don't mean it that way… It's just been a long few weeks. Months, actually… "

What a different answer than I'd have given six months ago. I didn't even ask if he loves her. I have always believed that love can make anything work – now I'm not so sure. He needs better than what I've told him.

I really try to think about my answer. If I had wanted someone to tell me what to do before Pete and I got back together, what would I have hoped they would say?

Finally, I say, "Do you love to talk to her? Are you excited to see her after a long time apart? Does watching her sleeping make you happy? Do you feel completed or more fully yourself when you are with her? When you imagine her building her life with someone else, does it fill you with cold fear? If those things are true, then it's worth trying, no matter what."

We stand up and walk back to the office, a cold wind blowing in our faces.

When I get home at 6:30, it is pitch dark, and Vanessa is already standing by the door, packed and ready to go.

Gracie toddles over to her, holds her little arms out to be picked up, waves at me, and says, "Bye, bye Mommy."

Vanessa gives me a meaningful stare and passes Gracie back to me.

"No, no, honey," I say. "Vanessa is going home to her house. You live here with Mommy and Daddy."

Gracie cries inconsolably as Vanessa goes out the door.

I feel my heart breaking.

29

We are high up in a fancy Boston Hotel, celebrating the upcoming holiday season with a crowd of infectious disease doctors and their significant others. As you can guess, the conversation is scintillating – especially if you are me, and you can barely remember the difference between a bacteria and a virus.

I grip my cocktail and tell myself that I will not take my anger at my husband out on his friends and colleagues. He's at work all the time anyway; the last thing I need is to have everyone think he needs to go to Africa to get away from me.

Since it is the departmental Christmas Party and I'm forced to stand here and make conversation with the very people who are responsible for Pete missing Christmas, it is hard work. The alcohol is helping somewhat.

I look around the room. Doctors truly do not know how to dress. Knowing this, I am wearing the same Derek Lam dress I wore during Fashion Week. No use buying something new. There is not one interesting outfit on a man – a few bow ties, yes, but they seem more an act of desperation than any attempt at a personal style. I wonder if the corduroy jacket with patches on the elbows will ever make a comeback on the runway... Really, they all seem to have just ducked out of their white coats. Are no woman doctors married to men who care about clothes? A little more interest among the women, but it is mostly rehearsal dinner wear with a few repurposed bridesmaid's dresses thrown in for good measure.

I do see one truly interesting woman. She is tall and thin with dark skin and a regal bearing. Her hair is in long braids and tied in a high ponytail. Her face is beautiful, but what I notice is the dress.

The dress is brown and has corset detailing on the bodice, and amazing decoration – the fabric is painted with red and light brown squiggles that could come from a modern art gallery or cave paintings with ochre. A few small shells are sewn on as symmetrical decoration, and she wears a choker made of several rows of the same shells.

She is lovely, and she looks like no one else here – perhaps no one I've ever seen.

I see a small girl holding her hand and I know instantly that this must be Dr. van de Berg's young Malian wife, the doctor whom he married who lives apart from him. Her eyes look unbearably sad, but that may be my imagination, or it may be boredom from holding her place in a receiving line. Her daughter is five with hair in twists and a frilly red velvet Christmas dress. The child talks quietly with her mother and smiles shyly at people who talk with her. She clearly has a great deal of experience in being the only child in the room.

I have sworn to myself that I cannot forgive Dr. van de Berg for ruining my Christmas, but I want to meet the woman wearing this dress.

I nudge Pete and ask him to introduce me, and we walk over together.

The doctor looks exactly as I remember – early sixties, but with a fit runner's body, steel grey hair, and a handsome face that has seen a lot of sun. His blue eyes are sharp, but they crinkle with laugh lines at the corners.

He clearly doesn't remember me because he shakes my hand heartily and says, "Delightful to meet you my dear, delightful. This is Mariam and our daughter Anouk."

"I love your dress," I say to Mariam.

"Thank you," she smiles.

I am about to ask her who made it when the doctor interrupts.

"I understand that you and Peter have children as well?"

"Yes," I say, "we have a boy who is three and a baby."

"And you are at home with them, yes?" he asks.

"No, no, I am a handbag designer and creative director for a small company. But we have a wonderful nanny."

Mariam looks at me with interest.

"Which firm?" she asks.

"Skyler Reed."

"Oh, I love Skyler Reed – not so small any more, if what I see in Vogue is true."

I shrug and smile. I have not quite learned how to describe Skyler Reed now that it is part of international conglomerate; especially because I'm not entirely comfortable with the transition.

"Do you like your nanny?" the doctor asks.

"Yes," I say. "It's interesting, I wouldn't have imagined that when I hired someone to look after my children I would get a friend, but we have a great relationship…"

Dr. van de Berg interrupts.

"I would be very careful, if I were you."

"Sure, sure," Pete says.

"No really, Peter, I mean it – years ago, in Geneva, there was a woman that I knew, very high up in the hospital. She hired a nanny who came very well recommended. An Englishwoman, I believe, which may explain some of it. At any rate, this woman watched the baby from his earliest infancy. One afternoon, after the woman had been with them a year, the mother came home early from the hospital to find the nanny pinching the baby mercilessly."

We all gasp.

"Of course, she was fired on the spot," he continues. "But it was many, many years of doctors, psychiatrists, everything they could think of. But the child never was quite right."

He puts his hand on his own daughter's shoulder.

"Children truly do belong with their mothers," he says.

I look at Pete in shock.

I don't know whether to laugh or cry.

Given that my baby is trying to leave home with the nanny, I think that pinching is the least of my worries.

"Don't listen to Gerard," Mariam says. "He has no idea what he is talking about…"

She smiles at him benevolently.

"Gerard thinks that because his beloved mother was at home with him, it is the only way to raise a child."

"But, my dear, you are home with Anouk. It the best way, is it not?"

"I'm home with Anouk because otherwise she would not see either of her parents," she says it sweetly, but it makes me think that Mariam is not unaware of her husband's absences.

"Of course, my love," he says.

Pretty free with the endearments, this one. Since he is old enough to be her father, perhaps her grandfather, it has an odd effect.

He pats her on the arm and looks a little embarrassed. As though they have had this conversation more than once.

"But you of course both understand the importance of my work…" He turns to Pete and me. "I think the mother's love is the most important in the early years, especially for a girl, don't you agree? As she ages, certainly, we shall bring her with us when we go back to Mali. But not now, she is too young. Perhaps we can convince Peter to come to Mali with us, and then Anouk might perhaps have playmates – the children are of an age, I believe?"

Great.

I know that the smile on my face looks stricken.

Mariam turns to me.

"Come; let's allow them to talk of doctor things. Now you tell me what you are planning for fall? What are you showing?"

I tell a little about the fairy tales that we are working on.

"Wonderful," she says. And she claps with happiness.

I like this woman a lot.

"Tell me," she says. "Why are you not doing the Creative Desk article any more?"

I must look surprised.

"Oh, I know more than you know – it is boring, being in Geneva with no one to see and nothing to do – playing with Anouk, that I love, but waiting and waiting for Gerard… Well, one must find things to do. So when I find out that anyone affiliated with the program is doing anything interesting, I follow it closely on the computer. I have been an admirer of yours since Peter started with the program. How could I not be?"

I blush.

"But I'm just a handbag designer. You're a doctor aren't you?"

"Shhhh," she says. "I hated it. I tease Gerard that I am home because he makes me be, but if I wanted to do anything, he would let me. For myself, I would love to make dresses."

"Did you make that one?" I ask. "I love it."

"Oh, no, no; this one is from a quite famous African designer who works in Paris – Alphadi. You have heard of him?"

I am embarrassed to say no, but I haven't.

"No matter," she says. "But tell me, what has happened to your feature on the web site? There is something there now, but it is stultifying…"

I decide to spare her the corporate details and tell her only that I have started a new one on my own. I tell her the title.

"I will have to look at it," she says. "Does anyone read it?"

"Shockingly, yes," I say. "I would hardly have imagined it. I enjoy it, but now it's added yet another thing that I have to do."

She smiles.

Anouk has been standing quietly during our conversation – something my children would never have done.

She pulls at her mother's hand and whispers something to her.

"Pardon me," Mariam says. "We will visit the powder room."

For the rest of the evening, I manage to drink steadily and to listen to boring doctor talk without starting any more conversations on my own.

30

"Okay, now hold your nose, and don't touch anything!" I say to Jake as I push the button in the nastiest elevator in Boston's subway system. And that is saying something.

Interestingly it is an elevator that connects a major subway line to the train to the airport. It is an open question why the MBTA believes that tourists and their bags should become acquainted with the distinct smell of an elevator that is used as a public restroom. Normally, I would never go within 50 feet of this elevator, but I am pushing a stroller with a backpack hanging off the handles, carrying a backpack myself and holding the hand of my three-year-old, so the escalator is not an option.

When we get off the elevator, I hear the rumble of our connecting train.

"Hurry up, let's hustle." I say to Jake. If we run, we can make it, and we're running late, so we should try to make it.

My three-year old and I start running through the tunnel with the stroller.

My backpack bounces and the stroller clatters. Jake holds onto one of the stroller handles and runs as fast as his little legs can manage.

Then, disaster –

Jake's foot hits the stroller wheel. He falls. I trip over him, and I fall. The stroller rolls to a stop ahead of us, unattached.

This being Boston, no one stops to help us up.

If Pete had been here, we would not have fallen.

While I am helping Jake up, we hear the train screech out of the station.

We walk to the platform, dejected.

The hustle must have shifted the weight in the backpack hanging off the stroller, because just as the next train pulls into the station, the stroller slowly tips over backwards, and poor little Gracie is flat on her back, held in place by her five-point harness, and wiggling her little arms and legs like a bug stuck to a slide.

I ignore the stares from passersby, right the stroller, take the backpack off of it, and now wear it on my front military style. We board the train this way – I'm ready for my deployment as an urban mom taking two kids across country by myself.

If possible, it gets worse at security.

Whoever made the rule that kids have to take off their shoes at security needs a special room in hell with a bunch of two- and three-year-olds refusing to remove their shoes.

Jake won't take off his sneakers.

He screams, he cries, he runs away. He hides under a table in a secure area.

Gracie's stroller is already on the belt.

"Excuse me," I ask the uniformed TSA official in front of me, "can you hold her? I have to go get him."

A line is now forming behind me and my enormous pile of stuff.

"We're not allowed to hold babies," the woman says brusquely.

"Fine, can you go get him?" I point at Jake.

"We aren't allowed to hold kids, either."

There are no other uniformed representatives.

If Pete had been here, I would not be outnumbered by children.

I can't ask the people behind me in line – they all have places to go, plus, they might walk off with my baby. This woman can't go anywhere. It's her job to stand right here being useless.

"Please, take the baby," I say through clenched teeth. I thrust her at the woman who finally takes her.

Gracie immediately starts screaming.

I hop to the other side of the security line and grab Jake, hoping that no alarms sound, and I march him back to the line.

I hold Jake under my arm, force his shoes off, take the baby back, and try to go through the metal detector holding both of them.

"The little boy needs to walk," the metal detector man says. Did he miss what just happened? Does the child meet any terrorist profile in the known world?

I tell Jake that if he doesn't behave himself and walk through the detector slowly, without touching anything, Santa won't be coming to Grandma's house. He pulls himself together and makes it through.

"Will Santa come now?" he asks after we've collected our things.

"I don't know," I say. "That depends on how quickly you put your shoes on."

I wish I'd thought of the Santa angle earlier – he's all obedience now.

We make it to the gate just as boarding begins and I can finally relax.

Finally we're on the plane. Gracie is on my lap, Jake next to me – our flight is going directly to Memphis. In just a few short hours, I'll be eating barbecue in the warm embrace of my family.

Speaking of warm, at that moment, I feel a warm wetness in my lap, and I think I might cry.

In the excitement, I have had no time to change Gracie's diaper, which has now overflowed and leaked all over her and me.

If Pete had been here, I would have gotten him to change the damn diaper.

I trudge back to the tiny airplane bathroom, kids in tow, embarrassing wet spot on my lap.

This airplane does not have a changing table in the tiny bathroom, so I balance Gracie on the sink while Jake stands behind me, wedged in next to the toilet. His hand almost touches the flight attendant call button before I stop him. Gracie leans her elbow on the faucet, spraying water on my blouse.

Of course I have changes of clothes for the children, but it never occurred to me to pack something for myself.

Hopefully the next week of festivities is more relaxing than the trip to get here.

I try not to resent Pete, or look at the empty seat next to Jake where Pete is supposed to be sitting.

Gracie is asleep in my lap and Jake is about to fall asleep next to me, when he suddenly opens his eyes and looks at me.

"Mommy, what happens if Santa comes down the chimney when there's a fire?"

"What do you think might happen?" I ask.

"Santa's bottom might get burned!"

"Really?"

"The reindeer might laugh," he says. And he smiles a great big smile and then falls asleep.

JANUARY

31

Christmas was painful, what with Pete's mom mourning his absence, the sad and horrible party with all of his friends and no Pete, and the children crying for Daddy.

But Santa did end up coming – he brought a toy assault rifle and five bushels of teeny tiny Polly Pocket paraphernalia – and at least it was over quickly.

During the extra week that the children stayed in Memphis, I have done nothing but work and if I have noticed Pete's absence it has been with a certain gratefulness that I am not charged with feeding him.

For myself, it's been Dunkin' Donuts coffee, soup from Au Bon Pain and a huge bag of baby carrots that the kids left. For the first time in my fashion career, I'm beginning to look fashionably gaunt. I'm pleased about that, but the dark circles under my eyes are much less charming.

Then, on the 8th of January, my kids come back, Pete comes back, Gretchen is back for what is supposed to be her last week with us, and I am back to failing at everything.

Monday morning, when I wake Jake, he looks at me with sad eyes.

"I want to see Gillian."

Gillian is my husband's brother's six-year-old. She and Jake have an amazing bond.

"Oh, honey, we'll see her this summer," I say.

He sits on the floor and weeps.

I realize that this is the first time he's met one of life's big emotions – finding a true friend and then missing her. Knowing that it will be a very, very long time before you can see someone again and longing for them. This is one he will meet again and again in his life, and I am here to see it.

I do, however, have an 8:30 meeting and I am supposed to be taking him to preschool, so we don't really have time to dwell.

"Come on, honey, we have to get ready for school."

"But, mommy," he says. "I'm so sad. Can you just hold me?"

I think about it for a minute… No, I really can't – people have flown in from New York for this meeting, Tom will be there, the whole marketing team, two representatives from an international company making licensed goods who are headed back to China tomorrow. If I'm not there Katrina will take over and I'm not giving her an inch of ground.

I hug him quickly and then pull him to his feet.

"C'mon, kiddo, if you want mommy to take you to school, you need to hustle."

"But I want to see Gillian," sniff, sniff.

"No time, let's get your clothes on."

He sinks to the floor sobbing.

I don't have time for this.

"Vanessa," I call out to the dining room where she's feeding Gracie, "you'll have to take Jake to school, I really have to go now."

I see her on my way out.

"Tess," she says, with a worried look in her eye, "Gracie doesn't seem quite herself. Do you think there's any chance she has that ear infection again?"

I look at Gracie. It's true, she doesn't look that hot – and she hasn't touched her breakfast, a sure sign that something's wrong, since most of the time, she's a champion eater.

If I don't have time for one of life's big emotions, I sure don't have time for an ear infection.

I feel Gracie's forehead.

It's definitely hot.

I simply can't take her to the doctor.

I think of Katrina's words so long ago – can't the nanny take her to the doctor? I remember my indignation, and can't waste any time worrying about it.

I find myself saying to Vanessa, "I'll call the pediatrician on the train and get an appointment; you can take her over after you drop Jake off at school. It's right on Centre Street."

"You want me to take her to the doctor?" Vanessa says.

"I don't know what else to do," I say.

As I run out the door, I feel her eyes on my back – judging me.

I enter the meeting two minutes late and find Katrina's eyes on me – judging me.

Can't win for losing.

The meetings are long and productive, but they suck up the whole day. I have a voice mail message from Vanessa confirming the ear infection and I buy the antibiotics over the phone so she can pick them up later.

There is also an email from Jake's school saying that the pet mouse died over the holiday break. The teachers have decided to tell the children that the mouse had gone to live with another family. This decision was made because some families were adamantly against telling the children about the mouse's death. We are all free to mention to our own children, should it be important to us, but the school is worried that the children might talk to one another about it.

Wow. On the one hand, this seems insane to me – what better way to introduce the children to the circle of life than through the death of Hugo the Mouse. On the other hand, do I really have time for an in-depth discussion of life and death? No. I decide that I'm not going to say anything about the mouse.

I take advantage of the fact that Pete is working a short day to stay late and finish a few things – let him be the one to put them to bed by himself for once.

I forget to ask Pete if Jake has mentioned Hugo the Mouse's absence.

FEBRUARY

32

My first indication that this Fashion Week is going to be categorically different from the last one is the car and driver that pick me up at the airport. The driver holds a placard with my name on it in the baggage claim area, and he insists on bringing my bags.

The second is that we're back at the Plaza – I just mentioned the wonderful service and comfortable beds and Lauren (who has just returned from maternity leave and is carrying the first generation Skyler Reed/Medela breast pump) got it done. I had to stop her from putting Katrina in the Ramada in Newark.

I am trying to build a respectful relationship with the demon bitch. Lauren told me that she is on a very low floor, next to a bank of rooms taken up with a group of gastroenterologists from Cleveland. No one could ever claim that was my fault.

The next indication is that unlike the last trip, I have not a moment to sit down or be still. From the minute I arrive, I feel like Eisenhower organizing the invasion of Normandy. There are just so many moving pieces that all must be in place before our show in the tents at Bryant Park.

For the first time, we are doing a full fashion show with all the attendant attention and publicity. Of course, Leo has done this dozens of times, and I've seen our bags in other designer's shows, but to be doing our own show, it's a whole other level of effort – and many, many people would like to see us screw it up.

I get the feeling that not all of those people come from outside the company.

In the four months since my restoration, I have noticed Katrina's sly and at times open attempts to disparage my knowledge, creativity or understanding. She likes to stand outside my office door and talk to junior design staff about how tidy desks demonstrate disciplined minds. My desk does bear a certain resemblance to a trailer park after a tornado, but I know where everything is – and besides, I thrive on controlled chaos. Katrina still holds Caitlin under her sway, and I swear that I've seen the former intern (recently promoted to Katrina's first assistant) taking notes in a little notebook – especially when I am late or can't find a piece of paper right when I'm looking for it.

Coming down the hallway, I hear Katrina talking to Caitlin about the upcoming show.

As I walk past, she raises her voice.

"Well it's Tom that I feel sorry for – really, what can he have been thinking? It's not as though she's ever done anything on this scale! When it is an unmitigated disaster, at least no one can claim it was my fault… I just hope we can redeem some of the brand value…"

If I'm the general during the day, I'm a socialite in the evenings. Suddenly, everyone knows who I am – I have people who I have seen for years but who have never troubled to remember my name, coming up to me to introduce themselves.

I didn't even have to pick my own clothes – Leo has outfitted me for every event. I have never been styled before, and it is an interesting experience – the clothes are things that I would have looked at but never worn (and that's saying something). I have to figure based on the fact that Leo thinks they'll look good, that they'll actually look okay. And they must, because I am swimming in compliments.

In my new insider view, I see lots of cool stuff that I have always been too self-conscious to notice before.

I am introduced to a famous actress and fashionista (on her request) and we talk about her first Skyler Reed bag, back in the early days. It turns out it was her first big purchase, and she had been friendly with Skyler in the intervening years. Skyler always managed our famous contacts – she loved that stuff, and she did own the company. The actress asks me if I've heard from her at the ashram.

I am embarrassed to say that I haven't. I hope that it is because she doesn't want to think about work. Maybe she isn't calling anyone.

"She left a message on my cell last week that she feels spiritually cleansed," the actress said. "She's thinking of coming to Hollywood to be a producer."

"I thought she wanted a less stressful life," I say.

The actress laughs. "We'll see."

I watch the actress as she talks to me. She is beautiful, but strangely unreal.

A young woman to my left wearing a party hat and a very short skirt unconsciously pulls a bit of food from between her teeth, and I know instantly that the actress has given up her ability to ever do that – anywhere. She is always watched, always photographed.

There's also the matter of the two or three very large men with earpieces who are unobtrusive, but always in view. What a strange life.

I look around the room, and I notice several faces veering away from eye contact, and I realize that they have been watching me too. It is similar to the feeling a youngish woman gets when she walks into a sports bar – a bunch of eyes sizing you up. The difference is that these people know who I am and where I work.

I knew it was true with Skyler, but I hadn't considered that it would happen to me. I'm not sure that I like it.

Finally, the day of our show comes and it is a marvel.

Leo has taken my ideas – about fairy tales, organic forms and natural materials – and transformed them into wonderful clothes that complement our bags, shoes and belts. The fabrics are beautiful, and I watch from backstage as the models walk out and back in his clothes. If I could, I would wear every piece. On the hangers, I knew that they were good, but on the models, they are magnificent.

Leo drags me out with him when he acknowledges the applause.

I am giddy.

The afterparty is in a private club that feels like a stylized luxury speakeasy, all red velvet banquets and throwback mixed drinks. I couldn't tell you the name of it for anything. I'm not sure how people who get around with a car and driver ever really know where they are. This is a life where you never have to Mapquest the directions.

I may not know where I am, but I sure know who I am – the belle of the ball.

I wear a dress that Leo picked out – it's a Badgley Mischka. It is long and flowing in shades of white and grey. It has a Grecian style, with bands at the bust and draping on the sleeves. It also dips low. Very low. Much lower than I am used to. Thankfully, I do actually own a bra designed to cope with such things. I look like a princess.

I am complemented by Tom (and a million other corporate types whose names I could not hope to remember), my design staff brings me drink after drink, and I get a double cheek kiss and a 'wonderful' from Hilda Adams the fashion critic.

Katrina sulks in the corner. I'm sure she's found something to criticize, but I refuse to let her ruin my night.

I sit down in one of the banquets to rest my feet for a moment when Leo slides in beside me. He puts his arm around my shoulders. I try to decide if this should be making me uncomfortable.

"Relax," he says. "You can finally relax… You own this town. I had so much fun working with you on this one. It may be the most fun I've had as a designer. We are good together."

I smile.

We sit there together for a minute. He smells really good.

I try to think about something other than arm around me. It's not like he's done anything inappropriate – it's just a brotherly arm over the shoulder, right?

Gabriela the Brazilian supermodel must not like it too much though, because a second later she is at his side telling him that she is bored and she wants him to take her to another party.

Soon afterwards I go home too (in my case back to my bed at the hotel).

MARCH

33

Fashion Week is over, reviews were great, clothes are selling, bags are selling, Corporate is happy. Things are supposed to be better for me at work, but they are not – now that Fall is over, we're in a tizzy for Resort...

Resort, you may ask, what the hell is resort?

That is certainly what Vanessa said when I attempted to explain why I would be late coming home because of yet another conference call.

"What could you possibly be talking about?" she said.

"Haven't you people said everything that could ever be said on the subject of a handbag?" Her tone is light, but I know her aggravation is real.

I try to explain to her that resort has grown into a full category of its own. It was originally designed for wearing on holiday vacation in tropical spots, but now is really the only reason that any of us can buy new clothes that are seasonally appropriate to the summer months, because otherwise when you realize you need a pair of khakis or a light cardigan, the stores would be filled with clothes for fall and winter.

Vanessa buys all of her clothes at the thrift shop, where they have no seasons. She is unsympathetic.

Gretchen is unsympathetic as well. She and Pete make jokes at dinner about resort. They can do this because although Gretchen has found her own apartment and is no longer living in our house, she is here almost every night. It is March. She came in September. I have no idea if she ever plans to find her own friends. Maybe she's just planning to move back in, waiting me out. She's started working for Dr. van de Berg, too, so she can see Pete all the time, I fear.

Pete and I are more like roommates than a couple now anyway. With so much work and so little time, when we barely have the energy to talk, we certainly don't have the energy for sex. When was the last time? November. Between Halloween and Thanksgiving, things were almost back to normal. But then he told me about Mali, and things got busy at work.

The only reason I haven't said anything else about Gretchen's constant presence is because I'm so rarely home at this point that I don't exactly have a strong argument. Most nights I come home to find that Gretchen has already made the children dinner. Something healthy and natural like greens or fish or couscous, and I can't convince anyone that I've tried and they truly won't eat anything like that for me.

Then, today, when I get home, Gretchen and Vanessa are whispering together.

"I'll take the children on a walk," Gretchen says, and I know that something is wrong. It is March – it is still cold and dark, and it is almost bedtime. There is no good reason for Gretchen to be taking the children out.

"I'm quitting," Vanessa says, without preamble.

"But no, but why, but you can't…" I cry. I feel like Mrs. Banks when Mary Poppins leaves because of the wind's change. "But we need you!"

"Yes, but it isn't meeting my needs," she says. "I started nannying to make money while I was working on my art, and that worked with your family for a long time – hell, Tess, I like you, I like the kids."

She shrugs.

"I'll miss them, but I have to do something else for me."

"We can figure something out," I say. "Gracie will be in preschool soon, you can have that time during the day; we can make it work, Vanessa, please don't go."

She shakes her head.

"It isn't good for them either, Tess, with both of you being gone so much."

"Well, I can't do anything about that!" I say, exasperated, and then I try to pull myself back. "Can't we do something for you?"

"No."

I try to be devious, we were her first family, maybe I can convince her that the grass isn't any greener...

"Won't you have the same issues with the new family?" I ask. "How do you know that they won't need you to work more than they say?"

"It's not like that – they only need me some evenings and on the weekends," she says. "It's a great deal, actually, because I will be living in a mother-in-law's apartment in their house, so I can let my apartment go. The kids are in preschool during the day, so I'll have time to do my own thing."

Wait a minute. This sounds familiar.

"Are you leaving us to go work for Raj and Mira?"

"They asked me not to tell you," she says.

"And they thought I wouldn't find out?"

"Don't be mad..." she says.

Mad, I'm not mad, I'm furious, crazed... You let somebody borrow your nanny and see what happens? Mira was my freshman roommate! I can't believe that they are doing this to me.

"I asked them if they wanted to hire me," she says. "I had already decided that I was quitting... It's not their fault that I think it would be easier to work for them."

I remember her whispering with Gretchen.

"Did Gretchen put you up to this?" It wouldn't surprise me – I have a feeling that Gretchen is looking for ways to make me be at home more. As though I don't already know that I've been spending too much time at work…

"No, no, I only told her today," Vanessa says.

I wonder whether to believe her.

"How long do I have?" I asked, resigned.

"Two weeks."

Great. Now I can look forward to interviewing nannies.

The horror show continues at dinner.

Gretchen has made a lovely dish of curried lentils. Pete and the children love it. The lentils are ashes in my mouth.

All during dinner, Gretchen talks about Dr. van de Berg and all the great work they are doing at his clinic in Mali.

"Hey, Pete," she asks. "Have you heard that Dr. Malik is leaving?"

I don't know who Dr. Malik is. Is this someone I've met? Someone I'm supposed to remember? No one enlightens me.

Pete nods.

"Why don't you put your name in?"

"I've been thinking about it." Pete looks at me. "It would be a great job – I mean being the medical director at the clinic in Mali would be awesome, but I don't think Tess would think much of moving to Africa right now."

When did we start talking about moving to Africa? Isn't this something you're supposed to mention to your wife first? I mean, I knew that he was questioning his career, he has said several times that the trip to Mali was mind-blowing, but I was expecting him to start pushing for more trips abroad, maybe look at some summer opportunities to be a doctor-in-residence, not that he'd be considering moving our family to the third world…

"But what a wonderful experience for the children," Gretchen says. "To grow up in another culture, to learn the world… They could even learn another language – what a gift for children to be fluent in French and Bambara…"

Okay, following the Christmas party and Pete's trip, I have finally found Mali on a map – it is in West Africa. I have found the designer of Mrs. Van de Berg's dress, his name is Alphadi and he is from West Africa, although he works in Paris. But I have no idea what Bambara is, and I honestly sort of resent being expected to know it. I'm not going to ask.

"Bambara is the main language in Mali." Pete says.

Now I resent having to be told.

"Daddy, would we see giraffes if we lived in Africa?" Jake asks.

"Sure, kiddo," he says.

"Peter, if you got the job, you could go to Mali with the children, while Tess stays here. She is so rarely home as it is, and I'm sure she could make the time to visit. It would be like a vacation."

She is wearing a smile I cannot read. Is she serious? Joking?

Evil?

"There are plenty of great infectious disease jobs here in Boston," I say. "There's no reason for Pete to think of going to Africa."

"Except for the reasons he went into medicine," she says, and she is deadly serious now.

I cannot believe I am having this discussion with this woman at my table, with my kids watching. I am as civil as I can be.

"Pete has made his decision about the kind of life that he is going to have while the children are small. We are not risking taking them overseas. It's too dangerous."

Safer ground when it's about the children, and not about me.

"Funny," she says. "People all over the world manage to raise children to adulthood. I'm sorry to hear that you think that your children, who have the benefits of wonderful medical care and vaccinations, and who would be living within an international community, are too good for the rest of the world."

My face is getting red…

"Hold on, hold on, everybody," Pete says. "We don't even know if there is a job – Dr. Malik may manage to sort out his personal life – how about we hold off on moving the family to Mali before we've even seen a posting."

I put the children to bed, while Pete and Gretchen load the dishwasher. I don't love seeing them doing something so couple-like together, while at the same time, I can't be with her for another minute.

My horrible day is not yet over, however.

Pete and I lie in bed together, having a whispered discussion about what we are looking for in a nanny.

"Should we get someone who lives in the house?" Pete asks.

"We don't need a live-in," I blurt out.

"Why not?" he asks. "Isn't that really why Vanessa quit? Because we need her more time than she's willing to give? With a live-in we wouldn't have that problem – if you have to work until 7:00 it's no big deal because she lives here anyway…"

"Where would we put her?" I ask. Gretchen in the spare room has been more than enough of an invasion of privacy.

"We could move," he says. "With your raise, we could afford a larger house. It would be a strain for a few months, but once I start making more, we would be fine."

I find myself getting angry and I'm not sure why. It's not like I've never thought about moving – four people in a 2+ bedroom condo would make a tight fit eventually. But something about this conversation is making me livid.

"We don't need a live-in," I say again, this time too loudly.

"Don't get mad, Tess. I'm just trying to talk about how we can make all this work. Why won't you consider it?"

I know that I must seem irrational. I just know what I'm feeling.

"Because I'm the mommy, we don't need another one," I finally whisper.

I feel like I'm about to cry.

Pete puts on his steadiest voice – it is the one he uses for patients who seem mentally deranged. If he were at work he'd be looking for a buzzer to call in the orderlies.

"Tess, you have your job, which is crazy-busy; I have my job, which is crazy-busy. How are we going to be able to both keep our jobs if we don't have somebody here to pick up the slack? We aren't like those people who have family in town. It's just us here."

"We did it okay before, back before Skyler sold," I say. "Just wait, it'll get better, you'll see. I'll be able to be home more."

Pete's patience finally breaks.

"Oh for crying out loud, Tess! You've been saying that to yourself and Vanessa for months – when will you finally realize that it's not true? It's not getting any better. In fact, I'll bet it's about to get worse. How long will it be before they want you to go to China with them? What will we do with the kids then? Something has to change – you made the choice to do this, you told me that this is what you wanted – that's fine with me, I just want you to be happy. But if you want this, you have to realize that you're going to have to give up on doing everything yourself. This is not the Mothering Olympics."

We fall asleep on opposite sides of the bed, and I make sure that even my feet can't touch him.

www.lifemotherhoodhandbags.com/home

LIFE, MOTHERHOOD & THE PURSUIT OF THE PERFECT HANDBAG

February 25 - I try to never read reviews, but wow, we did good!
So I really try not to pay attention to what people say about my company. We should do what we do and try not to worry about what people say. And yet… Yay!
Comments (57):

March 17 - Superhero Day?
My son's school has a Superhero Day, where the children are supposed to be costumed as superheroes they've made up themselves – nothing commercial and no weapons. This mentally & emotionally fulfilling preschool is killing me! Ideas?
Comments (12)
from Julia: And here you were whining about boring Halloween costumes! What about Cupcake Man?

About me
Since I was a little girl, I have dreamed about handbags… I am the lead handbag designer for a well-known firm. I am also married with a preschool son and a baby daughter. I am refusing to listen to the ongoing lobbying for a pet.

34

Two weeks later, I stand at the door, dressed and ready to go, and waiting on the new nanny.

I am by myself with the children –

Jake is adorable in his Cupcake Man costume. He loved Julia's idea. He has a large wrapper made of aluminum foil and we made him a glitter shirt with a big C on the front of it. He has on a purple cape, because every superhero needs a cape. I gave him a cupcake for dessert in his lunch too.

It's 7:30. Still no nanny.

I look at my phone – no messages.

7:45 – no nanny.

I call the number that she gave me. It has been disconnected.

I interviewed 10 nannies, and she seemed far and away the best: pleasant, good with children, and crucially, available to work until 6:30 or 7:00 every night.

But she has disappeared.

I call our back-up childcare. They are having trouble with the plumbing and are not taking any children today.

I can take Jake to school, but what in the world will I do with Gracie?

I call every friend I have, no one can take her.

I think about calling in sick. I haven't called in since Katrina Aspinwall and OmniBrands came into my life.

But no, not today – I have a standing design meeting, and Leo has come in from New York especially to meet with me, and Katrina is having some kind of big top secret thing that I want to keep my eye on.

I pack the diaper bag full of toys and decide to bring the baby to work. She's an easy baby, she entertains herself well, I have my own office and I can spend most of the day in there with her. The standing meeting with my staff is at 1:00, so I'll just roll her into the meeting, asleep in her stroller. If she isn't napping maybe no one will mind, I am the boss, right? Really, people all over the world have their children at work with them… How bad could it be?

My first indication of how bad comes when I step off the elevator to be met by Katrina and a crowd of women, all well-accessorized in scarves and earrings. Looking more closely, I see a few of men, most dressed all in black with silver necklaces and one older man with a paisley neck scarf. They are quite decorative.

Gracie in her stroller, hands and face grubby from Munchkins, draws stares of undisguised disgust. One pretty blonde with smooth hair and a boucle Chanel suit does smile at her and do a little wave. Gracie waves back, and I am grateful for the smile. The blonde looks familiar to me for some reason, although I can't say why.

Katrina looks at me. "What is that doing here?" she asks. I am unsure if she means the stroller or the baby.

I remember her lack of sympathy to nanny troubles, so I lie. "Just breakfast with Mommy, thought I'd show her the office..."

I trail off. It is an awful lie. There is such a thing as Bring Your Daughter to Work Day, but it is meant for 11-year-olds, not 19-month-olds.

It wouldn't have mattered – even if Katrina had been listening to me, which she isn't, she knows so little about children that she may not be aware of developmental ages. She is one of those people who complain in restaurants because two-year-olds cannot sit quietly in their chairs and eat like normal people.

Her eyes glance at me again, avoiding looking at Gracie – "If you don't mind," she says. "We would like to have you come into the large conference room at 10:00 to make a small presentation about the brand values. I have gathered a group of leading interior decorators and home magazine editorial staff and we are presenting the new home line. They were quite interested in seeing where all the fashion magic is made."

She smiles at them indulgently, and I can see how she has built a following – in this setting she can be quite charming.

A statement about brand values? Surely she has known about this for some amount of time? You would think that she would have given me more than an hour to prepare. I remember that it is Katrina, the evil bitch, and I am grateful to even have that long.

The home line is a group of licensed collections with several manufactures, and the company is banking on it going well. The sunglasses, jewelry and knickknacks have sold, and Corporate is hoping to transform Skyler Reed into a lifestyle brand. I could care less about sheets, towels and window dressing, but I try to think of something inspiring to say.

I set Gracie up with her toys on a blanket.

I decide to go with the old standard about brass tacks, simple fabrics, great lines, and timeless style.

I have a few close calls, like when I take Gracie with me to the bathroom and I almost run into Katrina's tour of the office, but everything seems to be going fine.

At 9:50, I see the flaw in my plan.

I'm keeping Gracie's presence here a secret, but I can't leave her by herself in my office.

I peek out my door. I know Therrien or Linette won't want to watch her, but they've known me for so long, surely they can do me this little favor. It will only be for a few minutes. Or Stacey, I can always depend on Stacey – I mean she wouldn't have gone into stationery if she wasn't the kind of person you could ask for a favor. If she does it, I swear that I will write her a thank you note.

Wait, Linette and Therrien are vacationing together in Aruba – they are both single this year and decided just to take off together before resort consumes them both.

I look down the hall toward Stacey's cube. I creep out the door and close it quietly, making sure that Gracie doesn't notice. She's too busy knocking over a tower of soft blocks. There is a note taped to Stacey's computer that announces she's at the dentist.

Should I ask someone on my staff? They all are getting ready for a meeting with me at 1:00. That seems very uncool.

I remember that Leo is here today. Leo can help me. I knock on the door to his office.

He stands and smiles at me.

Good Lord he is gorgeous.

"Hi, Leo, it's gotta be fast – can I ask you a favor?"

"Sure," he says.

"Come to my office."

I open the door. Gracie is right where I left her.

"Um, what's she doing here?" Leo says.

"Long story – listen, can you watch her for a few minutes? It won't be very long – I just have to go talk to Katrina's interior designer convention."

"Sure, I like kids," he says.

I introduce Gracie to Leo.

"We've met," he says.

I remember the day in the park last summer. She was so much smaller then. She hadn't even had her birthday.

"She may not remember," I say.

"That's okay."

Maybe she won't cry. She saw me leave and didn't cry. Separation anxiety peaks at this age, but everybody loves Leo. I'm sure it will be fine.

I am five minutes late to our meeting. Katrina glares at me.

I stand at the front of the room, talking about our brand values, when I notice that the eyes of the room are no longer on me.

The large conference room is fronted with windows that look out into the office, and our visitors are looking out of them.

I also hear a sound. Normally one I like, but not in this context – it is wild, childish laughter.

I very slowly follow their eyes out the windows, and there I see Leo pretending to run down the rows of cubes with Gracie toddling after him and screeching with laughter.

I force myself to look at Katrina. Her face has hardened into a tight mask.

She forces a smile.

"Thank you, Tess," she says. "I will excuse you to address your… situation."

I have no time to finish my remarks, but thank our guests and try not to run out of the conference room.

Caitlin follows me out. Katrina will soon have the full report on whatever happens next.

I pick up the baby and shush her, apologizing to the design staff who are all peeking over their cube walls to see what is happening.

I march Leo back to my office, trying hard not to explode at him – he was trying to do me a favor.

Life, Motherhood & the Pursuit of the Perfect Handbag

"Um, Leo, what were you thinking?" I say.

"I was keeping her busy while you were in the meeting," he says, as though nothing strange or untoward has happened.

"Leo, I meant for you to keep her quiet, and out of the way, in my office, where nobody could see her."

"Well you didn't say that, did you? She was crying, I just wanted to make her laugh…"

I don't say that there are million ways to make her laugh that don't involve disturbing the whole office.

I start packing up our things. There is no way that I can stay here now. I'll have to call Tom to do some damage control. I don't want to hear the message that Katrina is going to leave him. He'll be in the office next week, so I try to prepare myself for the worst. I'll call Lauren too. It can't hurt to have her on my side.

"What are you so worried about?" he says.

"Oh, I don't know, keeping my job?"

Sarcasm is not a great mode for Leo.

"What, you think they are going to fire you because I was playing with Gracie?" he asks. He looks wounded.

"We've made the advertising buys. Sheets, towels, pillowcases, curtains, et cetera, have been bought and ordered from factories in China, Malaysia and India. If we get a slam in Vogue Home, and the line doesn't perform as expected, all because I brought my kid into the office – no, no, I do not think my position at Skyler Reed is safe. Or worse, they could put me back under Katrina – I'd never survive."

"I don't think Tom would do that," Leo says. "Your work is so great; you are the heart of the brand."

I sure hope so.

I pass through the kitchen area, where the designers are grazing on a pan-Asian spread.

I would have loved to avoid the gauntlet, but it's the only way out of the office.

The blonde in the Chanel suit smiles at me. I notice that she is carrying the accordion bag from last season.

"What a beautiful child," she says. "And such a laugh – infectious!"

No one else is looking at me directly, although a few of the other people look like they think the baby might actually be infectious. I am glad that Gracie is corralled in the stroller – she has a gift for befriending people who dislike children.

"I have a little girl of my own, but she's with the nanny today, it was a treat to see yours," the blonde says.

I smile wryly and say, "She was supposed to be too."

"I know how it goes." She leans in and whispers, "Have you heard of Parents in a Pinch? They come in on short notice for just this kind of thing. You might think of calling them, if it happens again…"

I am about to ask if they are expensive, when I remember two things – first, where I am standing, and second, they now pay me enough that I can afford to pay for a high-priced nanny. In fact, if it could assure that incidents like today don't happen again,

Tom will probably let me expense it. Why didn't I think of it this morning?

The blonde puts out her hand. "I'm Corrine Downing Dailey."

I realize that I've heard her name before. She is Kerry's friend the interior decorator in Back Bay. That's why she looks familiar; I've seen her face in the party pictures at the back of Boston Magazine. In other circumstances, I would ask her if she's talked to Kerry lately.

I feel glad that I have at least one person in my corner. Although the other faces do not look promising.

Katrina follows me to the elevator.

She looks at me coldly.

"Don't imagine that I won't be calling Tom about this debacle," she says.

"Oh believe me, I don't have any doubt about that," I say.

"Did you think that we were running a day care here? I've said it from the beginning – you have no concept of what is involved in running a high fashion firm. Really, here we are attempting to convince the opinion-makers for home fashion design that we are a leader in the industry, that we are poised to leap into the stratosphere of brands, and you are playing games. You may not take this firm seriously, but I certainly do. Perhaps this time, Tom will finally see that I am correct. You are, fatally, I'm afraid, quite middlebrow. There is no future for you at Skyler Reed."

I have never hated our ancient elevator more.

Finally the doors close and Gracie and I are away.

Will Tom take her side? I suppose it will all depend on whether Skyler Reed Home is a bust or not.

I have forgiven Pete enough to tell him the story. He thinks I'm making too much of nothing and thinks it's hilarious that Leo (who he's never met) would have played tag with Gracie in the office.

He waits until I have a glass of wine to tell me that they've posted Dr. Malik's job.

"Are you going to put in for it?" I ask.

"You don't want me to."

"I want you to do what will make you happy," I say. In my heart, I beg him to say that staying here in Boston and living our half-way normal life is what will make him happy.

"I'm sure I won't get it. It wouldn't hurt to apply for it – then I'd see if I was well-qualified. You know, for the future."

"Sure," I say.

I lay my head on his shoulder.

I am not going to tell Pete what he has to do. I am not going to be responsible for keeping him from his dreams. I had just hoped that his dreams would include us too. And that they would not involve me having to move to Mali.

www.lifemotherhoodhandbags.com/home

LIFE, MOTHERHOOD & THE PURSUIT OF THE PERFECT HANDBAG

March 27 - Bicycles...

Since resort is in theory about people vacationing, this will be the season when I'll finally tackle the bicycle problem. Last year I saw a model biking home from Fashion Week, and I just knew she needed a bag. Bike messengers bags as a basis, perhaps? But you have to add some real interest to the strap; otherwise it's just ruining your outfit. If I had time, I would borrow a bike and ride around, just to remember what it feels like. But that would mean that I needed a vacation, because I'm not biking in nasty dirty snow. And if I took a vacation, how would the bike bag ever get designed? A conundrum.

Comments (11):

About me

Since I was a little girl, I have dreamed about handbags... I am the lead handbag designer for a well-known firm. I am also married with a preschool son and a baby daughter. We also have many stuffed animals. I am currently attempting to convince my children that these are an acceptable substitute for a real pet.

APRIL

35

I take Corrine Downing Dailey's nanny temp service advice, and by the next week, we have a new, hopefully more reliable nanny and Parents in a Pinch on speed dial.

Weeks pass, and still I've heard nothing from Tom about Gracie.

The only reason I know that Tom actually listened to his messages and knows anything about it is that Lauren made a joke to me on the phone about bring your baby to work day. But that's it.

I assume that this must be because wants to talk with me

about it in person and he hasn't had time. He's is rarely in Boston now, only two or three times a month, way down from the two times a week when we were first acquired.

A month passes, and still I hear nothing.

Maybe they are waiting to see how the Home Line sells.

The wait clearly bothers Katrina as well. She and Caitlin whisper loudly, but nothing seems to happen.

Then, near the very end of the day on I get a call to come into Tom's office.

I go with trepidation.

He stands up to shake my hand – and not in an I'm-about-to-fire-you kind of way.

"So Tess, I've been meaning to talk to you about something," he says.

I wait to hear about Gracie.

Instead he says – "You may not be aware, but it was never intended that I would be the President of Skyler Reed forever. I'm still the Executive Vice President for all our brands, so this has been an addition to my duties. My family is certainly ready to have me not go to Boston every week."

I look at the pictures behind his desk – two teenaged boys and a middle-school girl – and I think about how it must have felt for them to have him gone so much.

"When we first acquired the brand, we thought it was important for me to be in the leadership spot during the transition – just to assure that it held onto its intrinsic value while also showing the aggressive growth that we were depending on. And I think by any measure we can be said to have been successful – our growth has exceeded even our best expectations while we have kept your old customers (and the fashion press) happy – no small task."

I smile at him. I agree with these things, but I'm not sure what it has to do with me.

"Tess, I have called you in because I would like to make you the President of Skyler Reed."

"Excuse me?" I say. I'm not sure I heard him correctly.

"This can't be a surprise," he says.

Oh yes it can.

"Um, but aren't you upset about last month, you know, me having the baby at work?"

"The fact that a baby was in the Skyler Reed offices for several hours on a Monday would not be enough to make me reconsider everything you've done for the brand, Tess. Although I would ask that you not make a habit of it… In fact, just between us, the strength of Katrina's overreaction to it finally made me realize that she is not really cut out to be a manager of people – marketing, licenses, brands, certainly, but not a company full of people. But I can tell that you are the right person to lead Skyler Reed. That's why I'm offering you the job of President – you'd keep your Creative Director title, although you would have to give up leading handbags personally. The other design areas would remain the same, with Katrina leading a group working on our partnerships and licenses for growing that element of the brand. It'd be a

Life, Motherhood & the Pursuit of the Perfect Handbag

great opportunity for you, Tess."

He's offering to make me the President of Skyler Reed? Me, who didn't go to Parson's or the Wharton School? Me, the lucky post-grad who got hired to answer the phone for Skyler's crazy business idea all those years ago?

I can't believe it.

Wait until I tell Pete.

Oh shit. What am I going to tell Pete?

"Thank you, Tom, thank you," I say.

"Wait," he says. "There is one thing, and it's a big one. It made sense in the beginning to keep Skyler Reed in Boston, but now with this growth that we're seeing, we've decided to bring the brand to New York. You will still have your own space – a Skyler Reed domain if you will, but by moving the company to New York, it will be more tied into the corporation as a whole. Honestly, Tess, I know it will be hard to leave your home, but I think it would be a great move for you. The sky's the limit for you with OmniBrands."

I don't know what to say and it must be obvious on my face.

"You don't have to decide right now," he says. "Just think about it for a day or two. Only a few people know – my boss, of course, and Leo, because his contract says he has to be informed about major decisions. I haven't told Katrina, and I will wait until I have your answer."

I stumble out of the office in a daze.

President? President of Skyler Reed? This is what I always

hoped was going to happen, and now it did. And not because Skyler gave it to me, but because I earned it.

But New York?

And what about my family? I would definitely have to get an au pair if I'm going to be the President of the brand. Skyler Reed at four times the size is a different proposition than it was when Skyler was president – and she was very busy then.

I call Pete from my desk.

Amazingly he answers.

"I have crazy news," I say. "But I can't tell you now."

"That's weird, because I have news too," he says. "They offered me the medical director job in Mali. Can you believe it? Nobody gets that kind of an offer right out of fellowship."

I'm silent.

"Come on, Tess, what do you think?"

"Are you going to take it?"

"Oh honey, I don't know, but can't you just be happy for me for two minutes? This is what we've worked so hard for."

"Sure," I say. "I love you."

I hang up the phone.

Leo walks by and pulls me into his office.

"Did he tell you?"

I nod.

"Finally," he says. "I've known for a week, and it's been nearly impossible to keep my mouth shut. Can I buy you a drink?"

The words *wait, let me call Pete* almost leave my mouth, but then I think about the times that Pete has been home late without even calling. He's in clinic this week. There's no reason he can't be home by 6:00. Let him rush home for the nanny for once.

I do call him from the lobby to tell him that I'll be late.

Leo and I walk across Back Bay trying to decide where to go.

I look in the windows of the shops – Armani, Donna Karan, Burberry, BCBG – this is where we're headed. I imagine a Skyler Reed store on Newbury Street – with clothes and accessories and a beautiful window display.

Looking at the skyline, I decide. We have to go to Top of the Hub. It sits in the top of the Prudential Building (the second highest skyscraper in Boston) and from it you can see the whole city. It's kind of a cheesy place to take someone fashionable, but the food is great and I think Leo will enjoy the view.

My ears pop as we ride the elevator to the top.

We have a drink in the bar looking out on the city, and we talk about fashion.

It is fairly crazy to be sitting and talking to a man about fashion. Pete has never cared an iota about handbags.

As it gets dark, I take Leo around the restaurant to show him everything you can see – all of Boston spread out below you.

He stands next to me.

We look at the city together.

I feel him breathing beside me. I'm not sure that I've ever stood next to someone this attractive.

We are tucked in behind a palm, looking at the North End

while I tell him all about the Old North Church and Paul Revere's ride, when I feel Leo's hand on my lower back.

He smells really good. I resolve to not think about it.

He turns as though he's going to tell me something, but instead, he leans in and kisses me softly.

Now he smells really good.

I shock myself by kissing him back – I know I've had a few vodka tonics, but I have never believed that alcohol makes you do anything that you don't want to do anyway.

His arms are around me, and he's kissing me for real now.

I think about the room, all the people here, all the people eating dinner. I think suddenly, about my husband and my children – then I feel bad that I thought about people seeing before I thought about my family…

I pull away.

"Leo, what are you doing?"

"What do you think I'm doing?" he says, and leans in again.

This time, I manage not to be hypnotized by his beautiful eyes.

"No, I mean what about Gabriela? Your supermodel, remember?"

He shrugs slightly, apparently sending the girl of everyman's dreams back out into the dating pool. He looks at me intently.

"What I remember," he says, "is you telling me that the sight of her should make me happy; that I should feel more like myself when she's around; that she should complete me; and I don't feel those things for Gabriela – but I do feel that way about you, Tess. Why do you think I keep coming to Boston? They'd be happy to have me stay in New York – certainly James doesn't like how much time I'm away from my own operation, and don't think that Tom loves paying for a room at the Taj every time I come to town. I come to see you. I kept saying it was friends, but I don't think so. Tess, I want to be with you."

I attempt to defuse this situation – he's very sweet, it's all very winning, but we are still going to have to work together.

"Leo, I'm married – I have two kids. I can't just have a new relationship every time I meet someone whose company I enjoy."

"You know there's more than that, Tess. Just think about it – ask yourself, does your husband want to be with you the way that I want to be with you? Would he fight to keep you? Do you know the answer?"

I look in those green eyes, and I tell him the truth.

"No, no I don't know the answer. But I can't do this."

He takes my hand.

"I'm not saying you have to decide today – just think about it."

I turn to go.

"Tess, I know this isn't just about you – but I'm telling you, I love your kids. I love that you have kids. We could be awesome."

It is a lonely ride home in the cab.

36

I think about skipping Kerry's henna party Saturday night. She invited all her girlfriends to get our hands painted while she gets a design that will cover her entire enormous belly.

The baby is due any day.

I don't want to go.

I don't want to have my hand painted with henna.

I don't want to have to talk to my friends about everything that's been going on. There's so much, it could take up all the oxygen in the room, and tonight is supposed to be about Kerry.

I have no idea what to do – about the job, about my marriage, about Leo – and I'm afraid to ask anyone…

And I know that Mira will be there, and I especially don't want to see Mira. If I had been fired yesterday at least I would have had that to hold over her head – look, you stole my nanny and I got fired….

Kerry must sense my reluctance, because she calls mid-afternoon, just to make sure that I'm coming.

"You sound distracted, Tess," she says after a minute.

"Yeah, I've got a lot going on."

"Well I definitely know that, since you've pretty much disappeared for the last few months."

"Sorry about that," I say.

"Come tonight, and I'll forgive you."

So I go.

Since I just have to walk up the hill, I'm one of the first ones there. I get a glass of wine, fill my plate with cheese, look at the henna designs and try to decide if I should tell Kerry about my job, or Pete's job, or Leo.

I realize that the baby is due any day, and I have no idea what is going on with her and Kevin. Since I've stopped talking to Mira and Raj I have completely lost touch with all my friends' lives. Another failure.

"Where's Kevin tonight?" I say. Since there are women here who I don't know well, including Corrine Downing Dailey, I decide to be as innocuous as possible. I don't know how many people Kerry has told about their troubles.

We are in the dining room, where the henna painting will be done.

Kerry leans back in one of the arm chairs from the dining room suite, struggling to get comfortable.

"Take a look in that top left drawer," she says, pointing me to a sideboard against the wall.

I pull out a manila envelope.

Just then Mira walks in.

"Hey Mira, go sit by Tess, there's something I want you to see," Kerry says.

Arrrghhh, if I didn't know better I'd have thought she had planned this. She knows that we are both too polite to not do as we're told in a social setting.

Mira walks over and gives me a friendly but embarrassed smile that seems to be asking for forgiveness.

My face is stone.

I open the envelope very angry at both of them.

My anger transitions immediately to astonishment when I see what's on the pictures.

They are pictures of Kevin with the redhead – the same one from Kerry's phone.

Kevin arm and arm with her on the beach. More pictures of them biking. Kevin kissing her in the rain outside a hotel in New York. Kevin walking down Centre Street holding her hand. Walking down Centre Street in Jamaica Plain? What can he have been thinking? Anyone could have seen him. I turn to the next picture and quickly turn it over in shock. It's Kevin naked in bed with the other woman. But something seems familiar about the picture. I turn it back over and look at it hard, trying to ignore Kevin's back – who knew he had back hair? You would think that someone with that much money would do something about that. I finally see it – it's the bedspread in the bedroom in this house. Kevin not only walked this woman down Centre Street, he had sex with her

Life, Motherhood & the Pursuit of the Perfect Handbag

in his marriage bed. Yuck.

"Yuck," Mira says. She has been looking at the pictures over my shoulder. Funny that we would have the same thought.

"So, I'm not sure where Kevin is," Kerry says. "But I suspect that he's in consultation with his attorneys."

"Did you give him these?" I ask.

"I did. We were out to lunch so he could convince me once again that we should try one more time. After the last time, I decided the best thing to do was to hire a private detective to find out if he was keeping up his end of the deal. The answer would seem to be no. Right after I showed him, I got up and left. A minute later they came in to serve him with divorce papers. It was a pretty perfect scene. Especially because he decided to try to win me over in a very fancy and popular restaurant in the South End. I hope a few of the people there knew who he was. He's always asking 'don't you know who I am?' I bet he was wishing there were fewer people who do after that."

She laughs.

"You seem to be taking it all well," Corrine says. She has also seen the pictures.

"Denial. It's all denial," Kerry says.

I wonder if that's it. I want to ask about Liam, but I don't know the other women well enough to do so.

Later in the party, after I've had my hand painted, I get up to refresh my drink.

Mira catches me in the kitchen.

"I'm really sorry," she says.

"It's okay," I say brusquely.

"No it's not – it really isn't. It's just when Vanessa asked us, we didn't know what else to do. Things have been so crazy, Tess. I don't know how we could have made it work much longer. I actually lost a booking because I had to cancel at the last minute when Raj got called out of town. That can't happen. There's a long list of photographers that these people can work with. There aren't any second chances in this business…. Please understand. We never, never, never would have taken her from you. It was never our plan. She's just so great and it seemed like a good solution. I'm sorry."

I realize that we are both talking about Vanessa like she belongs to either one of us – Mira stole my nanny. I lost my nanny. Vanessa is her own person. She wasn't happy working for us; she hadn't been happy for months. Why should it matter to me if she goes to work for a friend of mine? And could I guarantee that I wouldn't do the same thing under the same circumstances? No.

"It's okay, really," I say finally.

She gives me a quick hug.

"We've really missed you guys," she says.

"Yeah, us too."

"So what's been going on with you?" she asks.

"Not much – OmniBrands wants me for Skyler Reed President in New York, Pete has a job offer in Mali, and Leo Magnusson thinks he's in love with me…"

Life, Motherhood & the Pursuit of the Perfect Handbag

Just then Kerry lumbers into the kitchen.

"Sit back down," I say. "I'll bring you a glass of water."

"Why is everyone acting like I have a broken leg? I'm just pregnant. I can get my own water. Besides, I just caught the end of what you were telling Mira, and I gotta know what's going on."

I slow down and explain it all to them.

"Have you talked to Pete?" Mira asks.

"No."

"Are you planning to tell him?" Kerry says.

"Which part – that I got the job offer, yes; he already knows about Mali; and I can't think of any good reason to tell him about Leo, because other than kiss, I haven't done anything wrong."

"Wait, you kissed him?" Mira says, her voice shocked.

"He kissed me."

"You kissed him back?"

"A little."

"How was the kiss?" Kerry asks.

"Um, nice," I say. "But that doesn't surprise me – I mean what's the likelihood that a man who looks like that was going to get to this phase of life without having some serious kissing instruction?"

"Do you know what you are going to do?" Mira asks.

"No. None. Any ideas?"

"Do you want to be the President of Skyler Reed?" Mira asks.

I think about that for a minute.

"Well I think it's pretty awesome that they offered it to me – I mean that's a big deal, President of a major brand at 35…"

"Well sure it's an honor, but do you want the job?" Kerry says.

"Well, I don't want to be gone all the time, and I don't particularly want to attend a million meetings with Corporate, and I don't want to move to New York, and I would really, really miss designing handbags."

"It sounds like you don't want it," Mira says.

"But I don't want nothing, either," I say. "And if I try to go do my same job for another company I'll just be in the same position – living in New York, working all the time, busting my ass, all with the long term goal of getting the job that I'd be turning down."

"Well what do you want?" Kerry says. Her voice is tough. She is truly my no-excuses friend.

I try to think about exactly what I want.

"Well, I'd like to be Creative Director for a smaller company that makes a manageable number of bags while also being big enough to have a staff so I'm not a one-woman shop. I really don't want to answer the phone, and I don't want to be the sales staff, and I sure as hell don't want a table at art festivals."

"So why don't you go to your boss and tell him that?" Kerry says.

"Tell him what?" I say. I'm confused.

"Go and tell him that you don't want to be the President of Skyler Reed, but you would like to start a small brand of your own – you have a record of success, and we'll write you a business plan. All they'd have to give you was the initial funding. It might make things easier for them since it would save the PR hit of closing the Boston office."

"But what happens if he says no?" I say.

"Then he says no."

"But then I'll have said I don't want the President's job."

"But you don't want the President's job," Mira says.

"I didn't say that."

"Yes you did," Mira says. "You said that you don't want to work all the time or to live in New York and that you want to keep designing handbags. If all that is true, you don't want the job. Shit Tess, Raj and I have found out the hard way what trouble you get into when you take a job because you think you should and not because you want it. Sure Raj likes his job, but he's miserable, he misses the kids so much."

"Is he going to quit?" Kerry asks.

"He's going to ask to go down to 75 percent. We'll see what they say. He'd still travel, but that way he'd be home one week in four."

"Well now we've got Tess' job worked out for her, now we have to fix her marriage. Is Pete really going to Africa?" Kerry says.

"I don't know," I say.

"Do you want him to go?" Kerry asks.

"No, of course not!"

"Have you told him that?"

"No."

"Why not?" Mira asks.

"Shouldn't he know already? Shouldn't he know that I want us to be together as a family? That I don't want him picking up and moving across the world?"

"Everything we do is a choice, Tess." Mira says. "And choosing to not choose is making a choice too."

"What do you mean?" I say.

"If you take this job, or let Pete move away, you are making the decision about your life and your marriage. Nobody is making you do this."

"You've been married long enough to know that there is no man on earth who can read your mind," Kerry adds, laughing.

"Okay, okay, I'll tell him," I say.

"When?" Mira asks.

"I don't know."

"How about tomorrow? Raj and I will take your kids– you go do something romantic together and talk. Take the whole day – you guys deserve it."

"But what if I tell him and he still wants to go? I don't want to be the one who crushes his dreams."

"Who said anything about crushing dreams?" Mira says. "You guys are on the 60-year plan here; tell him you'd be happy to think about going with him to Africa in 20 years when the kids have gone to college – hell by then, it may even be true."

"What should I do about Leo?"

Life, Motherhood & the Pursuit of the Perfect Handbag

"You don't want to be with him, do you?"

I think about his beautiful face and quite lovely body. Then I think about a life of talking about nothing but fashion all the time, and going to parties and events like the ones I attended during Fashion Week. I think of the spreads in Vogue that you see with famous designers' and artists' children – dressed up in amazing clothes, living in opulent spaces, surrounded by privilege. I realize that this is truly the last thing I want for my children. I want them to have a nice moderately-normal childhood, something that they can look back on with pleasant nostalgia with a good-sized chance of replicating something similar in their own lives.

Then I think about Pete – his crinkly smile, his messy hair, the kid he was when I met him, the man he is now. No, I don't want to leave Pete, but I do want our marriage back. I know that the past six months cannot be what the next six months or six years look like; because if it is, the next time one of us has the chance to stray, I don't think we would say no.

Kerry's phone rings.

She runs to pick it up. She steps into the playroom to talk.

"Who is that calling at 10:30 at night?" I ask after she hangs up.

"Oh, just Liam calling to make sure I haven't gone into labor. He calls every night to check on me and the little man."

"Wait a minute; you know it's a boy?" I ask. "I thought you were so insistent on waiting. Have you known all along?"

"Yes, the ultrasound tech found out by accident – I just didn't want to listen to Kevin go on and on about having a boy. I thought it might make Madison feel bad."

"That's awfully nice of Liam to call and check on you," Mira says with a smile.

"Well, he's volunteered to be my birth coach," Kerry says.

"Oh, is that all?" Mira says. "Wow... He must really like you."

"Kerry, that's kind of weird," I say.

"I think it's nice," Mira says.

"And weird," I say.

Kerry smiles sweetly.

"Liam says he wants my little boy to be met by a man who isn't a jerk – just so he can know that they exist in the world."

37

Sunday morning, Pete and I wait in line for brunch at the Centre Street Café. I feel like an imposter, drinking my coffee with all the childless couples and groups of friends who wait in the line. I can't believe that only four years ago that was us. We had no idea what was in store for us.

After a great breakfast, we walk around Jamaica Pond.

It is wall-to-wall children and dogs on the path around the pond, but our favorite bench is open.

It's in front of a little hill and the breeze blows down on us.

The very first desperate hints of spring are breaking through. The ice on the pond has mostly melted, and a few of the trees are showing tiny, tiny buds. The sun shines on us and I almost think about taking off my jacket.

We sit together in companionable silence.

Finally I tell him.

"Remember on Friday, when I said I had big news?"

He nods.

"They offered me the President of Skyler Reed. It'd be a big job, and they want me to move to New York."

"Are you going to take it?" he asks.

I almost ask him if he wants me to, and then I remember, I want this conversation to be about what each of us wants for ourselves and for our marriage and our family.

"Do you remember, months ago we were at dinner and you talked about how much you loved your time in Nigeria, before you came back, before you settled down. You said that you had to write notes to yourself so that you would remember to eat and sleep."

He nods.

"Well that's how the last few months have been for me at work. It has been all consuming and exciting and frustrating and wonderful, and I haven't had two minutes for myself much less for anyone else."

"I felt the same in Mali at Christmas," he says. "Isn't that what we're supposed to have? Work that we love, work that consumes us?"

I think about high school and about college, and yes, that was the message – work hard, do your all, and you can get a job that is world-changing, or you can be a leader – president of a company by 35. And there's nothing wrong with that – but nobody ever told me that when I had children I was going to have two small people who need me to live for them too. And there's only so much of me to go around.

Life, Motherhood & the Pursuit of the Perfect Handbag

I think about how much I've been gone from my family for the past six months. I think about the craziness of thinking I could bring the baby to work, and I tell Pete the truth.

"I love the work I've been doing. I love the design, I love being part of something that is really big and important, but if I could go back to my old Skyler Reed life, I'd do it in a heartbeat. I want to keep doing what I love, and I don't want to be selling handbags at flea markets, but I don't want to never see our kids either – I'm just trying to figure out how to do both."

He holds my hand and we sit there silently for a minute.

"What about you?" I ask. "Do you want to go to Mali? I didn't say it before, but I really don't want to go – and even more than that, I don't want you to go by yourself. I'm not Mariam van de Berg. I can't sit here all by myself with the children, waiting for your occasional visits."

"I know," he says. "Being around Gretchen just made me think about how fun that life was."

I feel my joy level dropping. Great, Gretchen, just who I want to think about.

"You know what's funny though, I had lunch with her after I found out about the job…"

I think about feeling jealous, and then I remember that I was out at Top of the Hub with Leo after I found out about my job offer.

"Anyway, we were sitting there, and she just mentioned how much she envies our life – the children, a home. She thinks we don't enjoy it enough. She says that we seem to just be taking it all for granted."

"Do you think she's right?"

"When was the last time we just sat with the kids and did nothing? Or did something that was totally about them and us being together, not just an excuse to keep them busy so we could get some more work done?"

I think about it hard, and the answer makes me really sad.

"The day after Thanksgiving, when we went sledding," I say.

"And before that?"

"I don't know."

"Yeah, me either."

"So what are you going to do about Mali?"

"I'm not going to take it," he says. "Even if you would go and we took the kids with us, I'd be too busy to see them or you; and if I went without you, that's nothing like the life I want. There's a job at the hospital that's a good one, it would get me home by 6:00 most nights, not too much call. There are always trips that I can go on."

I give him a huge hug.

"I promise, after they are grown, I will definitely seriously consider going with you to Africa," I say.

"Definitely seriously consider?"

"Okay, okay, I'll go."

We take advantage of the empty house to make love leisurely, without worrying about anyone screaming that they need a glass

Life, Motherhood & the Pursuit of the Perfect Handbag

of water.

I feel even more like an imposter.

Pete whistles in the shower.

"Hey, Pete," I call when he steps out of the shower. "I've been thinking about the conversation I'm going to have to have with Tom."

He dries his hair with the towel.

"What about it?" he asks.

"What if he says no?"

"He says no. We'll be okay."

"No, that's not what I mean. I think this is something I would like to do, even if he says no."

He smiles his crinkly smile.

"You mean do a start-up handbag company?"

I nod.

"Honey, we will have enough money to make our mortgage, not enough to start a handbag company… We don't know anybody with pockets that deep."

I think about it for a minute and then I remember.

"Yes we do."

"Who?"

"Skyler Reed."

I don't know how much Skyler got out of the company sale, but it was certainly enough to bank roll what I am imagining. It sounded like from what the actress said in New York that Skyler might be bored. Maybe she'd like to go in on something like this…

"But then I would have to call her…"

"So call her," Pete says.

"We didn't leave things on the best terms," I say. "Jesus, Tess, just call her. All she can do is say no."

So I sit down at the kitchen table and call Skyler's cell phone number. I hope she hasn't changed phones.

She picks up.

"Tess! How are you doing?" she says.

"Great," I say. My voice is falsely bright.

"How's everything at Skyler Reed?"

"Oh great, great," I say. "Are you in California?"

"Yeah. I'm thinking about producing movies, maybe."

"How's that?" I ask.

"Great, great…"

We sit there in uncomfortable silence for a minute.

I remember why I'm calling her.

"Um, Skyler, actually Skyler Reed sucks. Katrina is exactly as big of a bitch as she seemed, and they want to move the whole thing to New York. On the plus side, they want me to run it."

"Are you going to?"

"I don't really want to…"

"Yeah, California sucks too. This movie thing is not fun. They just want to spend my money and I don't get to do anything."

"How was the ashram?"

"Relaxing for about three days."

"After that?"

"God, I've never been more bored. I ended up going to Delhi and buying fabric for handbags."

"Skyler, you don't have a handbag company any more."

"I know! How sick is that?"

So I tell her my idea, and she says that if I can get Tom to get on board, she'll take a 25 percent ownership stake.

"Will you come work with me?" I say.

"For you, you should say," she says. "If it's your company, you'd have to be clear who works for who."

I think 'whom' and then I am so grateful that I am soon to be liberated from Katrina and her grammar policing.

"Absolutely. Will you come back and work for me?"

"I don't know Tess, I don't know if I want to get back on my gerbil wheel."

"I won't make you go back on the wheel," I say. "You were right before – I didn't understand how much work you were doing. I understand now. I'll handle all the President stuff, but I'd love to have your help on the marketing and design side."

"Well if we're making apologies," she says. "I'm sorry for not giving you the chance to be the President. Honestly, I was kind of jealous of your life – the kids and Pete and everything. I didn't want to think it was possible to do both."

"What do you think now?"

"I think that I don't know anything, but I'm willing to learn…"

That evening I go over to Kerry's and the two of us make a business plan for my presentation to Tom on Monday.

38

Monday, I walk into the office on shaking legs.

I am dressed like the businesswoman that I hope to become. I look like myself, only toned down a little – a crème colored Emporio Armani jacket with three-quarters sleeves and a thin black belt, worn over a black shift dress. My shoes and bag are black, but fabulous. For once I don't feel like an imposter in a suit. I love the Armani suits that Leo bought me, but they are so beautiful, and so expensive, I never really feel like they are mine.

I carry a portfolio under my arm with the business plan.

I have already emailed Lauren to let her know I'd like to see Tom and I'm the first person on his schedule.

I walk in, trying to look confident. I tell myself that I can do this.

Tom stands and shakes my hand.

"I hope that you have good news for me," he says. "Have you considered our offer?"

"I have, and I'm afraid that I'll have to decline," I say.

"Oh, Tess, I'm so sorry to hear that."

I stop him before he can go further.

"I do, however, have an offer for you."

I lay out the idea for him – a boutique line, based here in Boston, taking a few of the key people who I know won't want to move to New York, producing the bags out of the New Bedford factory. I tell him about Skyler's willingness to put in a 25 percent stake. I tell him about the blog and it's readership, which has grown exponentially. "Right now, it's anonymous, but I think if I say who I am, it might be a nice scaffolding to build the brand. Based on the name of the blog, most of the readers are women with children. Not that it would be the sole focus of the brand, but we could have that be our special bailiwick. We could move the Medela partnership over to the new brand, it's a bit of an orphan within Skyler Reed, and will be more so if I'm not here."

"Interesting idea," he says. "Why should we do it?"

"It builds on our existing infrastructure, so it's really not a large start-up cost; it lets you keep the small brand credibility while also taking Skyler Reed in whatever direction you want to take it in; and it keeps down the hue and cry about deserting Boston."

"And we get to keep you on board," he says.

"Well, yes, but I wasn't going to say that."

"Well if you want to start your own brand, you had better get used to tooting your own horn. I actually think it's a great idea. Let me have some internal conversations, and I'll let you know the answer soon. Hopefully by next week. I'll wait to make the announcement about the new President until after we know."

He looks down at the papers on his desk.

"If they say no, is there any chance you'd reconsider taking the President job?"

"No," I say. "But thank you."

I avoid Katrina's curious stare as I make my way to the office. I wonder if he's planning to give President to Katrina?

Leo is in New York today, so at least I don't have to face him.

It is over a week later when Tom finally gets me on a conference call with Corporate and we find out the terms of our deal. I'll be underwritten by Corporate, and they'll provide administrative support, but other than that, I'm largely on my own. My staff will be small, only about ten people, and we'll concentrate just on handbags for the first year.

I wonder how much of my staff will choose to stay.

The next day, Tom calls a big meeting in the office – his invitation says that there will be an important announcement.

I remember that first meeting when Katrina didn't introduce me.

I would love to have seen the look on her face when Tom introduced me today if I'd taken the President's job.

I sit with Stacey, Linette, Therrien and Leo, and we all whisper about what the announcement could possibly be. Of course, I have some idea what it's going to be about, but I have no idea who he's chosen. I just hope it isn't Katrina.

She must think it's her, because she's got a smug smile pasted on her face. She sits with Caitlin and a few of her other minions.

Finally, Tom stands, while Lauren runs the Power Point.

He goes over the things I already know, about how well we've been doing since the acquisition – how we are a credit to our parent company. We are meeting expectations, the shareholders are happy.

"Now I have a major announcement," he says. "We have chosen a new President for Skyler Reed. This is someone who has been with us since the beginning of the acquisition. Someone who's standing in the industry is matched by business understanding and a wonderful eye."

Katrina bestows smiles on those around her like the Queen of fricking England. God, I should have taken the job just so that she didn't get it.

"I am pleased to announce that the new President of Skyler Reed is..."

Katrina stands with a benevolent smile.

"Leo Magnusson," Tom says.

Leo stands up in his easy-going way as Katrina slams herself back down into the chair.

"That's embarrassing," Therrien says, loud enough that the people around us can hear.

The room erupts in applause. I think everyone sees the bullet that they just dodged. Not that Leo isn't great – but wow.

"Dudes," Leo says. "Thanks a lot. This is going to be

awesome…"

He sits back down.

"Why didn't you tell me?" I whisper.

"Didn't seem important," he says. "I wish you would have taken it."

"But don't you want it?"

"Sure, but I think you would have been great."

"How on earth are you going to manage to do all your different jobs?" I ask.

"I'll figure it out – I was ready for something new anyway. Been doing this indy fashion thing for a while. Maybe I'll like being a corporate warrior. Eye of the tiger, et cetera."

I laugh. I bet he'll be great.

After wrapping up on the wonders of Leo's resume, and how everyone else in the org chart will stay the same, Tom makes the announcement about the move to New York.

Many of the junior staffers look thrilled at the opportunity to work for a major designer in New York City. We have always struggled to convince designers to move to Boston. Others look very sad. They are the ones who have family or friends here and have been happy to have a first tier job but not to have moved so far from home.

Tom is upbeat.

"This is all a sign of Skyler Reed's success. We have outgrown our current quarters, and we have moved to the forefront of American brands. You should all be very proud of yourselves."

Life, Motherhood & the Pursuit of the Perfect Handbag

Then he asks me to step forward.

"In other news, Tess is going to be leaving us," he says.

There is a gasp, I think from Stacey.

"Leaving us, but not leaving handbags," he continues. "Tess is going to be starting her own small firm here in Boston."

I smile at everyone. I wonder if people think that I've been pushed out.

Tom and I have decided that today should be my last day in the office, in order to avoid confusion, so when the meeting is over, I grab some empty paper boxes and start packing my desk.

After a few minutes I feel someone's eyes on me.

It's Katrina.

"I knew that you wouldn't survive," she sneers. "You never were really ready to perform at the highest levels. You just aren't willing to make the requisite sacrifices, and that comes through very clearly to those who make the decisions. In this industry, you must dedicate everything to the work – anything less is simply unacceptable."

She's certainly recovered her self possession. I wonder if she even understands why Tom didn't make her President.

"You know they offered me the President job, don't you?" I say.

"They most certainly did not," she says.

"Yep, they did – but I said no."

She splutters.

"Do you know why?" I ask.

She glares at me.

"Because I knew that if I did, if I made the requisite sacrifices, I'd just end up a nasty bitter bitch like you. So good luck with everything, and I sure hope your job loves you back."

She storms out of my office.

That felt good.

Maybe I'll regret it if I need to get something from Skyler Reed later.

Naw, I don't think so.

I hear someone at the door. She can't be back.

It's Leo.

Still just beautiful.

He comes over to my desk and puts both hands on it and leans forward.

"So you're staying here in Boston, are you?" he says.

"Yeah, there's too much here for me to give up."

"Are you sure?" he asks. Even his breath is sweet. The man is like Apollo.

"Yes."

"Well good luck with everything – you know how to get in touch with me if you change your mind."

"Leo, she's out there, you know."

"What?"

"The girl who makes your heart sing, the one who will give you babies of your own."

"Pffffft."

"You might find her if you stopped looking at 19-year-olds. Not that you'll have any time to date now that you're the President of Skyler Reed."

"You sound like my mom," he says.

I come around the desk and we hug awkwardly.

Then I push him out the door.

"Get out of here. If I can get this wrapped up soon I'll be able to make it home in time for dinner."

www.tess-holland.com/home

TESS HOLLAND, INC

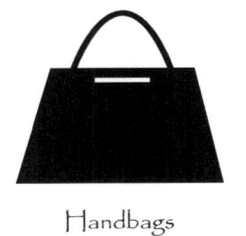

Handbags

Welcome!

May 1 - Whether you are finding us for the first time or have been redirected from lifemotherhoodhandbags.com, the pursuit of the perfect handbag continues at Tess Holland Inc.

Founder, Creative Director and Lead Designer – Tess Holland

Since I was a little girl, I have loved handbags. I'm all about making functional things beautiful. I call it the pursuit of the perfect handbag... I am the founder of Tess Holland, Inc. For the previous eleven years I worked as a designer and Creative Director at Skyler Reed+Boston. I've just moved to a big old house in the Jamaica Plain neighborhood of Boston with my husband Pete, my son Jake and my daughter Gracie. Yesterday, my husband came home with a kitten.

MAY

39

I'm at Wake up the Earth.

That's the name of my favorite of our neighborhood festivals. It happens at the beginning of May, right when it is beginning to look like spring may in fact arrive in New England for another year.

They close down Centre Street for the entire ten block business district. Starting from the Civil War Monument, a mass of people walk together to the corridor park that runs on top of the subway. It is a parade in which everyone can participate, where you see everyone you know, and it's all in honor of the spring. People walk down the street on stilts (always careful not to step in the abandoned trolley tracks), families push decorated strollers, masses of teenagers bang on homemade drums. It is a wonderful crazy thing. At the end, there is a street festival with bands and stands selling food and crafts.

We walk in the crowd together with Jake's preschool class, all of them with flags and shakers that they made at school. We see everyone that we know, and I'm reminded of why we love our neighborhood.

Raj and Mira are behind us, going steadily more slowly because the kids are walking together. Vanessa is with them, laughing at Amit's antics. Raj just got the confirmation last week that he can go to 75 percent time, so they all practically glow with happiness.

Ahead of us, Kerry holds baby Rowan in a wrap, while Madison walks between her and Liam, holding each of their hands. With Kerry's divorce final, today is their coming out party as a couple.

This is the first year that Pete has been off work to come.

It feels strange to show him the life that the kids and I have been living for the past few years that he has been largely absent from. I am excited to introduce him to our friends and our life, now that he's back in fully.

He has taken a job here in Boston that is supposed to be a normal working day, with only occasional call, and I promised to let him go to Africa next summer. It is funny, I am so excited about the small things – we'll be able to make dinner together, or watch a movie after work – for the first time since we've been married, we'll be like normal people.

The kids are so young, I wonder if they will even remember back when daddy used to be gone all the time.

Pete has taught Jake to whistle and the two of them improvise a little tune along with the drumming down Centre Street.

As for me, things are wonderful. My staff of ten has moved into a new space a block away from our old one, still in the heart of Back Bay. We have ten handbags coming out in the fall, along with two laptop bags and four diaper bags (including a diaper manbag). We've continued the partnership with Medela.

Skyler is the Chief Marketing Officer for Tess Holland, Inc.

And once a week, she comes in the office and is in charge, while I go back to taking Fridays off.

Acknowledgements

A special thank you to everyone who supported me as I worked on this book: my wonderful family – John and Valerie McNee, Elaine McNee Kemp, Gail and Fred Roberson; my JP moms – Enna Grazier, Samantha Overton, Shoshana Korn and Dana Clancy; my Chapel Hill moms – Dana Gelin, Jessica Sherrieb, Allison Ballew, Christina Chenet and Mandy Evans; my early readers and cheerleaders Camille Hemmer, Kirsten Sanford, Courtney Harness, Merideth McEntire, Hilary Roberto, Lauryn Zipse, Gail Roberson, Marci Benson and Somer Clark-Day.

I cannot say enough good things about Harriet Wu and Mandy Brannon, who helped make the whole thing real.

Thank you most of all to Russell and our wonderful sons, Will, John Henry and Grant.

Made in the USA
Lexington, KY
23 November 2011